U0032575

Taiwan

用英文說台灣

文庭澍、Catherine Dibello◎著

如何用英文描述台灣經驗？
《聯合報》教育版熱門專欄告訴你！

Everyday English in Taiwan

中英對頁編排，生字句型深度解析。
克漏字、選擇、翻譯、多元練習題。

隨書附贈ICRT DJ精心錄製 **2** CD

聯經

收穫的過程

2004年7月31日，一個太陽才剛露臉就已燠熱難當的夏天早上，和平時一樣，我一面吃著早餐，一面翻閱著報紙。翻到最後一頁時，一篇「民意論壇」上〈英文作文寫不出台灣……〉的讀者投書引起我的注意。當時，大學聯考才剛結束一個月，參與批閱英文考卷的交通大學教授廖柏森，針對大專聯考英文作文題目："Travel is the Best Teacher" 寫了下面這段讓我深有同感的文字：「……考生寫起外國城市、博物館、遊樂園、節慶和文化都還算流利；但寫到國內的旅行經驗，卻很難拼寫出對的地名和景點，描述本地風土民情也是左支右絀，可見學生對本土事物的英文字彙掌握不足，無法表達地方性的題材和生活經驗……」。咀嚼廖教授文中含義之餘，突然靈光一現，心想學生既然拙於描寫地方性的題材，何不自編教材，讓學生學會一些與台灣日常生活息息相關的用語？

這個想法隨著好友Cathy Dibello教授的來台，很快付諸行動。Cathy是賓州Shippensburg大學的英國文學教授，除了教學生欣賞文學之美，還以教英文作文見長。她曾在80、90年代兩度來台，任教於靜宜及東海大學，對台灣大學生學習英文時遭遇的困難有某種程度的了解。此番來台，Cathy將在東海任教兩年，她的背景、學養和經驗正是我合作編寫教材的不二人選。我認為

機不可失，在她剛下飛機、還頭昏腦脹分不清東西南北之時，要言不繁的說明我的計畫。我們很快且幸運地找到一片揮灑園地——《聯合報》文教版張錦弘先生答應為我們闢一專欄，為了使讀者一目了然，我們擬了一個開門見山的名稱「用英文說台灣」（Everyday English in Taiwan），每星期根據台灣節慶或發生的時事，適時寫一篇三段式短文。轉眼間春去秋來，忽忽已寫了40來篇。

為了每星期的專欄，我和Cathy一星期見面一次。Cathy和我都是教英文作文的老師，與我們教學生寫作文的方式一樣，通常先上天下地漫想各種可能的題目；鎖定題目後，分頭找與題目相關的文章；接著一人一語，想一長串與題目有關的生字或慣用語；最後敲定整篇文章的走向和每段的大意後便開始下筆。文章通常由Cathy執筆，有些如節慶等她不太熟悉的領域則由我擔綱。我們各自有繁重的教職在身，e-mail成為我們相互討論的工具，通常一篇文章成文後，來來回回相互修改不下五、六次，有時截稿前還不斷琢磨，我們這種寫作方式，不是以作品為取向（product-oriented）一次就定稿，而是以過程為取向（process-oriented），是不斷琢磨寫作方式的最佳範例。

專欄刊出後，我們常接到讀者來書，與我們切磋用詞遣字之餘，常問我們何時可以集結成冊，我們於是挑選專欄中的36篇，分成節慶、社會、教育、健康、科技、飲食、災難、宗教

八個議題，編纂成書。除了專欄原文之外，為了方便學生練習，還加了生字造句、課文重點分析，以及克漏字、詞類變化和翻譯的練習題。這些習題在書後都有所謂的「標準答案」（Answer Key），但讀者應該瞭解，英文翻譯常常不只一種說法。為了讓讀者複習從課文中剛學會的字句，答案常與正文相去不遠，讀者若另有巧思，歡迎來信與我們討論。我的e-mail地址是 tingshu.wen@msa.hinet.net，Cathy的則是：dibello2@thu.edu.tw。

我在學校教了25年英文，在課堂上常常得身當學生的活字典（walking dictionary），回答如「How do you say援交、網友、檳榔西施、鋼管女郎、詐騙集團……in English?」等的問題，但隨著變化快速的社會，有時學生問的詞彙連我也啞口無言，不知如何作答。這次與Cathy寫專欄的過程中，最先受惠的是我們兩人，她瞭解了許多台灣特有的風土民情，我則學會了許多時髦的用語，大大拉近與學生的距離。

另外，我們的專欄也嘉惠不少學寫作文的學生——我們每篇文章的立場相當中立，可是學生寫作文，尤其是寫論說文（argumentation essay）時，一定得有自己的立場（take a stand）。上作文課時，我們通常用某篇專欄文章，如 "Cram Schools" 為引子，在課堂上討論後，要學生寫出自己讀補習班的經驗及對補習教育的看法，這種讀和寫相輔相成的教法，提升學生寫作的信心。感謝《聯合報》記者張錦弘先生和聯經編輯何

采嬪小姐對專欄的支持，逢甲大學Tutorial Hour的學生不斷供應年輕學子愛讀的題目和想法，還有我的子姪Michelle, Jessica, Karen, Chris, Yvonne和 Miranda投注心力，幫我出習題，當然最感謝的還是讀者，多虧您們不斷的回饋，使這本書的內容增色不少。

文庭澍

Preface

My connection with this book began the night I arrived from the United States in August 2004. Although I was jet lagged and weary, when my good friend Wen Ting-shu excitedly asked for my help with the bilingual column in United Daily News that led to this book, I knew I could not say no, especially after she sat me at her dining room table and "ordered" me to write.

Immediately, we generated dozens of interesting topics about the way we live now in Taiwan. In fact, there seemed to be no end to the quirky things that make Taiwan so special. With its unique blend of cutting edge trends and centuries-old customs, Taiwan remains endlessly fascinating.

As the months went by and we explored more topics, I learned more and more about Taiwan. Not only did I read articles and ask Taiwanese friends for information, I also braved acupuncture treatments, enjoyed a spa massage, ate night market food, and watched Lantern Festival fireworks. Writing the columns thus strengthened my bond to Taiwan, which has become a sort of a second home to me in the twenty-five years that I have repeatedly visited the island.

Writing the book has also strengthened my bond of friendship with my co-author, my very dear friend, Wen Ting-shu. I could not ask for better collaborator than this disciplined, energetic writer. We both hope that *Everyday English in Taiwan* will give readers as much pleasure as it gave us writers.

序

第一次和這本書牽上線，是在2004年8月我剛從美國來台的晚上。那時我既有時差、又滿身疲憊，好友文庭澍興奮莫名地要我幫忙撰寫即將在《聯合報》刊登的雙語專欄，也就是這本書的前身。當時她讓我坐在她家的餐桌前，一聲令下，我簡直毫無招架餘地。

我們很快就想出許多與台灣生活相關的趣味議題。事實上，台灣之所以特別，正是在它層出不窮、千奇百怪，巧妙地融合頂尖的時髦玩意兒和百年來的老習俗，讓人永遠興味盎然！

　　幾個月來，隨著不斷嘗試新的議題，我對台灣的瞭解也與日俱增。寫專欄過程中，我不但閱讀與題目相關的文章，還詢問台灣朋友相關的資料。除此之外，我更身體力行，大膽嘗試針灸、享受Spa芬香按摩、遍嘗夜市小吃和觀賞元宵節繁華煙火。寫這個專欄，深化我與台灣的關係，25年來，我先後多次造訪這裡，台灣儼然已成為我第二個家。

　　寫這本書也使我和我的合作伙伴文庭澍的感情更上一層樓，我常想，像她這麼有紀律又精力過人的合作伙伴，夫復何求？我們都希望這本《用英文說台灣》帶給我們兩位作者的樂趣，也同樣能感染我們的讀者。

黎白露
Cathy Dibello

目次

I. *Holidays* 節慶

中秋節

II. *Social Issues* 社會議題

III. *Education* 教育

IV. *Health* 健康

V. *Disasters* 災難

手機響遍台灣

VIII. *Religions and Folk Beliefs* 宗教和民間信仰

Holidays
節慶

Traveling Abroad During the Spring Festival `CD1 Track1`

While most people in Taiwan see the New Year holiday as time to spend at home with their families, others choose to travel abroad₁. A good place to start planning your trip is with your travel agents₂. They help you purchase tickets and apply for₃ visas. But before they start the formalities, you need to decide whether a tour group or independent travel will suit you.

Many Taiwanese prefer a tour since everything is arranged, including your itinerary, accommodations, and meals. A tour guide will accompany you while you are sightseeing and sometimes even when you are shopping. Moreover, these trips often cost less because you are purchasing a package deal.

On the other hand₄, other people prefer the freedom of independent travel. You can choose whether to stay₅ in a luxury resort or a budget motel and whether to eat in five-star restaurants or "greasy spoons." Whether you like the ease of a tour or the freedom of independent travel, traveling₆ abroad is a great way to spend your New Year holiday.

春節出國行

　　多數台灣人視春節為回家與家人團圓的節日，然而有的人卻選擇出國旅遊。計畫旅遊先得與旅行社業務員一起計畫行程，他們會幫你買票和辦簽證，不過在辦這些手續前，你得決定跟團還是自助旅行比較適合你。

　　許多台灣人喜歡跟團，因為所有行程、住宿和餐飲都會打點好，導遊還會陪著你觀光，有時連「血拼」也跟著你。另外，跟團的花費通常較少，因為你買的是套裝行程。

　　不過，也有人喜歡自助旅行，你可以選擇住豪華的度假村或便宜的汽車旅館、在五星級餐廳還是小飯館用餐。不管你喜歡的是跟團的輕鬆，還是自助旅行的自由自在，出國旅遊都是最好過春節的方法。

✏ 生字 Vocabulary

1. Spring Festival 春節
   In Taiwan, most people visit their parents during the Spring Festival.
   在台灣大多數人春節時會回家看父母。

2. travel agent 旅行社業務員
   If you use a travel agent, planning your vacation will be easier.
   如果你靠旅行社業務員，規劃你的假期會比較容易。

3. visa 簽證
   Many countries require tourists to have a visa in addition to a passport.
   許多國家要求觀光客除了護照外還得加簽證。

4. formality 手續
   Applying for a visa is one of the formalities of travel.
   申請簽證是旅遊必經的手續之一。

5. tour group 旅遊團
   She still keeps in touch with the people from her tour group.
   她跟旅行團的團員還保持聯繫。

6. independent travel 自助旅行
   The young man preferred independent travel since he hated going places with a group of strangers.
   這位年輕人喜歡自助旅行，因為他很討厭跟一群不認識的人到各

個地方旅遊。

7. itinerary 行程
The itinerary for my trip to Japan includes Tokyo and Kyoto.
我的日本行程包括東京和京都。

8. accommodation 住宿
Because her business paid for her accommodations, she stayed in very expensive hotels on her trip to France.
因為她的公司付住宿費，她到法國可以住很貴的旅館。

9. tour guide 導遊
The tour guide spoke excellent English, which was very helpful for the tourists.
這位導遊一口超棒的英文對遊客的幫助很大。

10. sightseeing 觀光
We spent two weeks sightseeing in Europe.
我們花了兩星期在歐洲觀光旅遊。

11. package deal 套裝旅遊
You can save money on your ticket and hotel if you purchase a package deal.
如果你買的是套裝旅遊，可省下不少機票和旅館的費用。

12. luxury resort 豪華度假村
The newlyweds stayed in a luxury resort on their honeymoon.
這對新人在豪華度假村度蜜月。

13. budget motel 便宜汽車旅館

To save money, he stayed in a budget motel.
為了省錢，他住便宜的汽車旅館。

14. five-star restaurant 五星級餐廳
To impress his girlfriend, he took her to a five-star restaurant.
為了討好他的女友，他帶她去五星級餐廳。

15. greasy spoon 便宜小飯館
The poor student usually eats in a "greasy spoon."
這位窮學生通常在便宜小飯館裡用餐。

課文重點分析 Analysis

1. abroad（副詞）在國外，例如：

   go abroad 到國外

   study abroad 出國留學

   travel abroad 國外旅行

2. travel agency 是旅行社，travel agent 是旅行社的業務員。

3. apply for a visa 辦簽證，apply to a graduate school 申請研究所，apply for a job 申請工作，apply for a loan 辦貸款。
   application（名詞）例如：an application letter 申請工作的信函
   applicant（名詞）申請者。

4. 這篇文章比較參加 tour group（跟團）還是 independent travel（自助旅遊）哪個好。比較兩者的優劣，可以用 On the

one hand...(一方面來說)，On the other hand...(另一方面來說)，注意 "on the other hand..." 立場相反，與「另外」(in addition) 的意思不同。

5. 注意：住旅館要用動詞 stay in a hotel，因為是短期待在旅館，而不是長期住(live)在旅館裡。

6. traveling abroad 當主詞時，動詞 travel 要改為動名詞 traveling。

✏️ 克漏字 Cloze

> formalities, budget motel, tour group, travel agent, visa, five-star, itinerary, sightseeing, Spring Festival, package deal

1. My ＿＿＿＿＿＿＿ found a very cheap flight for me.

2. Everyone in this ＿＿＿＿＿＿＿ will be over 60 years old.

3. Some countries do not require visitors to have a ＿＿＿＿＿＿＿.

4. The ＿＿＿＿＿＿＿ restaurant was very expensive.

5. Buying a ＿＿＿＿＿＿＿ made her trip much cheaper.

6. My mother loves to go ＿＿＿＿＿＿＿ when she travels.

7. Buying a house involves many _____.

8. I changed my _____ so that I could stay in Paris longer.

9. A _____ is a much cheaper place to stay than a resort.

10. The _____ is Taiwan's longest holiday.

✐ 選擇適當的詞性 Multiple Choice

_____ 1. You can _____ your own roommates in that dorm. (a)choice (b)choose (c)chose

_____ 2. She _____ to go to Thailand for her last vacation. (a)choice (b)choose (c)chose

_____ 3. The new worker wasn't given a _____ about his schedule. (a)choice (b)choose (c)chose

_____ 4. I am taking a _____ of Japan this summer. (a)tour (b)touring (c)tourism

_____ 5. I can tell he is a _____ by the clothes he is wearing. (a)tourism (b)tour (c)tourist

_____ 6. For some countries, _____ is a major source of income. (a)tourism (b)tour (c)tourist

_____ 7. This restaurant's tables are too _____. (a) grease
(b) greasy (c) greasily

_____ 8. The worker's hands were covered with _____.
(a) grease (b) greasily (c) greasy

_____ 9. You should wear _____ clothing to this wedding.
(a) formally (b) formal (c) formality

_____ 10. For the boss's son, the job interview was just a
_____. (a) formally (b) formal (c) formality

_____ 11. The poor student cannot afford the _____ of
eating in a restaurant. (a) luxury (b) luxuriously
(c) luxurious

_____ 12. She lives in a _____ apartment. (a) luxury
(b) luxuriously (c) luxurious

翻譯 Translation

1. 我喜歡自助旅行而不喜歡跟團。

_____

2. 旅行社業務員會幫你辦簽證和買機票。

_____

3. 我討厭辦出國手續。

_____

4. 我覺得跟團比較適合我的父母。

_____

5. 他喜歡跟團，因為每件事都安排得很好。

_____

6. 她不喜歡觀光或購物時有導遊伴隨著。

_____

7. 你住過五星級飯店嗎？

_____

8. 我不能決定住豪華度假村好還是便宜的汽車旅館好。

_____

9. 即使(Despite)有跟團的輕鬆，我還是喜歡自助旅遊的自由。

_____

10. 每次外出用餐(dine out)，我總是選便宜的小餐館。

_____

2 Lantern Festival Fun CD1 Track2

After the five-day₁ springtime celebration, Taiwanese, stuffed₂ with holiday food and a few kilos heavier, return to their homes. Most people, however, are still absorbed in the holiday atmosphere until the end of the Lantern Festival, which falls on the 15th day of the first lunar month. Indeed, for Taiwanese, the Lantern Festival marks the end of the New Year celebration.

The festival gets its English name from the bright, decorative lanterns that people carry under the full moon. During the evening of this year's festival, the most popular lantern will be the rooster, this year's Chinese zodiac animal₃. Lion dances and fireworks₄ will add to the excitement, and people can have fun guessing riddles at lantern fairs.

Like every holiday, this one has its special foods. In particular, sticky-rice₅ balls, which symbolize family unity, are a customary snack. With its colorful traditions and tasty foods, this centuries-old festival still offers pleasure for the young and old alike.

2　歡樂在元宵

　　五天的年假一過，肚裡滿塞著年菜，暴增了好幾公斤的台灣人回到了自己的家。不過，大多數人還沈浸在年節的氣氛裡，直到過完了元宵節。沒錯，農曆一月十五日的元宵表示新年活動的結束。

　　元宵節的英文名字「燈籠節」取自於十五月圓時人們在月下提著亮晶晶、妝點漂亮的燈籠。今年的元宵節晚上，最有人氣的燈籠當然是今年的生肖——公雞。另外，舞獅和煙火增添節慶的歡樂，人們在燈會猜燈謎也十分有趣。

　　如同每個節慶一樣，元宵節也有它特殊的應景食物，湯圓，這個依慣例要吃的小點心，象徵全家團圓。元宵節雖有好幾世紀長，以其色彩繽紛的傳統和可口的食物，還是能提供老少咸宜的樂趣。

✏ 生字 Vocabulary

1. **be stuffed** 被塞飽了
   At the wedding banquet, the guests were stuffed with dozens of dishes of expensive food.
   在結婚喜宴時，賓客被許多價格昂貴的菜給塞飽了。

2. **holiday food** 節慶食物
   Most festivals in Taiwan are associated with special kinds of holiday food.
   許多台灣的節慶跟特別的節慶食物有關。

3. **be absorbed in** 沈浸
   The girl was so absorbed in reading her book that she didn't hear her mother call her.
   這個女孩沈浸在書裡，沒聽到媽媽在叫她。

4. **mark** 標示
   Teacher's Day marks Confucius's birthday.
   教師節是孔夫子的生日。

5. **rooster** 公雞
   The rooster crowed loudly every morning, waking up the farmer's family.
   公雞每天早上喔喔啼，喚醒農夫一家人。

6. **zodiac animal** 生肖
   Because she was born in 1952, her zodiac animal is the dragon.

因為她生於1952年，所以生肖是龍。

7. lion dance 舞獅

Many tourists came to Taipei to watch the lion dance.

許多觀光客來台北看舞獅。

8. fireworks 煙火

Special occasions in Taiwan are often celebrated with fireworks.

台灣特殊慶典活動會放煙火慶祝。

9. guess riddles 猜燈謎

Even school children like to guess riddles during the Lantern Festival.

連學校的小朋友都喜歡在元宵節猜燈謎。

10. lantern fair 燈會

His grandmother always goes to the lantern fair with her friends.

他的祖母總是和朋友趕燈會。

11. sticky-rice balls 湯圓

My mother makes delicious sticky-rice balls each February.

每年二月我的媽媽會搓湯圓。

12. symbolize 象徵

At the New Year's Eve dinner, families in Taiwan leave some of the fish to symbolize that they have food to spare.

除夕吃年夜飯時，台灣家庭留些魚肉不吃，象徵他們有多餘的食物留下(年年有餘)。

13. centuries-old 幾世紀之久的

A centuries-old violin was found in Los Angeles.
一把幾世紀之久的小提琴在洛杉磯找到了。

✎ 課文重點分析 Analysis

1. 在台灣年假通常連續5-7天，2005年的新年年假只有5天。
   五天的年假five-day是形容詞，後面的day不加s。其他用數
   字當形容詞的情形例子還有：a ten-story building, a seven-
   year-old girl, a three-meter-long road, a ten-centimeter-thick
   carpet。

2. stuffed with...是形容 Taiwanese 的子句，這句話將 who are
   省略。原句為：Taiwanese, who are stuffed with holiday
   food and a few kilos heavier, return to their homes.
   stuff(動詞)塞入，stuffed 被塞入、吃飽了，stuffing 填塞
   物。

3. 12 Chinese zodiac animals 依次如下：rat, ox, tiger, rabbit,
   dragon, snake, horse, goat, monkey, rooster, dog, boar。問
   人西洋星座是什麼要說：What is your sign? 若問人屬什麼要
   說：What is your Chinese zodiac sign? 你若屬鼠可以說：I
   was born in the year of the rat.

4. fireworks 煙火和 firecrackers 鞭炮不同，不過放煙火和放鞭
   炮的動詞卻一樣：set off fireworks 和 set off firecrackers。

5. sticky rice（糯米）是很黏的米，sticker（貼紙）是黏的紙。

🖉 克漏字 Cloze

> are absorbed in, fireworks, lantern fair, lion dance, mark, rooster, sticky-rice balls, symbolizes, was stuffed, zodiac animal

1. She loved to watch the _____ during the Lantern Festival.
2. _____ look beautiful against the night sky.
3. The _____ protected the other chickens.
4. A rose often _____ love.
5. Taipei has a very popular _____ each year.
6. She felt sick after she ate so many _____.
7. His _____ is the snake.
8. She changed her name to _____ her new life.
9. The children _____ watching television, so they don't hear their mother calling them.
10. After the boy ate all the snacks, he _____.

✎ 選擇適當的詞性 Multiple Choice

_____ 1. Donna likes to _____ her dumplings with pork and cabbages. (a)stuffed (b)stuffing (c)stuff

_____ 2. Our Christmas stockings are always _____ with goodies after Santa comes. (a)stuffing (b)stuffed (c)stuff

_____ 3. The _____ in my pillow(枕頭)is so lumpy that I cannot sleep. (a)stuffing (b)stuff (c)stuffings

_____ 4. Jane collects _____ and often trades them with her friends. (a)stick (b)stickers (c)sticky

_____ 5. The table was _____ after Nicholas knocked over the glue(膠水)bottle. (a)sticker (b)sticking (c)sticky

_____ 6. The sight of a mouse will easily _____ my cat. (a)excite (b)excited (c)exciting

_____ 7. There was so much _____ in the air as the parade started down the street. (a)excite (b)exciting (c)excitement

_____ 8. Turning eighteen was very _____ for Robert because it meant that he was an adult.(a)excited

(b) exciting　(c) excitement

_____ 9. Mark was so _____ about going on vacation that he couldn't sleep the night before. (a) excited (b) exciting　(c) excitement

_____ 10. Colleen loves pigs and has chosen to _____ her room in pig pictures. (a) decorating (b) decorating　(c) decorate

_____ 11. Lindsay hired an interior designer to pick out the _____ for her new house. (a) decorations (b) decorate　(c) decorating

_____ 12. The plate on the wall is only _____ as it serves no useful purpose. (a) decorative　(b) decorate (c) decorations

_____ 13. Sarah uses a towel to _____ the water leaking around the bathtub. (a) absorbing　(b) absorb (c) absorbed

_____ 14. John was so _____ in the TV show he was watching that he did not hear the doorbell ring. (a) absorb　(b) absorbed　(c) absorbing

✏ 翻譯 Translation

1. 我最喜歡的一道菜(dish)是糯米雞。

_____

2. 今年的年假放幾天?

_____

3. 元宵節是(fall on)農曆一月15日。

_____

4. 元宵節表示(mark)春節慶祝活動的結束。

_____

5. 她得到她的英文名字是從一個明星的中間名字取來的。

_____

6. 每當元宵節晚上,小朋友在滿月下提著燈籠。

_____

7. 元宵節你吃了湯圓了嗎?

_____

8. 去年的生肖是什麼?

_____

9. 你是屬什麼的?

_____

10. 我屬虎。

Tomb Sweeping Day
CD1 Track3

Unlike most traditional holidays which are based on[1] the lunar calendar, Tomb Sweeping Day follows the solar calendar—falling on April 5th. During this festival, as its name shows, the entire family (except for[2] married[3] daughters) goes to the tombs of their ancestors to "sweep" their burial grounds.

To complete this annual[4] task, family members have to carry a broom and a dust pan to sweep the dirt around the tombs, a shovel to dig out weeds, and pruning shears to trim the overgrown trees. One last touch[5] is to water[6] the plants with a barrel of water.

After the manual labor is done, the spiritual ritual begins. The family arranges bouquets of flowers in vases, sets up offerings in front of the tomb, and burns ghost money and incense. As family members pray for their ancestors' continued protection, they strengthen the bond between the living and the departed[7] family members.

清明掃墓節

四月五日清明掃墓節跟其他農曆的節慶不一樣，是過陽曆，這一天，正如節名所示，除了嫁出去的女兒外，全家人都到祖先的墳墓「掃」他們的墓地。

為了完成這一年一度的工作，家人需要提著掃帚、拿著畚箕將墓地周遭的塵土掃除一清，鏟子用來挖除雜草，剪子用來修剪茂長的樹，最後再用一桶水來澆花草。

動手的工作完成後，才開始神聖的儀式。家人把花束插在花瓶裡，祭品陳設在墓前，接著燒香和燒紙錢。當家人祈求祖先繼續保佑子孫之際，也強化了生者與死者間的凝聚力。

✏ 生字 Vocabulary

1. Tomb Sweeping Day 清明節
   On Tomb Sweeping Day, people pay their respects to their ancestors and clean family graves.
   清明節人們打掃祖墳，並向祖先致意。

2. solar calendar 陽曆
   Most international businesses use the solar calendar instead of the lunar one.
   大多數跨國公司用的是陽曆，而不用陰曆。

3. burial ground 墳地
   Her grandparents chose a burial ground outside of the city.
   她的祖父母在市郊選了一塊墳地。

4. annual 每年的
   Filing income tax is an annual duty for all citizens.
   報所得稅是所有公民每年一度的義務。

5. dust pan 畚箕
   My mother uses a dust pan when she sweeps.
   我的媽媽掃地時用畚箕。

6. shovel 小鏟子
   He bought a new shovel so that he could plant a tree.
   他買了一把新的小鏟子來種樹。

7. pruning shears 修樹的剪子
   The gardener used the pruning shears to shape the heavy

vines.

這位園丁用了一把修樹的剪子去修剪濃密的蔓藤。

8. a barrel of 一桶

The price of a barrel of oil is very high.

一桶石油的價錢很高。

9. manual 手的

The boy was determined to get a college degree to avoid a job that required manual labor.

這個男孩決心拿到學士學位，以免從事需要用手操作的工作。

10. spiritual ritual 神聖的儀式

Burning incense is an important part of this spiritual ritual.

燒香是神聖儀式的一部份。

11. bouquet 束（花）

Her boyfriend sent her a bouquet of roses for her birthday.

為了她的生日，男友送了一束玫瑰。

12. vase 花瓶

My mother has a beautiful vase that she keeps full of flowers.

我媽媽有個美麗的花瓶，裡面插滿了花。

13. bond 凝聚力

There is often a close bond between a mother and her children.

母親和兒女之間往往有一種親密的關係。

14. departed 離開的

His departed relatives left him a fortune.

他去世的親人留給他一筆財富。

✒ 課文重點分析 Analysis

1. base...on 和 be based on 根據、依據，是很容易混淆的兩個詞，請看例句，注意主詞的不同：

We based our decision on her recent detailed report.

Our decision was based on her recent detailed report.

我們的計畫是依據她最近的詳細的報告訂定的。

The director based his movie on her novel.

導演根據她的小說拍電影。

The movie was based on her novel.

這部電影是根據她的小說拍的。

2. except for 和 besides 是容易混淆的兩個字，except for 是除了……之外沒有，或是除了……之外，其他人都要；...besides 是除了……之外還有。例如：

Besides John and Mary, many people are interested in this activity.

除了John和Mary之外，還有許多人對這個活動有興趣。

（John和Mary和其他人一樣，都對這個活動都有興趣。）

Except for John and Mary, so far no one is interested in this activity.

除了 John 和 Mary 之外，到目前為止還沒有人對這個活動有興趣。（只有 John 和 Mary 有興趣，其他人都沒興趣。）

Except for John and Mary, all my friends are interested in this activity.

除了 John 和 Mary 之外，我所有朋友都對這個活動有興趣。（只有John 和 Mary 沒興趣，所有朋友都有興趣。）

3. marry 和 be married, get married 也常容易混淆，請看例句：

John married Mary two years ago.

John 和 Mary 兩年前結婚。

They got married two years ago.

他們兩年前結婚了。

Now they are a married couple.

現在他們是一對結了婚的夫妻。

marriage是名詞，例如：

They had a happy marriage.

他們的婚姻很美滿愉快。

4. annual(形容詞)，annually(副詞)

The Dragon Boat Festival is an annual holiday.

端午節是一年一度的節慶。

We celebrate this holiday annually.

我們每年都慶祝這個節慶。

5. the last touch 是最後一個步驟。touch 也可以當動詞，意思
   是感動；be touched 是被感動的；touching（形容詞）是動人
   的。例如：

   Her speech touched many people's hearts.

   她的演講打動許多人的心。

   I was touched by this novel.

   我被這本小說感動。

   The way he looked at her was very touching.

   他看她的眼神真動人。

6. 注意第二段最後一句的兩個water，前者是動詞（澆水），後者
   是名詞（水）。

7. the departed person是指逝去的人。

   departure是名詞，離去。例如：

   His sudden departure surprised me.

   他的突然離去讓我驚訝。

✏ 克漏字 Cloze

> annual, shovel, dust pan, pruning shears, manual, bouquet, bond, departed, a barrel of, Tomb Sweeping Day

1. The students gave their friend a _____ of flowers after her performance.

2. My father used the _____ to trim the bushes.

3. Lantern Festival is an _____ holiday.

4. She often thinks of her recently _____ grandfather.

5. She swept the broken glass into the _____.

6. He used a _____ to dig a deep hole.

7. The students felt a close _____ with their favorite teacher.

8. Even though he lives in Taipei, he always goes back to Tainan for _____.

9. She brought her family _____ oysters.

10. Many students do not want to do any _____ labor.

✐ 選擇適當的詞性 Multiple Choice

_____ 1. The old man is afraid of evil _____. (a) spirit (b) spirits (c) spiritual

_____ 2. The monk was the group's _____ leader. (a) spirit (b) spirits (c) spiritual

_____ 3. This ancient _____ is still practiced today. (a) rite

(b) ritual (c) ritually

_____ 4. She feels a close _____ with her sister. (a) bonding (b) bonded (c) bond

_____ 5. The roommates quickly _____ and became close friends. (a) bonding (b) bonded (c) bond

_____ 6. When will this train _____? (a) depart (b) departure (c) departed

_____ 7. We still remember our _____ relatives. (a) depart (b) departure (c) departed

_____ 8. Her _____ for Paris was unexpected. (a) depart (b) departure (c) departed

_____ 9. Do you know how to _____ that bush? (a) prune (b) pruning (c) pruned

_____ 10. This overgrown tree needs to be _____. (a) prune (b) pruning (c) pruned

_____ 11. My mother chose to _____ my brother in a beautiful cemetery. (a) buried (b) bury (c) burial

_____ 12. The _____ ceremony was very moving. (a) buried (b) bury (c) burial

✐ 翻譯 Translation

1. 我祖父天天用掃帚畚箕掃地。

   _____

2. 我用陽曆不用陰曆。

   _____

3. 除了我妹妹以外，今年每個人都去掃了我們祖先的墓地
   (burial grounds)。

   _____

4. 最後的工作(touch)是把一束花插在一個花瓶裡。

   _____

5. 昨天下午我們用鏟子除雜草。

   _____

6. 除了除草之外，我們還剪茂長的樹。

   _____

7. 我們祈求我們祖先的繼續保佑。

   _____

8. 他每天都用一桶水澆植物。

   _____

9. 你燒了紙錢和燒過香了嗎？

_____

10. 跟他不一樣，我喜歡做動手的工作。

_____

Row, Row the Dragon Boat CD1 Track4

Dragon Boat Festival, as its name suggests, is celebrated with exciting races of boats decorated[1] like dragons. On the fifth day of the fifth lunar month, teams row their boats to drum beats, racing to grab a flag at the end of the course.

Besides the spectacular boat racing, wrapping zong zi is a popular holiday activity. These sticky-rice treats memorialize[2] Qu Yuan, a minister and a poet during the Warring States Period. When he drowned himself after failing to end government corruption, people threw zong zi into the river to discourage the fish from eating him.

Other holiday customs include hanging medicinal herbs[3] on the front door and trying to stand an egg on its end at noon. Like so many other ancient traditions, these actions are supposed to[4] prevent evil and encourage good luck. Whether we believe in these customs or not, Dragon Boat Festival is a great beginning to the summer season.

划，划，划龍舟

端午龍舟節，如其名所示，以舉辦精彩的龍舟大賽來慶祝節慶，農曆五月五日當天，船隻妝點成龍身，隊員隨著鼓聲努力向前划，比賽搶水道終點的旗幟。

除了場面壯觀的賽龍舟，包粽子也是流行的節慶活動，這些糯米製的食物，是為了紀念戰國時期的一位大臣也是詩人，屈原。屈原無力挽回朝廷的腐敗，投江自殺，人們扔粽子到江裡，以阻止魚兒啃食屈原。

其他慶祝習俗還包括在大門口懸掛藥草和正午立蛋。如同許多其他古代傳統，這些活動都為了避邪納吉。不管我們信或不信，端午節一過，盛夏也隨之到來。

✏️ 生字 Vocabulary

1. **Dragon Boat Festival** 端午節
   Dragon Boat Festival is my brother's favorite holiday.
   端午節是我哥哥最愛的節日。

2. **decorate** 妝點、裝潢
   She decorated her new house before her friends came to visit.
   朋友來看她之前，她把新家裝潢一新。

3. **team** 隊伍
   All of the teams wanted to win the race.
   所有的隊伍都想贏得這場比賽。

4. **drum beats** 鼓聲
   The drum beats made the race more exciting.
   鼓聲使這場比賽更刺激。

5. **grab** 搶
   The child grabbed the candy from his mother's hand.
   這個小孩從媽媽手裡搶了糖果。

6. **course** 道
   The horses raced around the course.
   馬繞著跑道比賽。

7. **spectacular** 場面壯觀的
   Taipei 101 is a spectacular building.
   台北101是棟很壯觀的建築。

8. wrap 包

   Wrapping presents is always fun.

   包禮物總是很有趣。

9. Warring States Period 戰國時代

   During the Warring States Period, China was not unified.

   戰國時代中國分裂不統一。

10. corruption 腐敗、貪污

    The newspaper accused the police department of corruption.

    這家報紙指控警局貪污。

11. discourage 不讓、阻止

    He put new bars on his house's windows to discourage thieves.

    他把家裡的窗戶裝了新的鐵窗阻止小偷進入。

12. medicinal herbs 藥草

    Traditional Chinese medicine uses many medicinal herbs.

    傳統中藥用了許多藥草。

課文重點分析 Analysis

1. 這裡的decorated是被動 (passive voice)，指船被妝點成像龍一樣。These boats are decorated like dragons.

   decorate也可以用作主動 (active voice)。例如：

   He decorated his new house with lots of posters.

   他用海報裝潢他的新居。

2. memorialize 和 memorize 這兩個字常容易混淆，前者是紀念某人或某件事；後者是記住或背起來某首詩或某件事。例如：

Every year we should memorialize this disaster.

每年我們都應該紀念這個災難。

His sister memorized some Buddhist scriptures.

他的姊姊背下某些佛教經文。

3. medicine 藥(名詞)例如：take medicine 服藥。

medicinal 有藥效的、藥用的。例如：medicinal plants 藥性植物。

herb 香草、藥草。例如：Chinese herbs 中藥草。

herbal 藥草的。如：herbal tea 香草茶，如 peppermint tea 薄荷茶。

4. suppose 和 be supposed to 很容易混淆，suppose 想、認為，例如：

I suppose you are an expert in this field.

我想你是這方面的專家。

be supposed to 應該，例如：

I am supposed to finish all the work by June.

我應該在六月之前把工作做完。

克漏字 Cloze

> decorated, team, spectacular, wrapping, corruption, discourage, grab, Dragon Boat Festival, course, medicinal herbs

1. Students have a holiday from school on _____.

2. The thief tried to _____ the woman's money.

3. The business _____ its front window to attract customers.

4. Eastern Taiwan has some _____ scenery.

5. _____ is a problem in many governments.

6. My grandmother prefers to use _____ instead of Western medicine.

7. Video cameras in stores _____ thieves from stealing merchandise.

8. The German _____ won first prize.

9. The race _____ was very muddy from the heavy rain.

10. _____ dumplings takes some practice.

✐ 選擇適當的詞性 Multiple Choice

_____ 1. Did you _____ your room by yourself?
(a)decoration (b)decorate (c)decorated

_____ 2. The students are _____ the classroom for the
holiday. (a)decorating (b)decorate (c)decorated

_____ 3. The _____ on the cake was beautiful. (a)decorating
(b)decorate (c)decoration

_____ 4. Her children love to _____ presents. (a)wrapping
(b)wrap (c)wrapped

_____ 5. The clerk _____ the gift in fancy wrapping paper.
(a)wrapper (b)wrap (c)wrapped

_____ 6. _____ leftover food in plastic wrap keeps it fresh.
(a)Wrapping (b)Wrap (c)Wrapped

_____ 7. Teachers should not _____ students who are
doing their best. (a)discourage (b)discouraging
(c)discouraged

_____ 8. The bad news was _____. (a)discourage
(b)discouraging (c)discouraged

_____ 9. The doctor told him he must take his _____ every
day. (a)medical (b)medicine (c)medicinal

_____ 10. The clinic had a _____ smell. (a)medical (b)medicine (c)medicinal

_____ 11. The restaurant's food is delicious since the cook uses fresh _____. (a)herb (b)herbal (c)herbs

_____ 12. Many people in Taiwan prefer _____ medicine. (a)herb (b)herbal (c)herbs

_____ 13. I _____ that it will rain tomorrow. (a)suppose (b)supposed (c)supposing

_____ 14. They were_____ to clean the room, but they did not. (a)suppose (b)supposed (c)supposing

🖊 翻譯 Translation

1. 昨天我媽媽教我包粽子。

   _____

2. 我對台灣的慶典習俗不太熟悉。

   _____

3. 你看了電視上壯觀的龍舟大賽了嗎？

   _____

4.　哪一隊在水道終點搶到了旗幟？

_____

5.　端午節中午你成功地把蛋立起來了嗎？

_____

6.　她的家妝點得像皇宮。

_____

7.　派對上的每個人正在隨著鼓聲起舞。

_____

8.　小孩寫文章紀念他們的父親。

_____

9.　我的祖父常在山裡採(pick)藥草。

_____

10.　掛這幅圖在前門是為了避邪。

_____

5 Chinese Valentine's Day

CD1 Track5

Lovers in Taiwan are lucky because they have two romantic₁ holidays in one year. Besides₂ February 14th, Western Valentine's Day, they also celebrate Chinese Valentine's Day.

This holiday, which takes place₃ on the 7th day of the 7th lunar month, memorializes the cowherd Niu Lang's once-a-year reunion₄ with the weaver girl Zhi Nu. On this day some people go to matchmaker temples to pray for love and marriage.

Now, however, this traditional holiday has become increasingly commercialized₅. People often say that money can't buy you love, but owners of flower shops, candy stores, restaurants, hotels, and jewelry stores would disagree.

中國情人節──七夕

　　台灣的情人可真幸運，因為他們一年有兩個浪漫的節日。除了二月十四日西方的情人節外，他們還可以慶祝中國情人節。

　　這個節日是農曆的七月七日，為了紀念牛郎和織女一年一度的團圓。這天有些人會去月老廟祈求愛情與婚姻。

　　不過現在這個傳統的節日卻逐漸商業化了。人們常說金錢不能幫你買到愛情，不過花店、糖果店、餐廳、旅館和珠寶店的老闆可不同意這種說法哦。

✎ 生字 Vocabulary

1. **Chinese Valentine's Day** 七夕（中國情人節）
   Chinese Valentine's Day is a traditional Chinese holiday for lovers.
   七夕是中國傳統情人節。

2. **romantic** 浪漫的
   Sending flowers to your girlfriend is very romantic.
   送花給你的女朋友可真浪漫。

3. **besides** 除了……之外
   Besides being handsome, my boyfriend is also kind.
   除了英俊外，我的男友心地還很好。

4. **take place** 發生
   The concert takes place every summer.
   這個演唱會每年夏天都會舉行。

5. **the 7th day of the 7th lunar month** 農曆七月七日
   The seventh day of the seventh lunar month is a special time for lovers.
   農曆七月七日對情人而言是特別的日子。

6. **memorialize** 紀念
   They celebrate this holiday to memorialize their former president.
   他們慶祝這個節日以紀念他們的前任總統。

7. **cowherd** 牛郎

A cowherd takes care of cows.
牛郎照顧牛群。

8. once-a-year 一年一度的

A once-a-year event seems more special than something that happens every day.
一年一度的事件似乎比每天發生的事還特別。

9. reunion 團圓

After my boyfriend came back from the army, we had a happy reunion.
我的男友從部隊回來後，我們有個愉快的團聚。

10. matchmaker temple 月老廟

Women who are looking for husbands sometimes go to matchmaker temples.
女人想祈求姻緣時有時會去月老廟。

11. pray for 祈求

At these temples, women pray for love.
在這些廟裡，女人祈求愛情。

12. increasingly 逐漸地

Increasingly, men give women presents on Chinese Valentine's Day.
愈來愈多的男人開始在中國情人節送女人禮物。

13. commercialized 商業化

Traditional holidays sometimes become commercialized because businesses see them as a way to make more money.

傳統的節慶有時會變得十分商業化，因為商家把它們視為賺錢的大好機會。

14. owner 老闆

She is the owner of the Italian restaurant.

她是這家義大利餐廳的老闆。

15. jewelry store 珠寶店

He bought his girlfriend a ring at a jewelry store.

他幫女友在珠寶店買了一枚戒指。

🖉 課文重點分析 Analysis

1. romantic 羅曼蒂克（形容詞），romance 羅曼史（名詞）。例如：

He used to be very romantic, but now he seldom shows his love to his wife.

他過去很羅曼蒂克，現在卻很少向太太表達情愛。

He likes to boast about his romance.

他喜歡吹噓他的羅曼史。

2. besides 除了……外還有……

Besides having a scooter, she has a car.

除了摩托車外，她還有一輛車。

In addition to roses, he bought chrysanthemums for his girlfriend.

除了玫瑰外，他還買了菊花給他的女友。

except for除了……外沒有……

Except for roses, he didn't buy anything for his girlfriend.

除了玫瑰外，他什麼都沒買給他的女友。

3. It takes place on the 7th day of the 7th lunar month. 指這個
   節慶的日期。

   例如：Christmas takes places on December 25th.

   聖誕節是12月25日

4. once-a-year reunion。once-a-year 是形容 reunion 的形容
   詞。 例如：

   We see each other once a year.(副詞)

   我們一年見一次面。

   We held once-a-year reunion last week.(形容詞)

   上星期我們舉行一年一度的團聚。

5. TV commercials 電視廣告(名詞)，commercialize 商業化
   (動詞)，commercialized 商業化的(形容詞)，例如：

   This TV commercial shows a bias against women.

   這個電視廣告對女人有偏見。

   The school tried to commercialize its research projects.

   學校想將研究計畫商業化。

   His latest films have become increasingly commercialized.

   他最近的電影愈來愈商業化了。

✐ 克漏字 Cloze

> matchmaker, Western, besides, commercialized, jewelry store, romantic, memorialize, reunion, took place, owner

1. _____ being selfish, he is also very stingy.

2. Many events _____ in this little town last year.

3. The mayor set up his statue in front of the building to _____ his good deeds.

4. She has been a professional _____ for many years. Many couples have gotten married through her arrangement.

5. I bought a ring for my daughter's birthday present at a _____.

6. We hold a family _____ twice a year.

7. They like to dine out at a _____ restaurant with candles lit on each table.

8. Christmas Day has become more and more _____. Most people forget about its origin.

9. The _____ of that restaurant married my cousin

last Sunday.

10. I would rather take Chinese herbal medicine instead of going to see a _____ doctor.

🖉 選擇適當的詞性 Multiple Choice

_____ 1. Many people would like more _____ in their marriages. (a)romance (b)romantically (c)romantic

_____ 2. My boyfriend gave me a _____ Valentine's Day card. (a)romance (b)romantically (c)romantic

_____ 3. They wanted to _____ her birthday at an expensive restaurant. (a)celebrate (b)celebration (c)celebrated

_____ 4. The holiday _____ lasted for many hours. (a)celebrating (b)celebrate (c)celebration

_____ 5. Airline ticket prices usually _____ in the summer. (a)increasing (b)increased (c)increase

_____ 6. Raising children is _____ expensive. (a)increasing (b)increasingly (c)increased

_____ 7. The new movie was a _____ success.

(a)commerce (b)commercial (c)commercially

_____ 8. Even religious holidays like Christmas have become
_____. (a)commercial (b)commercialized
(c)commercialization

_____ 9. I _____ with your idea. (a)disagree
(b)disagreeable (c)disagreement

_____ 10. The couple had a _____ about how
to spend money. (a)disagree (b)disagreeable
(c)disagreement

✎ 翻譯 Translation

1. 我每年都會去月老廟祈求平安。

_____

2. 這家花店的老闆很羅曼蒂克。

_____

3. 我期待(look forward to having)一年一度的高中同學會
(reunion)。

_____

4. 除了他以外,我沒有別的男友。

_____

5. 我請媒人幫我找個理想的伴侶(companion)。

_____

6. 這家廟已經變得愈來愈商業化了。

_____

7. 他很幸運因為他的糖果店生意很好(good business)。

_____

8. 慶祝中國情人節還不太流行(popular)。

_____

9. 你曾經到廟裡去祈求婚姻嗎？

_____

10. 中國情人節是農曆七月七日。

_____

Dos and Don'ts during Ghost Month CD1 Track6

Every holiday₁ has its special customs. Taiwanese believe that in the 7th month of the lunar calendar₂, or Ghost Month, ghosts will come out from the Gates of Hell and wander around in the living world.

The best way₃ to treat these wandering souls₄ is to burn ghost money for them to spend and offer food and drinks as sacrifices for ghosts to dine on. In the middle of the month, water lanterns light the way for the souls of the drowned₅.

During this month, activities such as weddings, swimming, and moving should be put on hold until all the ghosts return to the underworld, and the Gates of Hell finally close.

鬼月該做和不該做的事

　　每個節慶都有它特殊的習俗。台灣人相信農曆七月（或叫做鬼月），鬼會從鬼門關裡跑出來，在人世間到處遊蕩。

　　招待這些孤魂野鬼最好的方法就是燒紙錢讓他們花，提供食物飲料當祭品供他們享用。七月中旬時，水燈點亮溺死鬼(回家)之路。

　　這個月諸如婚禮、游泳、搬家等的活動都得暫停，直到所有的鬼都回到陰曹地府，鬼門終於關上為止。

✎ 生字 Vocabulary

1. **dos and don'ts** 該做和不該做的事
Every culture has special dos and don'ts about how to behave.
每個文化都有教大家行為舉止的規範：什麼該做、什麼不該做。

2. **lunar calendar** 農曆
Many holidays in Asia are based on the lunar calendar.
許多在亞洲的節慶都是根據農曆來的。

3. **Ghost Month** 鬼月
Taiwanese believe that ghosts come to Earth during Ghost Month.
台灣人相信鬼月時鬼都來到人世。

4. **Gates of Hell** 鬼門關
When the Gates of Hell open, ghosts can come to Earth.
當鬼門關一開，鬼都來到人世。

5. **living world** 人世間（陽界）
During this month, ghosts can move about in the living world.
在這個月，鬼魂可以在人間遊走。

6. **wandering souls** 孤魂野鬼（也有人戲稱為 homeless ghosts）
We offer food to wandering souls or homeless ghosts because they have no family members to remember them.
我們給孤魂野鬼食物，因為他們沒有自己的家人記得他們。

7. **ghost money** 冥紙錢

We burn ghost money to give ghosts some cash to spend in hell.

我們燒紙錢給鬼魂一些「現金」在地獄花用。

8. sacrifice 供奉（動詞）、祭品（名詞）
People sacrifice food and drinks to please the ghosts.

人們供奉食物和飲料來「取悅」鬼魂。

9. dine on 享用飲食
Ghosts dine on the food that people set on special tables for them.

鬼魂享用人們為他們放在特定桌子上的食物。

10. water lantern 水燈
People light water lanterns to guide ghosts who died from drowning.

人們點亮了水燈指引溺水鬼（回家之路）。

11. souls of the drowned 溺死的鬼
During Ghost Month, many people avoid swimming because they are afraid that the souls of the drowned will pull them underwater.

鬼月時，許多人避開游泳活動，因為他們害怕溺死鬼會把他們拉入水中（淹死）。

12. wedding 婚禮
It is unlucky to have a wedding during Ghost Month.

在鬼月舉行婚禮很不吉利。

13. moving 搬家

Moving to another house is not a good idea during this month.

在這個月搬家不是個好的想法。

14. put on hold 暫停

Until this month is over, we should put our plans on hold.

我們應該暫停所有的計畫直到這個月結束為止。

15. underworld 陰間

After Ghost Month, ghosts have to return to the underworld.

鬼月一過，鬼魂必須返回陰間。

✏️ 課文重點分析 Analysis

1. holiday 可以當作假期 vacation，也可以做節慶 festival。

2. in the 7th month of the lunar calendar 是農曆七月的說法，和陽曆七月 (July) 說法不相同。

3. The best way to...them is to...for...to... 例如：

   The best way to educate them is to build a school for them to study in.

   教育他們的最好方式，是蓋一間學校給他們讀。

   The best way to please the ghosts is to offer sacrifices for them to dine on.

   討好鬼魂的最好方法，是供奉祭品讓他們饗用。

4. wandering souls 是指這些靈魂正在四處遊蕩。These souls are wandering about.

5. drowned 被淹死，the drowned 被淹死的人，the poor 窮人，
the rich 富人。

克漏字 Cloze

> ghost money, dos and don'ts, dine on, on hold, wandering, souls, underworld, wedding, lunar calendar, sacrifices

1. Many people are curious about what ghosts are doing in the
   _____.

2. Because of her mother's sudden death, she had to put the
   party _____.

3. After her mom's funeral, she burned a lot of _____
   for her mom to use in another world.

4. Many farmers in Taiwan plant their crops based on the
   _____.

5. She decided to cancel her _____ because she
   wasn't sure she had chosen the right person.

6. They have prepared an abundance of _____ for
   gods and goddesses in the temple.

7. Every weekend we _____ salmon and imported fruit.

8. The little girl was _____ about because she couldn't find her mom.

9. Some people believe if they have been good during their lives, their _____ will go to heaven.

10. Before you go on a job interview, here are some _____ you should know.

✐ 選擇適當的詞性 Multiple Choice

_____ 1. Be careful not to _____ in the lake. (a)drown (b)drowned (c)drowning

_____ 2. A stranger _____ in the river last summer. (a)drown (b)drowned (c)drowning

_____ 3. His religious _____ made him a better person. (a)believe (b)believed (c)belief

_____ 4. Do you _____ in ghosts? (a)believe (b)believed (c)belief

_____ 5. On vacations, he likes to _____ around without any specific plans. (a)wandering (b)wander (c)wandered

_____ 6. They spent the summer _____ around Europe.
(a) wandering (b) wander (c) wandered

_____ 7. She always _____ her grown-up children like kids. (a) treat (b) treats (c) treating

_____ 8. He is used to _____ his employees like slaves.
(a) treat (b) treats (c) treating

_____ 9. I don't _____ the same beliefs that he does.
(a) hold (b) held (c) holding

_____ 10. The romantic couple _____ hands in the park last night. (a) hold (b) held (c) holding

_____ 11. I _____ green tea every day. (a) drink (b) drank (c) drinking

_____ 12. He _____ too much wine last night. (a) was drinking (b) drunk (c) drank

翻譯 Translation

1. 當你考大學入學考試時，記住以下 (the following) 該做和不該做的事。

2. 因為颱風侵襲台灣，考試因而被延期。

_____

3. 他已經準備了許多祭品討神歡喜。

_____

4. 對待這些孤魂野鬼最好的方法是燒冥錢。

_____

5. 因為我病了，我得延後我的婚禮。

_____

6. 我上星期提供食物和飲料給鬼享用。

_____

7. 下個月鬼會從鬼門關出來。

_____

8. 水燈幫溺水鬼照亮路。

_____

9. 鬼正在人世間遊蕩。

_____

10. 鬼月時搬家應該暫停。

_____

The Moon Festival CD1 Track7

The Moon Festival, also known as the Mid-Autumn Festival, takes place on the15th day of the 8th lunar month. The most popular legend about this holiday tells the story of Chang E, the wife of the brutal$_1$ emperor Houyi. After Chang E stole and took$_2$ her husband's magical$_3$ elixir, she flew$_4$ to the moon.

On Moon Festival night, Taiwanese families like to get together to eat moon cakes and pomelos, a fruit that is in season$_5$ around this time. People also enjoy$_6$ looking at the full moon and imagining that they see Chang E dancing there.

Holding barbeques on this night is a popular new tradition. Everywhere in yards or in parks, people grill$_7$ chicken legs and pork chops on racks. These days, it seems that food is more important than the meaning of the festival!

中秋節

　　農曆八月十五日是中秋節，這個節慶最廣為人知的傳說是述說暴君后羿的妻子嫦娥的故事。嫦娥偷吃了丈夫神奇的長生不老藥後，飛上了月宮。

　　中秋節這天晚上，台灣家庭喜歡團聚在一起，吃月餅和當令的文旦，也喜歡一邊看滿月，一邊想像嫦娥在月宮跳著舞。

　　中秋夜晚舉辦烤肉活動也成了受歡迎的新傳統，在家中庭院或公園裡，人們在烤架上烤著雞腿和豬排。近年來吃似乎比節令的意義來得重要。

🖊 生字 Vocabulary

1. **the Moon Festival** 中秋節（又稱 the Mid-Autumn Festival）
   After the Moon Festival, the weather in Taiwan usually cools down a bit.
   中秋節後，台灣的天氣通常會稍微涼一點。
   Bakeries make a lot of money during the Mid-Autumn Festival.
   糕餅店在中秋節賺很多錢。

2. **legend** 傳說
   Parents often tell children legends about famous heroes.
   父母常常告訴子女有關英雄的傳說故事。

3. **Chang E** 嫦娥
   According to one version of the story, Chang E was a beautiful fairy.
   根據某個故事的版本，嫦娥是個美麗的仙女。

4. **brutal** 殘暴
   The brutal ruler ordered many people's deaths.
   這個殘暴的統治者判許多人死刑。

5. **Houyi** 后羿
   Houyi was an archer who once shot down nine suns.
   后羿是個射手，他曾射下九個太陽。

6. **take** 服（藥）(take, took, taken)

Kids will not take medicine because of its bitter taste.

小孩因為藥苦而不肯服藥。

7. elixir 長生不老藥

In many stories, a magical elixir is supposed to guarantee eternal life.

許多故事中神奇的長生不老藥可保證讓人永生不死。

8. moon cake 月餅

Moon cakes can have many different fillings.

月餅有很多不同的餡。

9. pomelo 文旦

Pomelos have a light green skin, a round bottom, and a pointed top.

文旦有淡綠色的皮，下圓上尖。

10. in season 當令的

Fruit will be fresher and cheaper if you buy it when it is in season.

買當令的水果比較新鮮便宜。

11. full moon 滿月

Gazing at the full moon can be very romantic.

遠望滿月可真羅曼蒂克！

12. hold barbeques 辦烤肉

Many families hold barbeques in city parks.

許多家庭在城市公園裡烤肉。

13. yard 院子

Children enjoy playing outside in their yard.

小朋友喜歡在外面院子裡玩耍。

14. grill 在火上烤

Grilled chicken always tastes especially delicious.

碳烤雞腿吃起來總是特別有風味。

15. pork chop 豬排

They ordered pork chops for dinner.

晚餐他們點了豬排。

16. rack 烤架、衣服架子

The best way to cook meat outside is on a rack.

最好燒肉的方法就是在烤架上燒烤。

課文重點分析 Analysis

1. brutal emperor，brutal（殘忍的）是形容詞，形容名詞 emperor。brutality（殘忍）名詞。

2. 注意英文某些名詞一定要跟某些動詞搭配在一起，例如：tell a lie（說謊）、take elixir 和 take medicine（服藥）、take a risk（冒險）。

3. magical elixir，magical（神奇的）是形容詞，magic（魔術）是名詞。

4. fly的動詞三態變化：fly, flew, flown。

5. fruit in season 和 seasonal fruit 都是當令的水果。

6. 有些動詞後面接不定詞（to＋動詞），有些動詞後面接動名詞（動詞＋ing）。例如：

I want to participate in the speech contest.

我要參加演講比賽。

I enjoy listening to hip-hop music.

我喜歡聽嘻哈音樂。

7. grill 烤肉架、grill 烤肉、grilled 被烤過的。

克漏字 Cloze

legend, pomelos, brutal, grilled, moon cakes, elixir, racks, take, barbeque, season

1. She told me all the details about the _____ murder case.

2. The emperor was longing for eternal life, so he asked his men to search for an _____ for him.

3. His newly released novel was based on an ancient Japanese _____.

4. Family members are holding a _____ in the courtyard.

5. It's better to eat vegetables in _____ because farmers don't use as much pesticide.

6. _____ chicken legs will go perfectly with beer.

7. They like to shop for cheap clothes hung on the _____ at the department store.

8. Don't eat too many _____ during the Moon Festival, or you may get a stomachache.

9. How many tablets of medicine should I _____ after each meal?

10. _____ are the most famous local product in Madou (麻豆).

✏ 選擇適當的詞性 Multiple Choice

_____ 1. The film is based on a Chinese _____. (a)legendary (b)legend (c)legends

_____ 2. _____ Even children know about this _____ hero. (a)legendary (b)legend (c)legends

_____ 3. _____ The police finally caught the _____ killer. (a)brutally (b)brutal (c)brutality

_____ 4. _____ He treated his enemy _____. (a)brutally

(b) brutal (c) brutality

_____ 5. It is fun to _____ food outside. (a) grilling
(b) grilled (c) grill

_____ 6. The little boy asked for more _____ meat.
(a) grilling (b) grilled (c) grill

_____ 7. Spring is her favorite _____. (a) season
(b) seasons (c) seasoning

_____ 8. My mother added more _____ as she cooked.
(a) season (b) seasons (c) seasoning

_____ 9. The student took the train because he couldn't afford
to _____. (a) fight (b) flew (c) fly

_____ 10. The bird _____ right by my window. (a) fight
(b) flew (c) fly

_____ 11. She has _____ to Hong Kong many times.
(a) flown (b) flew (c) fly

✐ 翻譯 Translation

1. 你要怎麼慶祝今年的中秋節？

2. 感冒（catch a cold）最好不要服藥。

_____

3. 后羿是個殘暴的國王。

_____

4. 根據中國傳說，嫦娥是個美麗的仙女。

_____

5. 我不喜歡那個月餅的口味（flavor）。

_____

6. 他正在烤架上烤豬排。

_____

7. 你打算在中秋節的晚上舉辦烤肉會嗎？

_____

8. 我不相信一個神奇的長生不老藥存在。

_____

9. 文旦是秋天的當令水果。

_____

10. 他昨晚飛去美國了。

_____

Social Issues
社會議題

High Teenage Suicide Rate in Taiwan CD1 Track8

According to the Department of Health's statistics, an average of 9 Taiwanese people per day dies by suicide[1]. Many of the victims are teenagers. Why would young people who seem to have a bright future commit suicide?

Although today's teenagers enjoy a higher standard of living than their parents had at their age, they often lack[2] guidance and emotional support. When problems with their studies, families, or relationships cause stress[3], this "strawberry generation" is not always able to deal with the pressure.

To reduce this generation's suicide rate, adults need to recognize the warning signs of depression[4] and suicide. By teaching teenagers how to handle stress and depression, the older generation can help prevent the tragic[5] waste of young lives.

台灣青少年的高自殺率

　　根據衛生署的統計數字，平均每天就有9個台灣人死於自殺，其中許多死者是青少年。為什麼這些看起來前途光明的年輕人會自殺呢？

　　雖然今日的年輕人比他們的父母在他們這樣的年齡時，享受更高水準的生活，可是他們生活上卻缺少指引，情感上也少了支柱。當他們在求學、家庭或交友各方出了問題，造成生活緊張時，這群「草莓族」總是無法應付。

　　為了減少這一代年輕人的自殺率，大人需要時時察覺他們憂鬱和自殺的前兆，藉由教導青少年如何處理心理壓力和憂鬱，上一代的人可以防範青少年無謂犧牲生命所造成的悲劇。

生字 Vocabulary

1. suicide rate 自殺率
   This year's suicide rate in Taiwan is the highest ever.
   今年台灣的自殺率最高。

2. statistics 統計數字
   Statistics show that women live longer than men.
   統計數字顯示女人比男人活得久。

3. average 平均
   An average of only 50% of the population votes in that country.
   在那個國家平均只有50％的人口投票。

4. die by suicide 死於自殺
   Each year, over 3,000 people in Taiwan die by suicide.
   在台灣每年超過3000人死於自殺。

5. victim 受害者
   The government has provided financial aid to earthquake victims.
   政府提供地震受災戶金錢補助。

6. commit suicide 自殺
   Some lonely older people are prone to commit suicide.
   有些孤獨老人常容易自殺。

7. standard of living 生活水準
   Taiwan's standard of living is much higher than it was 40

years ago.
台灣的生活水準比40年前高很多。

8. at their age 在他們的年齡
Parents often tell children how hard they had to work at their age.
父母總告訴子女,他們在兒女這個年齡時工作有多辛苦。

9. guidance 指引
Adults need to give young children a lot of guidance to teach them how to behave.
大人應該給小孩很多指引,教他們如何守規矩。

10. emotional support 感情支助
Parents can give their children emotional support when they are upset.
父母在孩子不開心時,可以給予感情支助。

11. relationship 交友(指感情方面)
His relationship with his girlfriend made him very happy.
他跟女友的交往讓他很開心。

12. stress 緊張、壓力
She took a vacation to get away from the stress of her job.
她去度假,以離開工作帶來的壓力。

13. strawberry generation 草莓族
Some people call today's young people the "strawberry generation."
有人稱今天的年輕人為「草莓族」。

14. deal with 應付

A high school teacher has to deal with many students.

一個高中老師得應付許多學生。

15. recognize 認出

I could recognize him because I had seen his picture.

我可以認出他來，因為我曾經看過他的照片。

16. warning sign 預警

Many diseases have warning signs.

許多疾病都有預警。

17. depression 憂鬱症

Depression is a common mental illness in many modern societies.

憂鬱症是許多現代社會中很普通的精神疾病。

18. tragic 悲劇的

The 921 earthquake was a tragic event.

921大地震是個悲劇事件。

✏ 課文重點分析 Analysis

1. die by suicide 死於自殺，die of a heart attack 死於心臟病，die in a car accident 死於車禍。注意介系詞的不同。

2. lack是動詞，例如：He lacks confidence in his leadership.
   他缺乏領導人的信心。（注意：lack 後不能加 of）
   lack 也可以當名詞，例如：

His lack of confidence has become a big problem.

他的沒信心成為一大問題。

3. stress 是名詞，例如：

Because she is a mother and the CEO(Chief Executive Officer)of a computer firm, she has a lot of stress.

因為她是母親又是電腦公司的執行長，她承受許多壓力。

stressful 形容生活緊張，例如：

Her life is stressful.

她的生活很緊張。

be stressed out 形容人的緊張，例如：

He was stressed out before the exam.

他考前很緊張。

4. depressed 是形容詞，例如：

After her dog's death, she was very depressed.

狗死後，她很憂鬱。

depression 是名詞，例如：

Her depression worried all of her friends.

她的憂鬱症令朋友擔心。

5. tragic 是形容詞，例如：

His tragic death has alerted the government to the soaring crime rate.

他悲劇性的死亡使政府警覺到不斷上升的犯罪率。

tragedy 悲劇

The recent tsunami in South Asia was a tragedy.

最近南亞的海嘯是個悲劇。

✎ 克漏字 Cloze

> tragic, committed suicide, recognize, warning signs,
> lacks, victims, stress, statistics, at your age, deal with

1. Last year many depressed unemployed workers

   _____.

2. Many crime _____ went to the organization asking
   for support.

3. Recently she has gone through a tremendous amount of

   _____.

4. _____, I'd already gotten married and had three
   children.

5. I could hardly _____ her after she changed her
   hairstyle.

6. There were no _____ of their sudden divorce.

7. This new teacher didn't know how to _____ picky parents.

8. According to _____, there are many people in the city suffering from serious depression.

9. What he _____ is confidence and self-discipline to finish his research paper.

10. We were shocked by the _____ news of his sudden death.

🖋 選擇適當的詞性 Multiple Choice

_____ 1. I will _____ you to the restaurant. (a) guidance (b) guided (c) guide

_____ 2. He needs a lot of _____ in order to finish this tough assignment. (a) guidance (b) guided (c) guide

_____ 3. He shows a lot of _____ every time his team loses the game. (a) emotions (b) emotion (c) emotional

_____ 4. He was very _____ at the funeral. (a) emotions (b) emotion (c) emotional

_____ 5. My mom always _____ my decision whether she agrees with it or not. (a) support (b) supports

(c) supportive

_____ 6. His family has been very _____ throughout his career. (a) support (b) supporting (c) supportive

_____ 7. My boyfriend is my biggest _____. (a) supporter (b) supporting (c) supportive

_____ 8. After 10 years away from home, he could barely _____ his own children. (a) recognizes (b) recognition (c) recognize

_____ 9. He received much _____ for his excellent book. (a) recognizes (b) recognition (c) recognizing

_____ 10. He was very _____ after his girlfriend broke up with him. (a) depressing (b) depression (c) depressed

_____ 11. _____ is a major cause of suicide. (a) Depressing (b) Depression (c) Depressed

翻譯 Translation

1. 平均每天有9個人死於自殺。

2. 草莓族無法應付生活的壓力 (life's pressure)。

_____

3. 他的死完全沒有一點前兆。

_____

4. 青少年應該知道如何處理壓力。

_____

5. 許多自殺的「受害者」都是青少年。

_____

6. 我需要大人的指引和感情支柱。

_____

7. 台灣的生活水準比從前高了許多。

_____

8. 我幾乎聽不出是他的聲音。

_____

9. 他的母親不知道如何應付他的憂鬱症。

_____

10. 根據官方的 (official) 統計數字，台灣學生有很多壓力。

_____

9 Going Under the Knife
CD1 Track9

In the past[1], only fairy tale characters could be magically transformed from beast to beauty. Now, thanks to[2] cosmetic surgery, over a million Taiwanese a year have improved their faces or bodies. The most popular procedure in Taiwan is double eyelid surgery, which makes eyes look larger and rounder. Other common types of plastic surgery include nose jobs, breast augmentation, and tummy tucks.

Why are so many Taiwanese going under the knife? Many women think it will enhance their social lives and increase their self-esteem. Some parents even give daughters cosmetic surgery as a graduation present. Taiwanese men, on the other hand[3], often see plastic surgery as a way to improve their career opportunities. They want features that will be auspicious according to traditional Chinese face reading.

What all these people have in common is the fairy tale idea that if you change your body, you can transform your life. In a world that values appearance, people seem to have forgotten that beauty is only skin deep.

動刀整形

　　過去只有童話裡的角色才有可能魔幻似的由野獸化身為美女，現在因為有整形手術的幫忙，每年超過一百萬的台灣人可以改善他們的臉蛋及身體。在台灣最流行的療程是讓眼睛看起來比較大而圓的雙眼皮手術，其他普通的整形還包括隆鼻、豐乳和縮腹。

　　為什麼這麼多的台灣人喜歡挨這一刀？許多女人認為整形可以改善她們的社交生活和增強自信心，有的父母甚至把整形當成送女兒的畢業禮物。台灣男人反倒把整形當成改事業運的手段，他們想要的是中國面相學上一些吉利的臉部特徵。

　　這些人相同的地方是持童話上一樣的想法：你若「變身」，生活也會隨之而改。今日世界處處重視外形，人們似乎忘了，美色本是皮相而已。

✎ 生字 Vocabulary

1. fairy tale characters 童話角色
   Children often dream of being fairy tale characters.
   小孩通常夢想自己是童話中的角色。

2. transform 改變外貌
   She told the doctor that she wanted to be transformed into a beautiful woman.
   她告訴醫生，她想讓自己變成一個美麗的女人。

3. cosmetic surgery 美容
   Cosmetic surgery is now more affordable than it used to be.
   美容比從前讓人負擔得起。

4. procedure 療程
   Stars like Michael Jackson have had many different surgical procedures.
   明星像麥可傑克森，經過了多次的手術療程。

5. double eyelid surgery 割雙眼皮手術
   In Asia, double eyelid surgery is especially popular.
   在亞洲割雙眼皮手術格外流行。

6. plastic surgery 整形
   Plastic surgery is the common term for cosmetic surgery.
   整形是美容通用的說法。

7. nose job 隆鼻
   In Western countries, most people who have nose jobs want

smaller noses while people who have the procedure in Asia usually want prominent noses.

西方國家大多數的人美容鼻子，是想把鼻子弄小一點；可是在亞洲，人們卻想把鼻子弄高一點。

8. breast augmentation 隆乳

Breast augmentation is very popular among women in the United States.

美國女人流行隆乳。

9. tummy tuck 縮腹

Women who have had several children sometimes have tummy tucks to get back in shape.

女人生過幾個孩子後有時會動縮腹手術使身材恢復原狀。

10. under the knife 挨刀

Although the man needed heart surgery, he was afraid to go under the knife.

這個人必須動心臟手術，但他卻怕挨刀。

11. enhance 改善

The government set up a new system to enhance water quality.

政府設新系統以改善水質。

12. social life 社交生活

Career women often lead busy social lives.

職業婦女通常忙於社交生活。

13. self-esteem 自信心

After he was accepted into a good university, his self-esteem

improved.
他被一所好大學錄取之後，自信心大增。

14. graduation present 畢業禮物

She wanted her parents to give her a trip abroad as a graduation present.
她希望父母給她的畢業禮物是出國旅行。

15. auspicious 吉利的

The couple wanted to pick an auspicious day for their wedding.
這對情侶希望選個良辰吉日結婚。

16. face reading 看面相

Face reading is a traditional Chinese method of judging a person's character.
看面相是傳統中國判定一個人個性的方法。

17. skin deep 皮相

My mother always declared that beauty is only skin deep.
我媽媽總說美麗只是皮相。

🖎 課文重點分析 Analysis

1. In the past...Now...是古今對比的句型。例如：

In the past many people used rice cookers to steam their packed lunch. Now they use a microwave oven to heat up the lunch they buy at the convenience store. 過去許多台灣人

用電鍋蒸便當，現在他們則在便利商店用微波爐熱午餐。

2. thanks to, due to 和 because of 都是「因為」的意思，但前者和後兩者有些微的不同。請看例句：

Thanks to convenience stores, life in Taiwan is very easy.（比較正面）

多虧便利商店，生活在台灣非常容易。

Due to the typhoon, the highway was closed.（比較中性）

因為颱風，高速公路禁止通行。

Because of her high salary, she bought many expensive clothes.（比較中性）

因為她收入高，她買了許多昂貴的衣服。

3. 學生常誤解 on the other hand 的意思，其實on the one hand 是一方面來說，on the other hand 是另一方面來說，兩者是相反的意思。例如：

On the one hand, I enjoy the conveniences the cell phone brings to us. On the other hand, I hate the noises cell phones make.

一方面來說，我喜歡手機給我們的方便，另一方面卻討厭手機的噪音。

on the one hand 通常可以省略掉。

✒ 克漏字 Cloze

graduation present, characters, auspicious, double eyelid surgery, self-esteem, face reading, transformed, plastic surgery, fairy tales, tummy tuck

1. How many _____ are there in this play?

2. Kids with high _____ usually feel good about themselves; therefore, they seem to have an easier time handling conflicts and resisting negative pressures.

3. He just went through a _____. Now his beer belly is all gone.

4. My boss is interested in _____. The way he hires people is based on some special facial features.

5. Most _____ have a happy ending.

6. Most Chinese like to choose an _____ name for their new-born baby.

7. The _____ I got from my parents when I graduated from college was an English dictionary.

8. After breaking up with his girlfriend, he decided to go through _____ to change his fate.

9. Computers have _____ the ways we do our jobs and the ways we live.

10. After having _____, her eyes look brilliant and bigger.

✎ 選擇適當的詞性 Multiple Choice

_____ 1. The doctor recommended a _____ procedure to treat my back pain. (a)surgeon (b)surgery (c)surgical

_____ 2. The _____ skillfully completed the operation. (a)surgeon (b)surgery (c)surgical

_____ 3. He had brain _____ to remove a tumor. (a)surgeon (b)surgery (c)surgical

_____ 4. She hoped the etiquette classes would _____ her son into a gentleman. (a)transformation (b)transform (c)transformed

_____ 5. The block of clay was _____ into a beautiful sculpture. (a)transformation (b)transform (c)transformed

_____ 6. I can't wait to _____ from college. (a)graduate (b)graduated (c)graduation

_____ 7. His whole family came to attend his _____ ceremony. (a)graduate (b)graduated (c)graduation

_____ 8. He was not very _____ and preferred to do activities by himself. (a)society (b)social (c)socialize

_____ 9. _____ tends to look down upon people who are unemployed. (a)Society (b)Social (c)Socialization

_____ 10. She dreamed of having a _____ wedding ceremony. (a)tradition (b)traditional (c)traditionally

_____ 11. It is a family _____ to have a picnic on the beach on the first day of summer. (a)tradition (b)traditional (c)traditionally

_____ 12. Women _____ had to stay home to raise children. (a)tradition (b)traditional (c)traditionally

✏ 翻譯 Translation

1. 我小時候讀了很多童話書。

_____

2. 去年這所職校(vocational school)轉型為大學。

_____

3. 雙眼皮手術後，她的眼睛變得大又圓。

_____

4. 你注意到他隆鼻了嗎？Did you notice...

_____

5. 為了增加她的自信心，她願意挨一刀。

_____

6. 他選了一個吉利的日子結婚。

_____

7. 你認為整形可以改善你事業的機會嗎？

_____

8. 所有這些女人的共通點是她們對隆乳沒興趣。

_____

9. 為什麼許多台灣人重視外表？

_____

10. 因為搬到都市，我開始有了自己的社交生活。Thanks to...

_____

10 Foreign Brides (CD1 Track10)

Approximately 25% of recent marriages in Taiwan involved a "foreign bride." Many of these 300,000 cross-cultural marriages were arranged by Taiwanese agencies. Some₁ of these men were unable to find a wife in Taiwan, but others₁ wanted a wife whom they thought would be more "submissive₂" than the typical Taiwanese woman.

Unfortunately, these marriages do not always go smoothly. The wives sometimes find themselves the victims of social prejudice and domestic violence. Because they face language, cultural, and legal barriers in Taiwan, they often feel like second-class citizens. Moreover₃, many of their children, the "new Taiwanese" also suffer learning difficulties.

To solve these difficulties, private groups and public social welfare organizations have begun several helpful programs. These organizations provide services like free Mandarin classes, child care workshops, legal aid, and hotlines. While₄ these professional efforts are extremely important, we can also help these foreign brides. We should treat these women with respect and recognize that they are now parts of Taiwan's increasingly international society.

外籍新娘

　　最近在台灣大約每百件婚姻中就有25人娶的是外籍新娘，這三十萬件的跨國婚姻多由台灣仲介安排，其中有些男人因為在台灣找不到太太，有的則希望娶他們認為比台灣女人來得「聽話」的太太。

　　可惜的是這些婚姻並非都很順遂，有些外籍新娘成為社會歧視和家庭暴力的受害者，又因為她們在台灣得面臨語言、文化、和法律各方面的隔閡，常使她們覺得自己是次等公民，她們生的「新台灣之子」也常遭遇學習困難之苦。

　　為解決這些問題，民間團體和公立社會福利機構已展開許多協助計畫，它們提供的服務有免費的中文課、育子研習班、法律協助和熱線等。這些專業的努力固然重要，我們每個人也能幫忙這些外籍新娘，尊敬她們，肯定她們現在是台灣愈來愈國際化社會的一員。

✏️ 生字 Vocabulary

1. **foreign brides** 外籍新娘
   Many of Taiwan's foreign brides come from Vietnam.
   許多台灣外籍新娘來自越南。

2. **cross cultural** 跨國
   Raising children in a cross-cultural marriage is difficult.
   養育跨國婚姻的小孩特別困難。

3. **submissive** 聽話、服從
   Traditionally, wives were expected to be submissive to their husbands.
   傳統上妻子得服從丈夫。

4. **social prejudice** 社會歧視
   Some people in Taiwan hold social prejudice against people from Southeast Asia.
   有些台灣人歧視東南亞人。

5. **domestic violence** 家庭暴力
   Because domestic violence involves husbands and wives, police sometimes do not want to get involved.
   因為家庭暴力涉及夫妻問題，警察因而不願置身事內。

6. **language barrier** 語言隔閡
   Many foreign workers face a language barrier in Taiwan because they do not speak much Mandarin.
   許多外勞在台灣面臨語言障礙，因為他們不太會說中文。

7. cultural barrier 文化隔閡
Sometimes cultural barriers make it difficult for foreigners to feel comfortable in Taiwan.
有時文化隔閡使外國人在台灣很難覺得舒服。

8. legal barrier 法律障礙
Because of legal barriers, newly arrived foreign brides cannot work for their first three years in Taiwan.
因為法律障礙，剛來台灣三年的外籍新娘不能工作。

9. second-class citizens 次等公民
For many years, Taiwan's aborigines were treated like second-class citizens.
許多年來台灣的原住民被當成次等公民。

10. new Taiwanese 新台灣之子
Many "new Taiwanese" develop language skills slowly.
許多新台灣之子語言能力發展遲緩。

11. social welfare organizations 社福機構
Social welfare organizations try to solve many different problems in Taiwan.
社福機構試著解決許多台灣難題。

12. Mandarin 中文
Mandarin is one of the most widely used languages in the world.
中文是世界上最多人使用的語言之一。

13. workshop 研習班

Many schools set up a series of stress-management workshops to help students deal with stress.

許多學校開壓力處理班來幫助學生處理壓力。

14. legal aid 法律協助

Some organizations offer legal aid to people who cannot afford a lawyer.

有些機構提供請不起律師的人法律協助。

15. hotline 熱線

People can call a hotline to get help with their problems.

人們打電話給熱線，請他們幫忙解決問題。

✎ 課文重點分析 Analysis

1. 列舉兩種不同的狀況時可用 some...; others... 例如：

Some volunteers helped foreign brides deal with domestic affairs; others taught them Mandarin.

有的義工幫外籍新娘處理家庭事務，有的教她們中文。

2. submissive 形容詞、submit 動詞、submission 名詞

She doesn't like being a submissive wife.

她不喜歡做個順服的太太。

She has to submit her report by Friday.

她必須在星期五之前交報告。

The city could be bombed into submission.

這個城市可能被炸得很慘，只好投降。

3. moreover(另外)是連接詞，與 in addition, besides 和 furthermore用法相同。

4. while是although的意思。

✏ 克漏字 Cloze

> Mandarin, social prejudice, hotline, legal aid, domestic violence, language barrier, submissive, legal barrier, second-class citizens, foreign bride

1. The injured woman is a victim of _____.

2. The American student came to Taiwan to learn to speak _____.

3. His mother wanted him to marry a _____.

4. Foreign maids are often treated like _____.

5. The depressed student called a _____ for advice.

6. Because her English was poor, she faced a _____ when she moved to Canada.

7. Foreign workers sometimes face _____ in Taiwan.

8. The poor man had to ask for _____ because he could not afford to pay a lawyer.

9. My grandfather believed women should be _____ to men.

10. Due to a _____, he could not work in the United States.

✐ 選擇適當的詞性 Multiple Choice

_____ 1. This medical treatment does not _____ any pain.
(a) involve (b) involving (c) involved

_____ 2. He did not want to get _____ in politics.
(a) involve (b) involving (c) involved

_____ 3. She wants to find a job _____ computer skills.
(a) involve (b) involving (c) involved

_____ 4. The literary _____ helped him publish his novel.
(a) agent (b) agency (c) agents

_____ 5. I used a real estate _____ to buy my house.
(a) agencies (b) agency (c) agents

_____ 6. Traditionally, children were supposed to be _____ to parents. (a) submission (b) submit (c) submissive

_____ 7. The army bombed the city into _____.
(a) submission (b) submit (c) submissive

_____ 8. They have been _____ for ten years. (a) marry
(b) marrying (c) married

_____ 9. Do you want to _____ your boyfriend? (a) marry
(b) marriage (c) married

_____ 10. My parents do not have a happy _____. (a) marry
(b) marriage (c) marring

_____ 11. Can you help me _____ my papers?
(a) organization (b) organized (c) organize

_____ 12. My younger brother is a highly _____ person.
(a) organization (b) organized (c) organize

_____ 13. This _____ is 30 years old. (a) organization
(b) organized (c) organize

翻譯 Translation

1. 他們的婚姻是經由一家仲介安排。

_____

2. 大約有30％的大學畢業生找不到工作。

_____

3. 他覺得自己好像一個次等公民。

_____

4. 我們對待外籍新娘應該予以尊重。

_____

5. 多少外籍新娘是家暴的受害者？

_____

6. 由於(due to)語言和文化很大的隔閡，他們終於離婚了(got divorced)。

_____

7. 許多新台灣人(New Taiwanese)在學校有(suffer)學習困難。

_____

8. 他只想娶個聽話的女人。

_____

9. 這個組織提供像法律協助和熱線的服務。

_____

10. 你要參加免費的中文班和育子研習班嗎？

_____

Telescams （CD1 Track11）

"If you want your child back, you'd better transfer NT$ 30,000 into my account immediately!" This phone message, accompanied by the sound of a child crying in the background₁, represents every parent's worst nightmare. But as the parents rush out to pay the ransom, they have been victims of a fake kidnapping.

Fake kidnapping is just one of many telephone scams that have become common in Taiwan. Another popular swindle involves₂ phone calls or text messages₃ informing people that they can collect tax refunds, prizes, or lottery money by entering their account number at an ATM. An even trickier method plays on people's fears of fraud. In this scam, a bogus text message claims that the victim's credit card or ATM card has been used by swindlers. Of course, the "correction" of the problem at the ATM is what actually gives the scam artists your money.

How can you avoid₄ being a gullible victim of a scam? Be very suspicious₅ about phone calls or text messages from strangers, and never, ever, touch that confirm button, or your savings will be transferred to a swindler's pocket in less than a minute.

電話騙錢術

「如果你想要孩子回來,最好馬上轉三萬塊到我的帳戶裡!」這通搭配著孩子哭聲的電話內容,十足代表每位父母最糟的夢魘。當父母急著付贖款的當兒,他們自己卻成了假綁架的受害者。

假綁架只是台灣許多普通電話騙錢的一種手法,其它的騙術還有利用電話或手機簡訊,通知人們到提款機輸入帳戶號碼以提領退稅金、獎品或樂透獎金。更巧妙的方法是玩弄人們怕被騙的心理,用假簡訊告知你的信用卡或提款卡已被騙子盜刷,當然,到提款機上做任何「更動」,你的存款就真的被騙子騙走了

如何避免成為容易相信別人騙術的受害者?你得懷疑陌生人的電話或簡訊,還有千萬不要按提款機上的「確認」鍵,否則你的存款在一分鐘之內就進了歹徒的口袋裡了。

🖉 生字 Vocabulary

1. telescam 電話騙錢

   Telescams have become common in many countries that rely on the telephone.

   許多靠電話通訊的國家中電話騙錢十分普遍。

2. transfer 轉帳

   I wanted to transfer money from my account to my landlord's to pay my rent.

   我想從我的戶頭轉錢到我房東的戶頭，來付房租。

3. account 戶頭

   She has had the same bank account ever since she was in college.

   她從大學起就用相同的銀行戶頭。

4. ransom 贖款

   The kidnapper demanded a huge ransom to return the victim.

   綁匪要求一大筆贖款才放人。

5. fake kidnapping 假綁票

   A fake kidnapping can be just as emotionally disturbing as a real one to the parents.

   假綁票和真的一樣，讓父母情緒上受到波動。

6. scam 騙錢

   Criminals have recently used telephones, ATMs, and the Internet to develop new scams.

歹徒最近利用電話、提款機和網路發展新的騙錢方法。

7. swindle 詐騙
The man was accused of swindling over 200 people in July.
這個人被控在七月詐騙了200多人。

8 text message 手機簡訊
High school students enjoy sending text messages to their friends.
高中生喜歡送簡訊給朋友。

9. tax refund 退稅
Every year, he spends his tax refund on new clothes.
每年他都利用退稅的錢買新衣。

10. trickier 較精妙、詭詐的
Because of new technology, scams have become even trickier to detect.
因為新科技，騙錢術變得更詭詐而難以偵測。

11. fraud 詐騙
Crime rings often use illegally obtained information to commit fraud.
犯罪集團常利用非法得來的資訊行騙。

12. bogus 偽造的
The swindler made a bogus prize offer to get people to reveal their bank account numbers.
騙子提供偽造的獎金，誘使人們透露自己的銀行帳號。

13. scam artist 騙子

Scam artists are always thinking of new ways to cheat people out of their money.

騙子總是想出新招來騙取金錢。

14. gullible 易上當的

Many scams target gullible elderly people.

許多騙錢的目標，鎖定易上當的老人。

15. suspicious 可疑的

If you receive a suspicious package, you have to immediately inform the police.

如果你接到一個可疑的包裹，你得立刻告知警察。

16. confirm button 確認鍵

The ATM will not let you withdraw money until you hit the confirm button.

提款機不讓你提款，除非你按確認鍵。

17. savings 存款

My grandfather is living on the money in his savings account.

我的祖父靠他活期存款戶頭裡的錢過活。

✎ 課文重點分析 Analysis

1. which is accompanied by the sound of a child crying in the background 是形容 this phone message 的子句。

2. involve 意指 include（包括）。

3. 什麼樣的 phone calls 或 text messages？下面的子句有交代：which inform people that they can collect tax refunds, prizes, or lottery money。

4. avoid後面的動詞＋ing，例如：avoid going home, avoid having eye contact。其他接動詞＋ing 的動詞還有 enjoy doing homework late at night，postpone getting dressed for the party，finish drinking coffee。

5. suspicious 可疑的、多疑的，是形容詞，如：

   suspicious behavior 可疑的行為，a suspicious nature 多疑的個性。

   suspect 是動詞，重音在第二個音節如：

   I suspected his intention when he suddenly offered me a job.

   當他突然給我一個工作時，我懷疑他的動機。

   suspect 嫌犯，是名詞，重音在第一個音節，如：

   The main suspect in this murder case escaped from jail last night.

   這個兇殺案的主嫌昨晚越獄了。

✏ 克漏字 Cloze

account, ATM card, gullible, ransom, scams, suspicious, swindle, tax refund, text message, transfer

1. She lost her _____, so she can't withdraw money from the machine.

2. The kidnapper asked for a million dollars in _____.

3. He has a lot of money in his bank _____.

4. _____ people are often cheated.

5. She wanted to _____ her money to a different bank.

6. My father was _____ of every stranger he met.

7. He received a _____ from his girlfriend on his cell phone.

8. Everyone hopes to receive a large _____ from the government.

9. The criminal had many ideas for new _____.

10. The businessman planned to _____ his customers.

📝 選擇適當的詞性 Multiple Choice

_____ 1. My lawyer will _____ me in court. (a)represented (b)represent (c)representing

_____ 2. The _____ of our school successfully finished the task. (a)represent (b)representation (c)representative

_____ 3. The economy was _____ last year than it is now. (a)worse (b)worsening (c)worsen

_____ 4. The storm may _____ tonight. (a)worse (b)worsening (c)worsen

_____ 5. The criminal plans to _____ the businessman's child. (a)kidnap (b)kidnapper (c)kidnapped

_____ 6. Twelve children were _____ last year. (a)kidnap (b)kidnapping (c)kidnapped

_____ 7. The old man wanted to _____ the bottles and cans. (a)collector (b)collected (c)collect

_____ 8. She has a stamp _____. (a)collector (b)collection (c)collect

_____ 9. The man's actions seem very _____ to me. (a)suspect (b)suspecting (c)suspicious

_____ 10. I _____ that the student had cheated on his exam. (a)suspect (b)suspected (c)suspecting

_____ 11. I had to show my passport to _____ my identity. (a)confirmed (b)confirm (c)confirmation

_____ 12. I wrote down my _____ number for my flight. (a)confirmed (b)confirm (c)confirmation

_____ 13. Doctors often _____ lives. (a)safe (b)save (c)saving

_____ 14. He has been _____ money for years. (a)safe (b)save (c)saving

✐ 翻譯 Translation

1. 請轉台幣10000元到我的帳戶裡。

_____

2. 如果你要小孩回來，最好付贖款。

_____

3. 他成了一件假綁架的受害者。

_____

4. 你可千萬(never, ever)不可以按確認鍵。

_____

5. 他的存款已被轉到一個騙子的口袋裡了。

_____

6. 在少於一分鐘之內,她的存款不見了。

_____

7. 老人(elderly people)常容易成為(gullible)騙術的受害者。

_____

8. 昨天我被通知去領退稅。

_____

9. 你曾接過假簡訊嗎?

_____

10. 你得懷疑(Be suspicious)陌生人的電話。

_____

Taiwan's Legislative[1] Election CD1 Track12

Now that the election is behind us and the campaign season is over, life will be quieter, if less exciting. Hoping to win seats in the legislature, pan-blue, pan-green, and independent candidates invested[2] enormous amounts of time and money. Colorful banners lined the streets, and the sounds of slogans filled the air as supporters held rallies for their candidates.

After months of being bombarded[3] with ads, Taiwan's citizens cast[4] their ballots at their local polling stations. Even though voter turnout was lower than expected, more than nine million people marked their ballots inside voting booths and then waited for officials to count the vote.

While[5] victorious candidates celebrated the election results, others felt disappointed. Despite[6] some accusations of vote buying, the election proceeded smoothly, and now we can resume normal life.

12 臺灣立委選舉

　　選舉已過，選季也隨之結束，我們生活雖少了點刺激，不過終歸平靜。為了爭立法院席次，泛藍、泛綠和無黨籍候選人無不投下大把金錢和時間，色彩繽紛的旗幟沿街插放，支持者在候選人的造勢集會上，口號響徹雲霄。

　　被競選廣告長達數月疲勞轟炸的臺灣公民，上星期六都在各地的投票所投下一票。即使投票率不如預期，還是有九百多萬人在投票廂中圈選了心目中的人選，接著等候選務人員計票。

　　贏的候選人為選舉結果慶祝，落選者則難掩失望。不過，除了少數買票案子外，整個選舉過程還算順利，現在我們終於可以回復正常的生活了。

✎ 生字 Vocabulary

1. **legislative election** 立委選舉
   The legislative election did not attract as many voters as did the presidential election.
   立委選舉不像總統選舉一樣吸引大批選民來投票。

2. **campaign season** 選季
   During the campaign season, politicians from different parties held rallies to accuse other candidates of wrongdoing.
   選季開始時，許多不同政黨的政治人物舉行造勢活動，指控對方的不是。

3. **seat** 席次
   Each major party was hoping to win more seats in the legislature.
   每個主要的政黨都希望在立法院贏得較多的席次。

4. **legislature** 立法院
   Taiwan's legislature is composed of representatives from throughout the island.
   台灣的立法院是由全島選出來的代表組成。

5. **pan-blue** 泛藍
   Pan-blue candidates managed to keep a slim majority in the legislature.
   泛藍候選人在立法院保住些微多數。

6. **pan-green** 泛綠

President Chen helped campaign for pan-green candidates.

陳總統幫泛綠候選人站台。

7. independent candidate 無黨籍候選人

Independent candidates can take away votes from the major political parties.

無黨籍候選人會吸走一些大黨的選票。

8. banner 旗幟

Political banners are decorated with their party's colors.

各政黨用自己政黨專屬顏色來妝點選舉旗幟。

9. slogan 口號

As elections approach, trucks with loudspeakers broadcast political slogans.

接近選舉時,卡車上的大喇叭高聲播放政治口號。

10. rally 集會

Many candidates attended rallies held by their supporters.

許多候選人參加支持者辦的(造勢)活動。

11. (be)bombarded 被砲轟

Sometimes people feel bombarded by all the political advertisements.

有時人們覺得被政治(宣傳)廣告疲勞轟炸。

12. citizen 公民

All of Taiwan's citizens who are 20 years old or older are eligible to vote.

所有台灣年滿20歲的公民都有權投票。

13. cast their ballots 投票
Some people had to stand in line to cast their ballots.
有些人得排長龍投票。

14. polling station 投票所
The neighborhood polling station was crowded on election night.
投票當晚鄰近投票所擠滿了人潮。

15. voter turnout 投票率
Sometimes voter turnout can be influenced by the weather.
天候有時會影響投票率。

16. mark their ballots 在選票上圈選
In the 2000 presidential election in the United States, many voters in Florida made mistakes when they marked their ballots.
2000年美國總統大選期間，佛羅里達州許多選民圈選有瑕疵。

17. voting booths 投票廂
The curtain in voting booths gives the voter privacy.
投票廂的布簾讓選民保有隱私。

18. count the vote 計票
In Taiwan it usually only takes a few hours to count the vote.
在台灣只花幾個小時票就統計出來了。

19. victorious candidate 當選的候選人
Victorious candidates held large parties after the votes were counted.

選贏的候選人在選票統計出來之後，舉辦大派對（慶祝）。

20. election result 選舉結果

The election results surprised some people.

選舉結果讓人跌破眼鏡。

21. vote buying 買票

Officials claim that vote buying is less common than it used to be.

官員說買票情形沒有過去普遍。

22. resume 回復

Having dropped out of school for two years, he resumed his studies at the same college.

休學兩年後，他回原來的大學繼續求學。

✐ 課文重點分析 Analysis

1. legislative 立法的（形容詞），legislation 立法、制訂法令（名詞），legislator 立法委員（名詞），legislature 立法院（名詞）。legislature 立法院也可以叫做 legislative Yuan。legislator 立法委員也可以叫做 lawmaker。

2. invest 投資（動詞），investment（名詞）。例如：

I invested some money in the stock market.

我在股市投資了一些錢。

My investment in the stock market is not that big（I'm still

talking 5 digits).

我在股市投資的錢不大，不過也有五位數字。

3. bombard 主動：People bombarded her with questions.人們質問她問題。

   be bombarded 被動：He was bombarded with all kinds of questions by the audience. 他被觀眾不停質問了各式各樣的問題。

4. cast動詞三態變化為 cast, cast, cast。

5. 當要描寫一個對比情況；一勝一負，可以用While...開頭，注意：while在這裡不是「當」的意思。

6. despite（雖然、不顧）就是 in spite of 的意思。注意後面只能接名詞，如果要接句子，要用 despite the fact that...。例如：

   Despite his parents objections, he insisted on marrying the woman he loved.

   不顧父母的反對，他執意娶他所愛的女人。

   Despite the fact that I didn't have a college degree, I still could find a high-paying job.

   雖然我沒有大學學位，我還是找到了高薪的工作。

克漏字 Cloze

banners, bombarded, cast their ballots, citizens, count the vote, election results, independent candidates, polling station, rallies, voter turnout

1. After he voted, he waited eagerly to hear the _____.
2. The street was decorated with brightly colored _____.
3. _____ was much larger than expected.
4. _____ do not want to be connected with a political party.
5. She attended many campaign _____ for her favorite candidate.
6. The reporter _____ the president with questions.
7. American _____ are warned not to visit some countries.
8. The students were eager to _____ for the first time.
9. There is a _____ in my neighborhood.
10. In some large countries, it takes days to _____.

🖋 選擇適當的詞性 Multiple Choice

_____ 1. He raised his hands in _____ when he crossed the finish line ahead of the others. (a) victor (b) victory (c) victorious

_____ 2. The Boston fans let out a _____ cheer when the Red Sox finally won. (a) victor (b) victory (c) victorious

_____ 3. The candidates all campaigned heavily during the _____. (a) elected (b) elect (c) election

_____ 4. Though _____ by most voters, the mayor's approval rating gradually declined. (a) elected (b) elect (c) election

_____ 5. Citizens are encouraged to contact their _____ to share their views on various issues. (a) legislators (b) legislations (c) legislates

_____ 6. The _____ is responsible for making laws. (a) legislative (b) legislation (c) legislature

_____ 7. Many parents cannot wait until their children become _____ and move out of the house. (a) independence (b) independency (c) independent

_____ 8. Many college students take advantage of their newly gained _____ by staying out late. (a) independence (b) independency (c) independent

_____ 9. Many of Taiwan's citizens _____ their ballots yesterday. (a) casted (b) cast (c) casting

_____ 10. The troops _____ the city and killed a lot of people. (a) bombards (b) bombarded (c) bombarding

翻譯 Translation

1. 下次的立委選舉在什麼時候？

_____

2. 你猜無黨籍候選人會在立法院贏得幾席？

_____

3. 支持者幫他們的候選人舉辦（造勢）活動。

_____

4. 我們還得被競選廣告轟炸幾天？ How many more days...

_____

_____

5. 這次選舉的投票率只有43％。

_____

6. 今天下午四點以前你一定要到當地投票所投票。

_____

7. 他們什麼時候開始計票？

_____

8. 我不知道他們什麼時候宣布（announce）選舉結果。

_____

9. 這位候選人被控告買票。

_____

10. 選季時色彩繽紛的旗幟沿街插放。

_____

13 Lottery Fever (CD1 Track13)

Have you ever₁ dreamed of becoming₂ instantly₃ rich? This dream of easy money attracted many different kinds of people to Taiwan's Big Lotto. These people were not just buying lottery tickets; they were also buying hope. Although₄ the odds of hitting the jackpot were very slim, people always like to take a chance.

As lottery fever swept the island, many types of people stood in line at lottery stalls to buy tickets. Big Lotto players included housewives, businessmen, professional gamblers, and even very poor people. They used many different methods to pick what they hoped were lucky numbers. While₅ traditional people prayed at temples, some modern types let a computer pick numbers at random.

What all these people had in common was the hope of striking₆ it rich. The weak economy made this dream especially appealing. Even though Big Lotto players knew their chances of winning were small, the size of their dream was very large.

13 彩券熱

你曾經夢想一夕致富嗎？這種想獲取容易錢的美夢吸引許多不同的人去買台灣大樂透。他們不單是買彩券，還想買個「希望」。雖然得大獎的機會微乎其微，人們還是喜歡試試手氣。

當「彩券熱」橫掃台灣時，不同類型的人在投注站排隊買彩券。大樂透的玩家包括：家庭主婦、生意人和職業賭徒，連生活窮困的人都來參一腳。他們用不同的方法選他們希望的「明牌」。比較傳統的人在廟裡祈求明牌，一些觀念現代的人士則靠電腦隨意選號。

大家有志一同的是希望一夜致富，在疲弱的經濟下，這種夢想特別吸引人，雖然大樂透玩家知道獲勝機會很小，他們的夢可非常大。

生字 Vocabulary

1. **easy money** 得來容易的錢
   Everyone dreams of getting easy money without working for it.
   每個人都夢想贏得來容易的錢，卻不想努力賺取。

2. **Big Lotto** 大樂透
   Taiwan's Big Lotto always gives away a fortune to people in need.
   台灣大樂透總是捐出錢來給需要的人。

3. **lottery tickets** 彩券
   Some people borrowed money to buy lottery tickets.
   有些人借錢買彩券。

4. **odds are slim** 贏的機率很小
   Even though people know the odds are slim, they still hope to be the winner.
   即使人們知道中獎機率不高，他們還是希望自己會成贏家。

5. **hit the jackpot** 中頭獎
   If you choose the winning number, you will hit the jackpot.
   如果你下注下對了，就會中頭獎。

6. **take a chance** 試試手氣、冒險
   Gamblers love to take a chance.
   賭徒都愛冒險。

7. **lottery fever** 彩券熱

People referred to the excitement about the Big Lotto as lottery fever.

人們指稱，這種對大樂透的興奮的現象叫做「彩券熱」。

8. sweep 橫掃(sweep, swept, swept)

Whenever a lottery offers a large prize, interest will sweep the country.

每回彩券提供大獎時，人們對彩券的興趣會遍掃全國。

9. stand in line 排隊

Because he hoped to win the lottery, he was willing to stand in line to buy a ticket.

他因為想贏樂透，所以甘願排長隊買一張彩券。

10. lottery stall 投注站

Most people bought their tickets at lottery stalls.

大多數的人在投注站買彩券。

11. lucky numbers 幸運號碼(明牌)

Everyone hoped that their lottery ticket would have the lucky numbers.

每個人都希望他們買的彩券會有幸運號碼。

12. pray 祈禱

Some people prayed for good luck.

人們祈求好運。

13. temple 廟宇

Many people in Taipei went to Long Shan temple to pray that they would win.

許多在台北的人到龍山寺去祈求贏（大獎）。

14. pick numbers 選號

Using a computer to pick numbers is a modern idea.
用電腦選號是現代的觀念。

15. at random 隨意地（=randomly）

If you don't want to choose your own numbers, a computer program can choose them at random.
如果你不想自己選號的話，電腦可以幫你任意選號。

16. strike it rich 一夜致富（strike, struck, struck）

My brother bought five lottery tickets because he is dreaming of striking it rich.
我的哥哥買了五張彩券，他夢想一夜致富。

17. appealing 吸引人

The cold drinks were especially appealing on a hot day.
冷飲在大熱天特別吸引人。

✎ 課文重點分析 Analysis

1. Have you ever dreamed of...

   問別人經驗時用現在完成式。例如：

   Have you ever read this novel? 你讀過這本小說嗎？

   Have you ever seen this movie? 你看過這部電影嗎？

2. 介系詞 of 後面的動詞 become 要改為動名詞 becoming；

   the hope of striking it rich 也是同樣情形，strike 改為動名詞

striking。

3. instant（立刻）是形容詞，如：instant noodles 泡麵，instant food 速食，instant coffee 即溶咖啡。不過修飾形容詞或動詞時，要改用副詞 instantly。例如：

He was instantly attracted to her.

他立即被她吸引了。

He felt warm instantly.

他立刻覺得暖和起來。

4. although = though（雖然）Although he didn't go to school, he still managed to read and write. 他雖然沒有上過學，他還是會讀和寫。（＊注意 although 後面不能加 but,「雖然……但是……」是中文的表達法。）

5. while..., ...這是比較兩種不同類型的說法，例如：

While he likes watching TV, I prefer listening to music.

他喜歡看電視而我喜歡聽音樂。

While some students play basketball after school, others hang around in the Net Cafe.

有的學生放學後打籃球，而有的卻在網咖混。

6. strike 是打擊的意思，棒球場上的三振叫 three strikes。課文中 strike it rich 的 strike 是動詞，strike it rich 是個片語，意指突然致富，例如：

His mom struck it rich in the fast food business.

他的媽媽突然在速食業這行賺了大錢。

✎ 克漏字 Cloze

> lottery, swept, slim, pray, random, striking, jackpot, temple, stall, fever

1. The chances of her getting this job are very _____.

2. I wonder why so many people are standing in line at the lottery _____.

3. Many people believe if they go to the _____ more often, gods will bless them.

4. The winner will be the first person drawn at _____.

5. The clock was _____ eight when we walked into the classroom.

6. If I hit the _____, I will buy a brand new car.

7. Let me know who won the _____.

8. I am satisfied with what I have right now. I have nothing to _____ for.

9. When the storm _____ across Taiwan, it caused

chaos to the country's transportation network.

10. Taiwan's political _____ seems to be cooling down.

✎ 選擇適當的詞性 Multiple Choice

_____ 1. Her whole family was always _____. (a) luck
(b) lucky (c) luckiest

_____ 2. He hoped that he would have better _____ this
year than last year. (a) luck (b) lucky (c) luckier

_____ 3. He was hoping he would _____ it rich that day.
(a) strike (b) struck (c) striking

_____ 4. Ever since he was young, he had dreamed of
_____ it rich. (a) strike (b) struck (c) striking

_____ 5. Few people have actually _____ it rich in Las
Vegas. (賭城) (a) strike (b) struck (c) striking

_____ 6. Many students eat _____ noodles. (a) instantly
(b) instant (c) instance

_____ 7. When he saw the young woman, he _____ fell in
love. (a) instantly (b) instant (c) instance

_____ 8. Riding a bicycle is _____. (a) easily (b) ease
(c) easy

_____ 9. Although he did not study much, he passed his exam with _____. (a)easily (b)ease (c)easy

_____ 10. Action movies do not _____ to me. (a)appeal (b)appealed (c)appealing

_____ 11. The ad for the resort was very _____. (a)appeal (b)appealed (c)appealing

_____ 12. Taiwan's _____ is better now than it was a few years ago. (a)economy (b)economics (c)economist

_____ 13. Taking a bus is more _____ than taking a taxi. (a)economy (b)economical (c)economist

翻譯 Translation

1. 即使中獎的機會很小，大家還是排隊買彩券。。

_____

2. 我從來沒有玩過大樂透。

_____

3. 我想試試手氣看能不能中頭獎。

_____

4. 我祈求神幫我通過考試。

_____

5. 彩券熱去年橫掃台灣。

_____

6. 你的彩券是在這家投注站買的嗎？

_____

7. 他隨便選了一個學生當班長(the class leader)。

_____

8. 我從來不夢想我可以很快致富。

_____

9. 你上星期買了一張樂透彩券了嗎？

_____

10. 贏一大把錢的想法真吸引人。

_____

14 Betel Nut: Taiwanese Chewing Gum (CD1 Track14)

Betel nut, a mild narcotic[1], has been widely used in Asia for centuries. It is popular because of its cheap, pleasant buzz, and it's one of Taiwan's major cash crops, contributing enormously to the economy[2].

However, betel nut also has many critics. Environmentalists claim that growing so many betel palms causes erosion. Doctors claim that betel nut is responsible for Taiwan's high rate of oral cancer, and many people dislike seeing the red-stained saliva where it has been spit[3] on the sidewalk.

But the loudest objection to Taiwan's betel nut industry is to "betel nut beauties," the young girls who sell it. Because these girls wear skimpy[4] clothing and sit exposed[5] in glass booths, politicians contend they give Taiwan a sleazy image. Owners, however, insist that this is a decent job for these girls and argue that sexy images are used to sell many products today. With millions of Taiwanese chewing[6] betel nut, the controversy is not going to go away anytime soon.

檳榔：台灣口香糖

　　檳榔這種藥性溫和的「麻醉品」在亞洲廣為人食用已有好幾世紀的歷史，它廣為人喜愛的理由是價格不高但讓人覺得興奮。它是台灣主要的經濟作物之一，對台灣經濟成長貢獻很大。

　　不過批評檳榔的人也不少，環保人士聲稱廣栽檳榔造成水土流失，醫生也怪台灣的高口腔癌罹患率的始作俑者是檳榔，其他人則不喜歡看到嚼檳榔的人在人行道上亂吐紅色檳榔汁（唾液）。

　　不過反對檳榔業最高的聲浪矛頭卻指向賣檳榔的年輕女郎「檳榔西施」，她們大膽的穿著在玻璃屋中亮相使政治人物指稱她們給台灣一個惡質形象，檳榔攤老闆卻堅持檳榔西施的工作正當，她們的大膽的形象正是賣點。台灣有百萬以上的檳榔人口，看來這個爭議一時還不得止息。

✎ 生字 Vocabulary

1. **betel nut** 檳榔
   Betel nut was grown by Taiwan's aborigines long before any Chinese arrived here.
   台灣原住民種植檳榔遠在漢人來到這裡之前。

2. **narcotic** 麻醉品、上癮的
   Betel nut has a narcotic effect.
   檳榔有讓人上癮的效果。

3. **buzz** 興奮
   Drinking a whole pot of strong coffee gave the student a slight buzz.
   喝了一整壺的濃咖啡後,這位學生有些興奮。

4. **cash crop** 經濟作物
   Rice is a major cash crop in many Asian countries.
   稻米是許多亞洲國家的主要經濟作物。

5. **critic** 批評者
   The book critic attacked the new novel in his newspaper column.
   書評家在他報上開的專欄裡批評這本新的小說。

6. **environmentalist** 環保人士
   Environmentalists are concerned with Taiwan's air and water pollution.
   環保人士關心台灣空氣和水污染的問題。

7. erosion 水土流失
The typhoon caused severe erosion on the mountainside.
颱風造成山邊嚴重的水土流失。

8. oral cancer 口腔癌
Taiwan has a higher rate of oral cancer than Japan does.
台灣的口腔癌罹患率比日本高。

9. stain 漬
A coffee stain ruined the man's new shirt.
一塊咖啡漬弄髒了這位男士的襯衫。

10. saliva 唾液、口水
Chewing betel nut increases your saliva.
嚼檳榔使你的口水增多。

11. spit 吐痰
Spitting in public places can spread disease.
在公共場所吐痰會傳播疾病。

12. sidewalk 人行道
Because so many motorcycles were parked on the sidewalk, she had to walk in the street.
因為有許多摩托車停在人行道上，她得在大街上行走。

13. betel nut industry 檳榔業
The betel nut industry is an important part of Taiwan's economy.
檳榔業是台灣經濟的一大重要部分。

14. betel nut beauty 檳榔西施
Taiwan is famous for its betel nut beauties who wear sexy outfits.

台灣以穿著大膽的檳榔西施出名。

15. skimpy clothing 暴露衣著
Her mother told her that she couldn't leave the house in such skimpy clothing.

她媽媽告訴她不可穿著暴露的衣著走出大門。

16. expose 暴露
The reporter wanted to expose the politician's secrets.

記者想揭發這位政治人物的秘辛。

17. glass booth 玻璃屋
Many betel nut beauties work in glass booths beside the road.

許多檳榔西施在路邊玻璃屋裡工作。

18. sleazy 低劣的
Her mother wouldn't let her watch such a sleazy movie.

她媽媽不讓她看這麼「沒水準」的電影。

19. decent 正當的
Her father felt that his daughter's position in a KTV parlor was not a decent job.

她的爸爸覺得女兒在KTV的工作「不太正當」。

🖉 課文重點分析 Analysis

1. narcotics 是容易使人上癮的「毒品」，betel nut 雖然算不上是毒品，不過也能使人上癮，是一種興奮劑 stimulant。narcotic 是名詞，也是形容詞。

2. economy 經濟（名詞）、economic 有關經濟的（形容詞）、economist 經濟學者、economics 經濟系、economical 經濟的、省錢的。

   The current sluggish economy probably won't improve anytime soon.

   目前衰頹的經濟近期內大概不會有何改進。

   The government has implemented a new economic policy.

   政府訂定了新的經濟政策。

   She is a renown economist.

   她是位有名的經濟學者。

   He majored in economics.

   他大學讀的是經濟系。

   My car is economical on gas.

   我的車很省油。

3. spit是名詞也是動詞。例如：

   Don't spit on the sidewalk.

   不要在行人道上吐痰。

His spit was stained dark red.

他吐的痰被染成深紅色的。

4. skimpy 是很少的意思，如 skimpy clothing 衣服穿得少、很暴露。Your essay is skimpy. 你的文章寫得太短。sexy clothing 跟穿得少無關，你可以穿得很多，不過看起來卻很 sexy。

5. expose（主動），be exposed to（被動），例如：

The news reports exposed government corruption.

新聞報導揭發政府貪污。

Children are often exposed to colds in their classes at school.

兒童容易在學校班級受到傷風的感染。

有些人喜歡 expose themselves，這種人我們稱為exhibitionist（暴露狂）。

6. 我們對食物的感覺有酸（sour）、甜（sweet）、苦（bitter）、辣（hot）、鹹（salty）、有嚼勁（chewy）、沒什麼味道（bland）、味道重（spicy）。例如：

Squid is chewy.

烏賊（小管）吃起來很有嚼勁。

注意：chewing（動名詞）是咀嚼，chewy（形容詞）是有嚼勁，兩者不同。

✎ 克漏字 Cloze

> betel nut, oral cancer, environmentalists, sleazy, erosion, critic, stain, decent, cash crop, narcotics

1. Many _____ are against the law.

2. Her mother did not think that modeling was a _____ job.

3. The film _____ did not like the new movie.

4. _____ is chewed in many Asian countries.

5. Corn is the main _____ in many parts of the United States.

6. _____ were happy about the new pollution regulations.

7. The _____ magazine contains pictures of naked women.

8. I don't know how to remove the coffee _____ on the tablecloth.

9. The coast was being worn away by _____.

10. Even though he had _____, he wouldn't give up chewing betel nut.

✏ 選擇適當的詞性 Multiple Choice

_____ 1. This computer is our company's best-selling _____. (a)product (b)production (c)produce

_____ 2. My company hopes to _____ three new models in the upcoming year. (a)product (b)production (c)produce

_____ 3. The _____ of each new car involves hundreds of people. (a)product (b)production (c)produce

_____ 4. The topic of abortion has always been very _____. (a)controversy (b)controversial (c)controversies

_____ 5. No matter how hard we tried, we couldn't resolve the _____. (a)controversy (b)controversial (c)controversies

_____ 6. This pill is taken _____. (a)oral (b)orally (c)orality

_____ 7. Nancy is preparing for an _____ test in her English class tomorrow. (a)oral (b)orally (c)orality

_____ 8. I'm still full because my lunch was _____. (a)enormous (b)enorm (c)enormously

_____ 9. Ben liked Sarah _____. (a)enormous (b)enorm (c)enormously

_____ 10. Everyone hoped that the _____ would improve in the upcoming year. (a)economics (b)economy (c)economist

_____ 11. The new war caused an _____ crisis. (a)economic (b)economy (c)economics

_____ 12. The _____ predicted the drop in the stock market. (a)economic (b)economy (c)economists

_____ 13. The high-tech _____ has grown a lot recently. (a)industrial (b)industrially (c)industry

_____ 14. Many people dislike the new _____ park that opened next to the school. (a)industrial (b)industrially (c)industry

🖎 翻譯 Translation

1. 你嚼過檳榔嗎？

2. 電腦在世界上 (throughout the world) 廣為人使用。

3. 種類繁多的水果對台灣經濟的貢獻很大。

4. 環保人士聲稱種植這麼多的檳榔樹(betel palms)造成水土流失。

_____

5. 台灣的高口腔癌罹患率已讓醫生擔心。

_____

6. 米是台灣主要的經濟作物之一。

_____

7. 檳榔攤(stalls)老闆堅持檳榔西施是正當的工作。

_____

8. 這位西施檳榔穿得很少正在一間玻璃屋裡工作。Wearing skimpy clothing...

_____

9. 不要在行人道上吐痰。

_____

10. 嚼檳榔的爭議一時不會止息。

_____

Happily Ever After (CD1 Track15)

Even though men in Taiwan no longer have to present large sums[1] of money to their future wives' parents, getting married still involves many rituals and expenses. In fact, the younger generation seems increasingly interested in traditional weddings that cost a fortune.

Before wedding preparations begin, the man must pop the question[2]. After his girlfriend accepts his proposal, he will ask her parents for permission[3] to marry her. Once the couple becomes engaged[4] at the engagement party, they have to spend money on wedding photographs and renting a formal wedding gown and suit for the bride and groom to wear at the wedding banquet. Fortunately[5], the guests' cash-filled red envelopes help pay for the food.

Even after the banquet, the newlyweds will still face the expenses of a honeymoon. While it may take years to pay all the bills, many couples feel that the special memories and the dream of living happily ever after are worth every penny.

永浴愛河

　　即便台灣男人不再需要出聘金給他未來的岳父母，結婚還是免不了許多禮數和花費。事實上，年輕一代似乎對花費不貲的「傳統」婚禮興趣愈來愈大。

　　準備婚禮之前，男方得先求婚，等女友接受他的求婚後，他開始跟女方的父母提親。一旦這對新人在訂婚宴訂了婚，他們開始花錢拍婚紗攝影和租新娘和新郎在喜宴需要穿著的正式結婚禮服和西裝，幸運的是，好在有來賓的裝滿現金的紅包可以用來付喜宴開銷。

　　喜宴之後，新人還得花錢度蜜月，雖然這筆帳得花好幾年才付得清，許多夫婦還是覺得這種永浴愛河的記憶和美夢，讓每一毛錢都花得值得！

✏️ 生字 Vocabulary

1. **happily ever after** 永浴愛河
   In many children's stories, the characters live happily ever after.
   許多兒童故事裡的角色都永遠過著快樂幸福的生活。

2. **ritual** 儀式、禮數
   Even modern weddings still have many rituals that the couple must follow.
   即使是現代的婚禮還是有許多新人需要遵照的儀式。

3. **cost a fortune** 所費不貲
   His new car cost a fortune.
   他的新車很貴。

4. **pop the question** 求婚（動詞）
   The man was very nervous on the day he planned to pop the question.
   求婚當天，這位男士非常緊張。

5. **proposal** 求婚（名詞）
   Her boyfriend's proposal was very romantic.
   她男友的求婚可真浪漫。

6. **a couple** 一對夫妻
   The couple had many interests in common.
   這對夫妻有許多共同的興趣。

7. **engaged** 訂婚

She became engaged on Valentine's Day.
她在情人節當天訂婚。

8. engagement party 訂婚宴
Many people were invited to their engagement party.
許多人受邀參加他們的訂婚宴。

9. bride 新娘
The bride selected several beautiful new outfits.
這位新娘選了許多漂亮的新衣服。

10. groom 新郎
The groom looked very happy at the party.
在派對上這位新郎看起來真開心。

11. wedding gown 新娘禮服
The bride's wedding gown was made of silk.
這位新娘的禮服是用絲做的。

12. wedding banquet 喜宴
The wedding banquet was held in a large restaurant.
結婚喜宴是在一家大飯店舉行的。

13. red envelope 紅包
While wedding guests are expected to bring presents in the United States, in Taiwan they are supposed to bring red envelopes filled with money.
在美國參加婚禮的客人要帶禮物，台灣吃喜酒的客人則要帶裝了錢的紅包。

14. newlyweds 新婚夫婦

The newlyweds were going to live with the husband's family.

這對新婚夫妻要跟夫家住在一起。

15. honeymoon 蜜月

They planned to go to Hawaii on their honeymoon.

他們計畫到夏威夷去度蜜月。

16. worth every penny 值回票價

The woman felt that her expensive new house was worth every penny.

這位女士覺得她價格昂貴的新家物超所值。

✏ 課文重點分析 Analysis

1. large sums of money 指的是男方出的聘金。「聘金」英文沒有完全對等的字，嫁妝的英文字則是 dowry。

2. pop the question 求婚是 make a proposal 和 propose 比較口語化（colloquial）的說法。例如：

If you propose to someone, you ask him/her to marry you.

He proposed to me last night.

昨晚他向我求婚了。

He popped the question last night.

昨晚他向我求婚了。（注意：這裡通常不會說向誰求婚，大家都心知肚明。）

3. permit 是動詞也是名詞，動詞重音在第二音節，名詞重音在第一音節。work permit(名詞)工作證。

Foreigners need a work permit in order to work in Taiwan.

外國人在台灣工作需要一個工作證。

permit(動詞)允許。

The immigration office doesn't permit foreigners to work here without a work permit.

移民局不准外國人沒有工作證在此工作。

permission(名詞)允許。

He can't sell this house without his wife's permission.

不經過他太太的允許，他不能賣這棟房子。

4. get engaged 和 become engaged 訂婚。engage 還有吸引的意思，例如：

Online games have engaged her for hours.

網路遊戲吸引她玩了好幾小時。

engage 牽涉，例如：

She tried to engage a shy person in conversation.

她試著讓一個害羞的人加入談話。

5. fortune(名詞)、fortunate(形容詞)、fortunately(副詞)，例如：

The wedding has cost him a fortune.

婚禮讓他花了不少錢。

He was fortunate to marry a wise woman.

他很幸運和一個有智慧的女人結婚了。

Fortunately, he found a teaching job despite his old age.

他很幸運地在這麼大的年紀還可以找到一個教書的工作。

克漏字 Cloze

> proposal, engaged, bride, groom, wedding gown, newlyweds, honeymoon, engagement party, worth every penny, rituals

1. The _____ looked beautiful on her wedding day.

2. The _____ were saving their money to buy their own house.

3. Her _____ fit her perfectly.

4. The _____ seemed very nervous when he proposed.

5. She had always wanted to spend her _____ in Japan.

6. They sent out 50 invitations to the _____.

7. On many holidays, people still follow ancient _____.

8. She was hoping to become _____ soon.

9. The young woman wasn't sure if she wanted to accept her boyfriend's _____.

10. The man thought his trip to Europe was _____.

🖉 選擇適當的詞性 Multiple Choice

_____ 1. Ben _____ to Jennifer during dinner. (a) proposes (b) proposal (c) proposed

_____ 2. They have been _____ for four years now, and they still haven't gotten married. (a) engaging (b) engaged (c) engage

_____ 3. They broke off their _____ because Ben decided that he wasn't ready to settle down after all. (a) engaging (b) engagement (c) engage

_____ 4. She tried to _____ her son with toys. (a) engaging (b) engaged (c) engage

_____ 5. My father won't _____ me to go to the party. (a) permit (b) permits (c) permission

_____ 6. You need the teacher's _____ to speak in class. (a) permit (b) permitted (c) permission

_____ 7. This stamp is _____ a lot of money. (a)worth (b)worthy (c)worthless

_____ 8. This fine gentleman is _____ of your respect. (a)worth (b)worthy (c)worthless

_____ 9. This _____ of Christina does not look like her at all! (a)photography (b)photographic (c)photograph

_____ 10. Brian became very interested in _____ after getting a new camera. (a)photography (b)photographic (c)photograph

_____ 11. The _____ loved taking pictures of animals. (a)photography (b)photographic (c)photographer

_____ 12. This _____ equipment is very expensive. (a)photography (b)photographic (c)photograph

_____ 13. It's nearly impossible to find a bad picture of your sister because she's so _____.(很上相)(a)photography (b)photogenic (c)photograph

🖊 翻譯 Translation

1. 你們什麼時候訂婚的？

   _____

2. John上星期跟我求婚了。

   _____

3. 我無法決定是否要接受他的求婚。

   _____

4. 新娘和新郎剛剛租了正式的結婚禮服和西裝。

   _____

5. 這對新婚夫妻決定到香港去度蜜月。

   _____

6. 即使他們的婚禮所費不貲，但他們覺得它（婚禮）花的每分錢
   都值得。

   _____

7. 每個人都夢想跟他／她的愛人永遠快樂地生活在一起。

   _____

8. 我花了三年才把婚禮的帳單付完。

   _____

9.　這對新婚夫妻花了很多錢照婚紗照。

_____

10.　傳統的婚禮有(involve)許多禮數新人得遵守。

_____

Plastic Money (CD1 Track16)

While Taiwanese used to rely on cash, now "plastic money" offers convenient but risky alternatives[1]. Credit cards let you charge purchases and pay later. Debit cards instantly deduct money from your account when you make a purchase. Cash cards allow you to borrow money through ATMs.

All these cards are very handy. You no longer have to carry much cash, and you never have to worry about having enough money for an emergency. If you use these cards wisely[2], you should never have a problem.

However, irresponsible use can lead to serious financial problems and even bankruptcy. Credit cards often have high interest rates, making spending sprees expensive if you don't pay off the entire balance. Cash card abuse has caused so many problems that the government recently passed stricter rules to regulate[3] their advertising and use. While these new rules can help, what we have to remember is that the cards don't cause debt; people do.

16　塑膠錢

　　過去台灣人靠現金，現在則有「塑膠錢」提供方便卻有風險的選擇。信用卡讓你買東西先賒帳，後付款。金融扣帳卡立刻將你每一筆消費從戶頭中扣除，現金卡則讓你從提款機「借」錢。

　　所有這些卡都很便利，至少你不需要帶太多現金，也不需要擔心緊急情況時沒有足夠的錢，如果你善用這些金融卡，絕不會出問題。

　　不過，如果隨意亂刷卡會使財務出問題，甚至破產。信用卡通常利率高，如果你不一次付清全額簽帳款，就會使大採購變得更花錢。亂用現金卡(借貸)也造成許多問題，最近政府才通過嚴格的法令，管制現金卡打廣告和它的使用方法，新法規當然有用，不過我們得記得，卡不生債，人生債！

🖊 生字 Vocabulary

1. plastic money 塑膠錢
   Credit cards are sometimes called plastic money.
   信用卡有時被稱為塑膠錢。

2. cash 現款
   My grandmother still pays for everything with cash.
   我阿嬤什麼東西都付現。

3. credit card 信用卡
   The average Taiwanese adult has four credit cards.
   平均每個台灣成年人有四張信用卡。

4. debit card 金融扣帳卡
   Many shops now accept debit cards.
   許多商家都收金融扣帳卡。

5. cash card 現金卡
   Cash cards are very easy to get.
   現金卡很容易申請。

6. charge 預支
   She used her credit card to charge her plane ticket.
   她用信用卡預支機票錢。

7. deduct 扣除
   The bank can automatically deduct payments from my account.
   銀行可以自動從我帳戶扣除我的消費額。

8. account 戶頭

She never has much money in her account.

她從來沒有很多錢存在戶頭裡。

9. make a purchase 購物

She used her Visa card to make a purchase.

她用她的Visa卡購物。

10. ATM 自動提款機 (Automated Teller Machine)

Most convenience stores in Taiwan have an ATM.

台灣大部分的便利商店有自動提款機。

11. handy 方便好用

Cell phones are very handy in an emergency.

手機在緊急狀況時很方便。

12. bankruptcy 破產

When his business failed, he had to declare bankruptcy.

當他生意失敗時得宣布破產。

13. interest rate 利率

She refuses to use a credit card since interest rates are so high.

她不用信用卡，因為卡的利息太高了。

14. spending spree 大採購

When she got her first job, she went on a spending spree.

她第一次找到工作時，上街大採購了一番。

15. pay off 一次付清

He has to pay off the money that he borrowed to go to college.

他得付清為了進大學借的款項。

16. entire balance 全額簽帳款

I pay off the entire balance of my credit card each month.
我每個月都付清信用卡的全額簽帳款。

17. regulate 管制、規定

The university cannot regulate what time students go to sleep.
大學不能管制大學生上床睡覺的時間。

18. debt 債

He was in so much debt that he had to sell his house.
他負債累累，必須售屋還債。

🖋 課文重點分析 Analysis

1. alternative 另一種選擇，是名詞。形容名詞要用形容詞 convenient 和 risky，不能用名詞 convenience 和 risk。

2. "If you use these cards wisely, you should never have a problem." 這句所提到作為一名 wise cardholder（聰明的持卡人），如果你每個月都 pay off the entire balance（將所刷卡的全額簽帳款一次付清），而不只是 make the minimum payment each month（每個月只付基本費），你就不需要擔心信用卡的 high interest rate（高利息），也不必擔心會 be in debt（負債）、have financial problems（導致財務出問題）或 go bankrupt（破產）。

3. regulate（動詞）、regulation（名詞）。

His mom regulated how much time he could watch TV.

他的媽媽控制他看電視的時間。

The teacher's regulation, forbids students from eating breakfast in class.

這位老師的規定，禁止學生在課堂上吃早餐。

克漏字 Cloze

> cash, charge, handy, bankruptcy, interest rates, spending spree, account, credit cards, regulates, plastic money

1. The college student already has two _____.

2. She used her tax refund to go on a _____.

3. He likes to _____ all of his major expenses.

4. The government _____ many aspects of our lives.

5. He keeps all of his money in one bank _____.

6. _____ seem to be getting higher again.

7. I don't like to carry much _____ on a crowded bus.

8. Convenience stores are very _____ places to shop.

9. My older brother calls credit cards ＿＿＿＿＿＿.

10. She owed so much money that she had to declare ＿＿＿＿＿＿.

✐ 選擇適當的詞性 Multiple Choice

＿＿＿＿ 1. She had been saving money in the same bank ＿＿＿＿ for many years. (a)accountant (b)account (c)accounting

＿＿＿＿ 2. I hired an ＿＿＿＿ to do my taxes. (a)accountant (b)account (c)accounting

＿＿＿＿ 3. He studied ＿＿＿＿ in college. (a)accountant (b)account (c)accounting

＿＿＿＿ 4. Some bank accounts will pay ＿＿＿＿ on your savings. (a)interesting (b)interested (c)interest

＿＿＿＿ 5. Taiwan's history is an ＿＿＿＿ subject. (a)interesting (b)interested (c)interest

＿＿＿＿ 6. He is not ＿＿＿＿ in politics. (a)interesting (b)interested (c)interest

＿＿＿＿ 7. The company went ＿＿＿＿ because the manager was secretly stealing money. (a)bankruptcy (b)bankrupt (c)bankrupting

_____ 8. Many people think declaring _____ is very disgraceful. (a)bankruptcy (b)bankrupt (c)bankrupting

_____ 9. The telephone company will _____ my bill from my bank account. (a)deduct (b)deducted (c)deduction

_____ 10. In Taiwan, if you rent your house, you can claim a tax _____.(稅的扣除額)(a)deduct (b)deducted (c)deduction

_____ 11. The school has the power to _____ many parts of students' lives. (a)regulatory (b)regulate (c)regulation

_____ 12. Foreign workers must follow many _____ in Taiwan. (a)regulatory (b)regulates (c)regulations

翻譯 Translation

1. 如果你沒有足夠的現金，可以用信用卡付帳。

2. 銀行會自動從你的戶頭裡扣錢。

_____

3. 現金卡讓你經由自動提款機借錢。

_____

4. 有了一卡在手，你不再需要帶很多現金。

_____

5. 如果你聰明地使用你的信用卡，你應該不會有問題。

_____

6. 信用卡通常有很高的利率。

_____

7. 每個月當我收到信用卡帳單，我付清全額簽帳款。

_____

8. 上個月他只付了基本費。

_____

9. 政府通過更嚴格的法規來管制信用卡打廣告。

_____

10. 他中了樂透後，馬上瘋狂大採購。

_____

Education

教育

Placement Results Posted
CD1 Track17

Being admitted₁ to college in Taiwan used to₂ be very difficult. In the past₃, everyone who wanted to go to a university had to take the Joint College Entrance Exam (JCEE). Many students' test scores were too low. Some₄ could not attend college at all; others had to attend a school they did not like or major in₅ a subject that they did not select.

Now students have several options. They can apply to₆ the university that they prefer. Students with special talents can be admitted by a recommendation from their high school. If a student is still rejected, he or she can take an exam. This year, the placement lists showed that a record number of students, 87%, were admitted.

In spite of₇ this high entry rate, some students, parents, and teachers are unhappy with the system. Many students are still not accepted₈ by their top choices, and some departments are having problems attracting enough students. Perhaps it is impossible to find a college entrance method that makes everyone happy.

放榜了！

以前，在台灣被大學錄取非常困難。以往，任何想進大學的人都得參加大專聯考，許多學生考試分數太低，有的根本無法進大學；有的則進了自己不喜歡的學校，或讀的系不是自己選擇的。

現在，學生有許多選擇：他們可以申請自己喜歡的大學；具有特殊才能的學生可以經由他們高中學校的推薦而錄取。如果某個學生(推甄或申請時)被拒絕於大學門外，他(她)還可以參加考試。今年榜單顯示87%學生被錄取，創了歷年新高。

錄取率雖然高，有的學生、家長和老師卻對這個制度還是不滿，許多學生無法滿足自己最高志願(進自己想進的學校或系)，有的系卻招不足學生，看來想要找到一個皆大歡喜的大學招生方法，似乎不太可能。

🖋 生字 Vocabulary

1. **placement results have been posted** 分發結果公布了（放榜了）
   Students who take the college entrance exam are nervous until placement results have been posted.
   參加大學入學考試的學生很緊張，直到放榜了才鬆了口氣。

2. **being admitted** 被錄取
   In Taiwan, more students than ever are being admitted to college.
   在台灣比以往更多的學生被大學錄取。

3. **Joint College Entrance Exam（JCEE）** 大學聯考
   Until a few years ago, the only way to get into college was to make a high score on the Joint College Entrance Exam (JCEE).
   直到幾年前，進大學唯一的方法還是只有在大學聯考得高分。

4. **test scores** 考試分數
   Students worry about whether their test scores will be high enough to get into college.
   學生擔心他們的學測成績是否高到能讓他們進大學。

5. **attend college** 進大學
   Her mother wants her to attend college.
   她的母親希望她能進大學。

6. **major in** 讀⋯⋯系

She wanted to major in history because it was her favorite subject.

她想讀歷史系，因為歷史是她最喜歡的科目。

7. option 選擇

Students have many more options than their parents did.

學生的選擇比他們父母（那個時代）來得多。

8. apply to 申請（學校）

Students can now directly apply to the college of their choice.

學生現在可以直接申請他們自己選擇想進的學校。

9. prefer 喜歡

If you are lucky, you will get into the college that you prefer.

如果你運氣好的話，可以進你喜歡的學校。

10. special talent 特殊才能

A college may accept a student who is an artist because of her special talent.

一所大學可能錄取一名藝術家型的學生，因為她的特殊才藝。

11. recommendation 推薦信

I asked my high school teacher to write a recommendation for me.

我請我高中的老師幫我寫推薦信。

12. take an exam 考試

If you can't get into college by other means, you can take an exam.

如果不能用其他方法進大學，你還可以參加考試。

13. placement lists 榜單

The placement lists are published every August.

榜單每年八月印出來。

14. record number 破紀錄的數字

A record number of students own motor scooters.

學生擁有摩托車的數字破紀錄。

15. entry rate 錄取率

This year's college entry rate is the highest it has ever been.

今年大學錄取率創新高。

16. department 系

It is important to study in a department that interests you.

讀你有興趣的系是很重要的。

📝 課文重點分析 Analysis

1. be admitted to 被(某個學校)錄取，可以進某個學校。例如：

   I was admitted to Chenggong University. 我被成大錄取了。

   如果要把 be admitted...當成主詞，就須要把動詞名詞化 being admitted。

   be accepted by 也是被(某個學校)錄取，＊注意：be admitted to 和 be accepted by 意思雖相同，後面的介系詞不同。

2. used to 過去的情況。例如：

I used to ride a bicycle to school, but now I drive to school.

used to 和 be used to 意思和用法完全不同，be used to 習慣
於。例如：

I am used to walking to school. 我習慣走路上學。＊注意：
be used to 後面動詞要加 ing，指習慣走路上學(walking to
school) 這件事情。

3. In the past...Now...這是一個時間對比的用法。例如：

In the past, people used dial phones, but now most people
use cell phones.

4. Some... ; others...有些人...有些人...。例如：

Some ordered coffee; others ordered black tea.

如果是三種不同型態的人，One..., another..., still another...

如果是三種不同型態的人群，Some..., others..., still others...

5. major in(動詞)讀某個系，major(名詞)某個系。例如：

I'm majoring in electrical engineering.

我讀電機系。

I selected art as my major.

我選美術當我讀的系。

6. apply to 申請學校，apply for 申請工作。例如：

I want to apply to a graduate school near where I live.

我想申請一家靠近我住的地方的研究所。

If you want to apply for a job, you need to know if you meet the requirements for that job.

如果你想申請工作，你得先知道自己是否符合那個工作的條件。

7. in spite of＝despite不管、雖然，後面接名詞。例如：

In spite of the terrible weather, the game continued.

不管天氣有多惡劣，比賽繼續舉行。

despite the fact that...後面接句子。

Despite the fact that she was so ill, she still came to the class.

雖然她病得很重，她還是來上課。

8. be accepted 和 be rejected 被接受和被拒絕。例如：

She was accepted by this college.

她被這所大學錄取了。

Unfortunately, she was rejected by this renowned university.

她不幸被這所著名的大學給刷下來了。

✍ 克漏字 Cloze

> test scores, placement, attend, recommendations, options, top choice, record number, entry rate, admitted, take

1. I have to get three _____ to support my application for this teaching job.

2. Getting married is not my _____. I need to pursue a master's degree in accounting first.

3. She was thrilled after hearing that she had been _____ to a renowned university.

4. Though my _____ were not high, thanks to my special talents, I managed to get into the college.

5. The high college _____ doesn't guarantee that you will be able to get into the college you prefer.

6. Which college does your son _____?

7. Before studying abroad, she has to _____ the TOEFL.

8. When she couldn't find her name on the _____ lists, she burst into tears.

9. Regarding job opportunities, I don't have many _____.

10. A _____ of participants, 124000, took the General English Proficiency Test this year.

✐ 選擇適當的詞性 Multiple Choice

_____ 1. He was thrilled to be _____ to the university. (a) admit (b) admitted (c) admission

_____ 2. The university only _____ a small percentage of the applicants. (a) admits (b) admitted (c) admission

_____ 3. The _____ process is quite rigorous. (a) admit (b) admitted (c) admission

_____ 4. The low acceptance rate to the university should not discourage you from _____ anyway. (a) apply (b) application (c) applying

_____ 5. Don't forget to complete your _____ in time for consideration. (a) apply (b) application (c) applying

_____ 6. Your _____ in music could get you admitted into a good music school. (a) talented (b) talents (c) talent

_____ 7. You are a _____ musician and with proper training could become a top performer. (a) talented

(b) talents (c) talent

_____ 8. In the end, you will still have to make a _____.
(a) chose (b) choice (c) choose

_____ 9. Often it is difficult to _____ where you will be
happy, especially if you have not visited the place.
(a) chose (b) choice (c) choose

_____ 10. He _____ a good spot to picnic in the shade
from the sun. (a) chose (b) choice (c) choose

_____ 11. She wrote a new _____ in her diary. (a) enter
(b) entry (c) entrance

_____ 12. The _____ to the exhibit is on your left after
the ticket booth. (a) enter (b) entry (c) entrance

翻譯 Translation

1. 你讀什麼系？

_____

2. 不管我的考試的分數有多高，我的媽媽還是不高興。

_____

3. 今年考大學入學考試的學生破了紀錄。

_____

4. 我是1970年進大學的。

_____

5. 因為他的特殊才能,所以被台大錄取了。

_____

6. 我還不知道放榜的結果。

_____

7. 你什麼時候要去申請那所研究所?

_____

8. 我沒有其他選擇,只好念歷史系。

_____

9. 你考過幾次大專聯考?

_____

10. 那所大學不是我的第一選擇。

_____

18 The GEPT Obsession[1] (CD1 Track18)

On January 8th, a record-breaking 124,000 people, from ages 6-76, took the General English Proficiency Test. What is the GEPT and why did people from all walks of life take it? This standardized test is offered at five levels, elementary, intermediate, high-intermediate, advanced, and superior. Each year, all over Taiwan, more companies encourage their old staff and require new recruits[2] to pass the test.

Like all tests, this one has both advantages and disadvantages. For Taiwan to be competitive[3] in this age of globalization, English skills are obviously important. The test gives employers standard criteria, so that hiring is not based solely on personal connections. Moreover, the GEPT encourages life-long learning since anyone can take it at any age.

Critics[4], however, claim that the test encourages teachers to "teach to the test." Also, many parents are pushing their children to take the test too early. This time, for instance, 30,000 elementary school students took the GEPT. Thus, while this test is a powerful tool in Taiwan's effort to build English proficiency[5], like any tool, it should be used wisely.

18 全民英檢熱

　　1月8日，從6歲到76歲共有12萬4千人報考全民英檢，真是破紀錄！什麼是全民英檢？為什麼各色各樣的人都來應考？這個標準化的考試分為初級、中級、中高級、高級和優級五級，全台灣每年都有更多的公司鼓勵老雇員和要求新雇員通過這項考試。

　　像其他的考試一樣，這個考試也有其優、缺點，為了讓台灣在全球化時代保有競爭力，英文能力顯然重要。全民英檢讓雇主在聘用新人時有個基準，不必單靠個人關係。另外，任何人在任何年齡都可以報考全民英檢，鼓勵全民終身學習。

　　不過，批評者卻認為這個考試讓老師為考而教，父母也逼小孩太早參加考試，以這次為例，居然有三萬小學生考全民英檢。這個考試固然是台灣努力建立英文能力強而有力的工具，不過就像任何工具一樣，得善加利用才行！

🖋 生字 Vocabulary

1. record-breaking 破紀錄的
   A record-breaking number of people entered the singing contest this year.
   今年參加歌唱比賽的人數破了紀錄。

2. General English Proficiency Test（GEPT）全民英檢
   Some companies require their employees to take the General English Proficiency Test（GEPT）.
   有的公司要求員工考全民英檢。

3. all walks of life 各行各業
   People from all walks of life love to swim.
   各行各業的人都愛游泳。

4. standardized test 標準考試
   Many people think standardized tests are the best types to give since they are fair.
   許多人認為統一標準考試公正無私，是最好的測驗方式。

5. elementary 初級
   The elementary level of the GEPT is designed to test the English of a junior high school graduate.
   初級全民英檢是設計給國中畢業生考的。

6. intermediate 中級
   Her father promised her a new cell phone if she could pass the intermediate level of the GEPT.

如果她通過中級全民英檢的話，她的父親答應給她一台新手機。

7. high-intermediate 中高級

The high-intermediate level of the GEPT was much harder than she expected.

全民英檢中高級遠比她想的難。

8. advanced 高級

To get a promotion, he had to pass the advanced level of the GEPT.

想升遷的話，他得通過高級全民英檢。

9. superior 優級

To pass the superior level of the GEPT, your English needs to be nearly as good as that of a native speaker.

要通過優級全民英檢，你的英文（程度）得和英文是母語的人相近似。

10. new recruit 新聘員工

Many new recruits had problems fitting into the company.

許多新進員工有公司適應的問題。

11. competitive 競爭激烈的

Recent presidential elections have been very competitive in several countries.

最近許多國家的總統大選競爭都十分激烈。

12. globalization 全球化

Because of globalization, the products we buy are made all over the world.

因為全球化，我們才能買到世界各地的產品。

13. criteria 標準（複數形；單數作criterion）
The criteria for the job were explained clearly in the company's website.

錄用人的標準都在公司網站上說明得清清楚楚。

14. connection 關係
She was hired because of her connections; her father is the boss's best friend.

她被錄用是靠關係，她的父親是老闆最好的朋友。

15. life-long learning 終身學習
Because she believes in life-long learning, she started studying Japanese even though she is 70 years old.

她相信終身學習（的好處），所以到70歲才開始學日文。

16. critic 批評者
Critics of nuclear power don't want Taiwan to build any more nuclear power plants.

批評核能的人不希望台灣再多建任何核能電廠。

17. "teach to the test" 為考而教
If our society emphasizes test scores too much, teachers may feel pressured to "teach to the test."

如果我們的社會過份強調分數的重要，老師也許會被迫為考試而教學。

18. English proficiency 英文能力
Her English proficiency improved remarkably after she'd

spent the summer listening to English radio programs every day.

她花了一個夏天每天聽英文收音機節目，英文程度突飛猛進。

🖉 課文重點分析 Analysis

1. obsession 是名詞，迷、熱中，例如：

   She has an obsession with anything purple.

   她對任何紫色的東西都著迷。

   be obsessed with 迷上，例如：

   He is obsessed with collecting toy cars.

   他迷上收集小汽車。

2. old staff 和 new recruit 是新舊員工的一個對比。

   recruit 也可以當動詞。例如：

   The company has recruited an experienced executive.

   這家公司新聘了一位主管。

   be recruited 被徵召。例如：

   My son was recruited into the army last month.

   我的兒子上個月被徵召入伍。

3. competitive 形容詞，競爭激烈的。例如：

   Taiwan's graduate school entrance exams are very competitive.

   台灣的研究所入學考試競爭十分激烈。

competitive 具備競爭力的，例如：

To be competitive on the job market, you need a good education.

要讓自己在職場具備競爭力，良好的教育是必需的。

compete 動詞，競爭，例如：

She likes to compete with others.

她喜歡跟人比。

competition 名詞，競爭，例如：

Everyone knew that the competition between them was severe.

大家都知道他們之間的較勁意味很嚴重。

competitor 名詞，對手，例如：

Her husband is her lifelong competitor.

她的先生是她一輩子的競爭對手。

competitiveness 競爭力，例如：

The country's competitiveness remains strong.

這個國家的競爭力還是很強。

4. critic 名詞，批評者(反對者)，例如：

Will a movie critic's review influence your decision to see the movie?

影評人的影評會影響你選片嗎？

critic 也是寫的評論(review)，例如：

From 2000 to 2003 I wrote movie critics for a local newspaper.

我在2000到2003年為一份地方報紙寫影評。

criticism 名詞，批評，例如：

Her constructive criticism helped me finish the project.

她建設性的批評助我完成這個企畫案。

criticize 動詞，批評，例如：

I don't like the way you criticize my friend.

我不喜歡你批評我朋友的態度。

5. 常聽學生謙稱自己英文能力不好時說： "My English ability is poor."

其實下面兩種說法比較正確：

My English is poor.

My English proficiency is poor.

如果說：我的英文聽力太差，可以用下面句子：

My English listening proficiency is poor.

✏️ 克漏字 Cloze

> all walks of life, connections, criteria, critics, competitive, globalization, life-long learning, new recruit, record-breaking, standardized tests

1. The _____ was eager to get his first paycheck.

2. The student liked _____ because she was good at guessing correct answers.

3. Because he knows the boss, he is able to use his _____ to get a higher salary.

4. _____ did not like the author's new book.

5. People from _____ came to the festival.

6. A _____ number of books were sold this year.

7. He needed a college degree to be _____ on the job market.

8. _____ can keep your brain active.

9. He wasn't sure what the _____ were for this position.

10. Some people think _____ is bad for the local

economy.

✏ 選擇適當的詞性 Multiple Choice

_____ 1. My teacher is _____ in five languages.
(a) proficient (b) proficiently (c) proficiency

_____ 2. This test measures your math _____. (a) proficient
(b) proficiently (c) proficiency

_____ 3. A radio is _____ equipment in most cars today.
(a) standardize (b) standard (c) standardization

_____ 4. I wish the company would _____ its dress sizes.
(a) standardize (b) standard (c) standardization

_____ 5. I have _____ English courses for many years.
(a) teaching (b) teached (c) taught

_____ 6. The new _____ had trouble adjusting to
the army's many rules. (a) recruiter (b) recruited
(c) recruit

_____ 7. She was _____ to be the new head of the
company. (a) recruiter (b) recruited (c) recruit

_____ 8. He has a hard time accepting _____. (a) critic
(b) criticize (c) criticism

_____ 9. The book _____ spends most of his time reading.
(a)critic (b)criticize (c)critical

_____ 10. That teacher is too _____ of his students.
(a)critic (b)criticized (c)critical

_____ 11. She has been an _____ of this company for twenty years. (a)employ (b)employee (c)employed

_____ 12. My mother wanted to _____ a foreign maid.
(a)employ (b)employee (c)employed

✐ 翻譯 Translation

1. 你考了全民英檢的中高級嗎？

_____

2. 全台灣各行各樣的人都迷 (be obsessed with) 這本書。

_____

3. 他年齡太小而不能考全民英檢。

_____

4. 你準備好全球化時代了嗎？

_____

5. 不要逼你的小孩去考初級全民英檢。

___

6. 新雇員的英文能力不夠好。

___

7. 我的英文口語(oral)能力只有中級程度(at the...level)。

___

8. 靠著跟老闆私人的關係，他得到這個工作。

___

9. 這家公司沒有用人(hiring)的基準。

___

10. 許多雇主要求員工參加(participate in)終身學習。

___

19 Cram Schools CD2 Track1

All over Taiwan, you can encounter weary₁ teenagers trudging home from cram schools late at night, carrying their bulky schoolbags. In our test-oriented₂ society, most young Taiwanese attend these private, after-hours schools that "cram" facts and testing tips into their brains.

Many students resent₃ going to a cram school after they have already spent a full day in class. They complain that they have no free time for hobbies or relaxation. Other students, however, like the air-conditioned₄ classrooms, helpful teaching assistants, fun new classmates, and articulate teachers. Moreover, this intensive₅ training often does improve students' test scores.

But while cram schools can be beneficial and even enjoyable, we must remember their limitations₆. As their name suggests, these schools only cram students with the "food" teachers feed them. If students only receive this canned knowledge, they can't be active, independent learners.

補習班

　　台灣到處可見疲累的學生夜晚背著笨重的書包、拖著蹣跚的步伐從補習班回家。在這個考試掛帥的社會裡,多數年輕台灣人上過私人辦的課後輔導班,這些班級把課本內容和考試要點強行塞入學生腦袋裡。

　　許多學生討厭上了整天課之後還要去補習班,他們抱怨沒時間做自己之所好,也沒空休息。不過也有學生喜歡補習班的空調教室、熱心助人的「班導師」、好玩的新朋友、和能言善道的老師,另外,密集式的訓練方法的確能夠提高學生的考試成績。

　　補習班雖然會帶來助益又好玩,不過我們得記得它們的侷限。如其名所示,補習班由老師塞給學生「食物」,如果學生只接受這類「罐頭」知識,他們不能成為主動又獨立的學生。

🖉 生字 Vocabulary

1. **cram school** 補習班
   Almost every child in Taiwan goes to a cram school.
   台灣幾乎每個小孩都進補習班。

2. **encounter** 遇到
   I didn't expect to encounter my mother at the new bookstore.
   我沒想到會在這家新書店遇到我的媽媽。

3. **trudge** 步履艱難地走著
   Trudging uphill, the hikers had to slow down.
   拖著步伐走上坡時，爬山人的腳步需要慢下來。

4. **bulky** 沈重
   After he went shopping, he had several bulky packages.
   他買完東西後，手裡提了好幾個重重的袋子。

5. **test-oriented** 考試掛帥的
   Taiwan's educational system is very test-oriented.
   台灣的教育制度以考試掛帥。

6. **after-hours** 放學後、下班後
   Late at night, the after-hours bar did an excellent business.
   夜深了，人們下班後去的酒吧生意特別興隆。

7. **cram** 塞
   The hungry dog tried to cram food into its mouth.
   這隻餓犬狼吞虎嚥。

8. tips 要點、秘訣
The magazine offered tips for losing weight.
這本雜誌提供減肥秘方。

9. resent 討厭
The clerks resent having to work such long hours.
店員討厭工作時間這麼長。

10. air-conditioned 有冷氣的
The old building did not have air-conditioned classrooms.
這棟舊的大樓沒有空調教室。

11. articulate 能言善道
Many people admired the articulate speaker.
許多人佩服能言善道的演講人。

12. intensive 密集式
Summer school classes are very intensive.
暑期班都是密集式的課程。

13. score 分數
She made a high score on her college entrance exam.
她大學入學考試分數很高。

14. beneficial 有益的
Drinking green tea is beneficial to your health.
喝綠茶對健康有益。

15. limitation 侷限性
Although this store is large, it has some limitations.

這家店雖大,但有些侷限性。

16. canned 罐裝的
Pubs and coffee shops often play canned music.
小酒館和咖啡館通常播放罐頭音樂。

✎ 課文重點分析 Analysis

1. weary(形容詞)、wear(動詞),例如:

The weary office workers like to go to the gym for relaxation.

疲憊的辦公室員工喜歡到健身房輕鬆一下。

Writing this book really wore me out.

寫這本書把我累壞了。

wear 的動詞三態變化為 wear, wore, worn。

wear 也有用舊的意思。如 a pair of worn-out jeans 一條舊牛仔褲。

2. orient(動詞)確定⋯⋯方向。例如:

When she got lost, she used the sun to orient herself.

當她迷路時,她用太陽來確定方向。

...-oriented 以什麼為取向,例如:

market-oriented management 以市場為取向的管理方式
test-oriented teaching style 以考試為取向的教學方式
money-oriented values 唯利是圖的價值觀

orientation（名詞）新生訓練

如 freshmen（大一新生）或 new recruits（新聘人員）進來時，學校或公司都會給他們一個 orientation，讓他們先熟悉環境及業務。

3. resent（動詞）、resentful（形容詞）、resentment（名詞），例如：

Students usually resent taking tests every day.

學生痛恨每天考試。

They are resentful of this kind of educational system.

他們很氣這種教育制度。

Their resentment toward education has influenced their learning attitude.

他們對教育的憎恨影響他們的學習態度。

4. air conditioner（冷氣機）、air conditioned（裝了冷氣的）、air conditioning（冷氣），例如：

My house is air conditioned.

My house doesn't have an air conditioner.

My house doesn't have air conditioning.

5. intense（形容詞）極端的、強烈的，如：intense heat 熱度極高

intensify（動詞）加強，如：intensify her training 加強她的訓練

intensive（形容詞）密集式的，如：an intensive class 密集班
intensive care 是加護病房。

6. limit（動詞）、limit（名詞）、limited（形容詞）、limitation（名詞），例如：

Don't limit your chances.

不要劃地自限。

Is there a time limit to this test?

考試有限時間嗎？

My money is limited.

我的錢有限。

He has many limitations.

他有一些侷限（不足之處）。

克漏字 Cloze

tips, weary, encounter, limitations, articulate, hobbies, beneficial, resents, bulky, intensive

1. His only ＿＿＿＿＿ were watching television and sleeping.

2. The new book gave ＿＿＿ for finding a husband.

3. Her ＿＿＿＿＿ coat made her look fat.

4. The _____ politician won the debate.

5. The poor man _____ the way rich people treat him.

6. The old computer program had some _____.

7. Walking up so many stairs made the old woman _____.

8. This _____ course teaches many concepts in a short time.

9. Successful businesses are _____ to Taiwan's economy.

10. I was happy to _____ one of my students in the library.

✎ 選擇適當的詞性 Multiple Choice

_____ 1. After a long day at work, she was very _____.
(a) wear (b) wearing (c) weary

_____ 2. I _____ a dress to work every day. (a) wear
(b) wearing (c) worn

_____ 3. He _____ a very expensive jacket. (a) wearing
(b) wore (c) worn

_____ 4. I have _____ that scarf many times. (a) wear

(b)wore (c)worn

_____ 5. The _____ fish did not taste as good as the fresh fish. (a)can (b)canned (c)caning

_____ 6. She bought a _____ of tomatoes in the supermarket. (a)can (b)canned (c)caning

_____ 7. Only a _____ number of those books are available. (a)limiting (b)limit (c)limited

_____ 8. The mother planned to _____ the number of hours her son could watch T.V. (a)limitation (b)limit (c)limited

_____ 9. The building's lack of an elevator is its only _____. (a)limitation (b)limit (c)limited

_____ 10. They _____ having to do extra work for no extra pay. (a)resent (b)resentment (c)resentful

_____ 11. The angry girl gave me a _____ look. (a)resenting (b)resentment (c)resentful

_____ 12. The _____ heat and humidity of Taipei's summer weather made her miserable. (a)intensive (b)intensify (c)intense

_____ 13. This _____ course is very demanding.

(a)intensive (b)intensify (c)intense

_____ 14. The top students in this class are _____ competitive. (a)intensively (b)intensify (c)intensely

_____ 15. Experts predict that fighting between the two countries will _____ next year. (a)intensive (b)intensify (c)intense

翻譯 Translation

1. 補習班雖對學生有益，但它們有它們的侷限性。

   _____

2. 補習班只是把一些考試秘訣塞到學生腦袋裡。

   _____

3. 今天我已待在學校一整天了。

   _____

4. 我討厭考試掛帥的教學方式。

   _____

5. 他雖然是補習班最能言善道的老師，他有他的侷限。

   _____

6. 我不喜歡這家咖啡館的罐頭音樂。

---

7. 學生抱怨他們沒有自由時間輕鬆一下。

---

8. 我受不了(can't stand)這間冷氣教室的強冷冷氣。

---

9. 如果你只靠(rely on)補習班老師，你永遠不會成為主動又獨立的學生。

---

10. 這種密集訓練的確改善了學生考試分數。

Health
健康

Taiwan Buffs Up! `CD2 Track2`

What happened to the delicate maiden and the meditative scholar who once represented the Chinese ideal? They've gone to the gym to work out$_1$. Now that Taiwan prefers healthy, toned$_2$ women and energetic, muscular men, fitness centers have gained popularity$_3$ throughout the island.

Appealing to$_4$ a wide population, gyms offer a way for everyone from high school students through grandparents to get in shape, reduce stress, have fun, and meet new friends. Some of these centers are extremely expensive, featuring$_5$ a luxurious environment, deluxe spa services, and free personal trainers. Other gyms attract different customers with their flashing lights, high-energy music and brightly colored$_6$ walls.

Most fitness centers schedule many group exercise classes, including yoga, aerobics$_7$, and Latin dance. Other common equipment includes weight machines and treadmills. They also have a swimming pool, sauna, Jacuzzi, and steam room. Finally, the children's classes, family days, and playrooms that many gyms provide encourage a future generation of buffed$_8$ Taiwanese.

台灣，勇起來！

　　纖細的仕女，深思的士大夫這些中國的理想人物現在都怎麼了？他們都上健身房去練身體去了！因為現在的台灣人喜歡健康結實的女性和精力十足的肌肉男，健身中心因而在島上大行其道。

　　為了吸引民眾，健身房提供從高中生到阿嬤級的顧客來健身、減壓、找樂子和交新朋友。有的中心收費昂貴，設備十分豪華，有頂級的療程服務和免費的私人專屬訓練師。有的健身房則以閃爍燈光、熱力四射的音樂和色彩繽紛的牆飾，招徠不同的顧客。

　　多數的健身房都安排許多團體運動課程，包括瑜伽班、有氧和拉丁舞蹈課。其他一般的設備有舉重機和走路機，並設有游泳池、三溫暖、按摩池和蒸汽室。許多健身房還有兒童課程、家庭日和遊樂室，讓台灣下一代也能強健起來。

🖊 生字 Vocabulary

1. **buff up** 強壯起來
   Some magazine articles offer tips for young women who want to buff up before their weddings.
   有的雜誌裡的文章提供婚前想強健起來的年輕女性一些秘方。

2. **delicate** 纖細
   Delicate dishes are easily broken.
   精細的碟子容易破。

3. **maiden** 仕女
   Many old novels feature an innocent maiden as their main character.
   許多舊小說中都有一個天真浪漫的小姐當主角。

4. **meditative** 冥想沈思的
   The woman had a meditative expression on her face.
   這位女士有股沈思的表情掛在臉上。

5. **work out** 鍛鍊身體
   Many women like to go to the fitness center to work out.
   許多女性喜歡上健身房去鍛鍊身體。

6. **toned** 結實
   Many women want to look toned, not muscular.
   許多女人希望看起來結實，卻不喜歡自己看起來太多肌肉。

7. **fitness center** 健身中心
   Fitness centers have become popular places for young people

to have fun.

健身中心是年輕人找樂子的熱門場所。

8. get in shape 健康、苗條

Swimming every day helps me get in shape.

每天游泳使我健康。

9. deluxe spa 豪華療程

The fitness center offers deluxe spa services like massage with essential oils.

這家健身中心提供像用精油按摩的豪華療程。

10. personal trainer 私人專屬訓練師

Many celebrities have personal trainers who help them stay in shape.

許多名流有私人專屬訓練師，幫他們瘦身。

11. yoga 瑜伽

Yoga helps people increase flexibility and relieve stress.

瑜伽幫人們增加彈性和紓解壓力。

12. aerobics 有氧舞

If you take an aerobics class, you can burn many calories.

如果你上有氧舞蹈，可以燃燒許多卡洛里。

13. Latin dance 拉丁舞

Latin dance is a popular group exercise class in Taiwan.

在台灣拉丁舞是很熱門的團體運動課。

14. weight machine 舉重機

Many weight machines are designed to work individual muscles.

許多舉重機設計成可以鍛鍊個別單塊的肌肉。

15. treadmill 走路機

Some people like to watch television while they are running on a treadmill.

有的人喜歡邊看電視邊在走路機上跑步。

16. sauna 乾的蒸氣室（烤箱）

The dry heat of the sauna relaxes tense muscles.

烤箱中乾的熱氣使緊繃的肌肉鬆弛。

17. Jacuzzi 按摩浴池

The swirling, hot water in the Jacuzzi was good for his sore back.

按摩浴缸裡的漩渦熱水對他酸痛的背有益。

18. steam room 濕的蒸氣室

She loved to spend time in the steam room after she exercised.

她喜歡運動後花些時間在蒸汽室裡。

✎ 課文重點分析 Analysis

1. work out 動詞，workout 名詞

   I work out in the gym three times a week.

   我一星期去健身房運動三次。

   I don't like a vigorous workout.

我不喜歡激烈的運動。

2. 用兩個形容詞將男女雙方的形象作一對比：healthy, toned women and energetic, muscular men。其他描寫形象的用法還有 loyal, diligent office workers；a timid, fragile boy；an outspoken, aggressive woman。

3. popular 形容詞，popularity 名詞。
Fitness centers have become popular. 也可以說 Fitness centers have gained popularity.

4. 如果要句子寫得有變化，可以多用現在分詞片語或過去分詞片語。appealing to 是現在分詞片語，原來的句型結構為：
Gyms appeal to a wide population.
Gyms offer a way for everyone to get in shape.
兩句合而為一：Appealing to a wide population, gyms offer a way for everyone to get in shape.

5. featuring 包括，指 some expensive fitness centers include the following features: 有的高價位的健身中心包括下面一些特色。

6. bright colors 鮮豔明亮的色彩。colored walls 被上色的牆壁，形容過去分詞 colored 要用副詞 brightly。

7. aerobic 原本的意思是激烈的，如：
Tennis is aerobic exercise.

網球是很激烈的運動。

aerobics(有氧舞蹈)原名是 aerobic dance，現在人提起有氧
舞蹈都用複數：aerobics，如：

I went to aerobics today.

我今天去跳有氧舞了。

8. buff 當名詞時是對某件事情很有興趣且十分在行的人，如 a
movie buff, a history buff, a wine buff。

buff 當動詞時是擦拭的意思。

🖋 克漏字

> aerobics, delicate, fitness center, personal trainer,
> sauna, toned, treadmill, weight machines, work out,
> yoga

1.　She doesn't want bigger muscles; she just wants to look

　　_____.

2.　Whenever it rains, he runs on a _____ instead of
　　running outside.

3.　After she exercises, she loves to relax in the _____.

4.　A _____ can show you how to exercise properly.

5.　He uses _____ three times a week to

build his muscles.

6. _____ is an ancient Indian form of exercise.

7. The new _____ is very luxurious but also very expensive.

8. He likes to _____ early in the morning.

9. _____ classes burn many calories.

10. The _____ vase was kept in a glass case.

✎ 選擇適當的詞性 Multiple Choice

_____ 1. The _____ necklace looked as if it could easily break. (a)delicately (b)delicate (c)delicacy

_____ 2. That seafood dish is the restaurant's most famous _____. (a)delicately (b)delicate (c)delicacy

_____ 3. The island was not _____ until recently. (a)populate (b)population (c)populated

_____ 4. Taiwan's _____ is quite high. (a)populate (b)population (c)populated

_____ 5. The monks _____ every day. (a)meditate (b)meditation (c)meditative

_____ 6. She practices _____ every day. (a)meditate

(b)meditation (c)meditative

_____ 7. My younger brother is a wine _____. (a)buffed (b)buffing (c)buff

_____ 8. He _____ his car to make it shiny. (a)buffed (b)buffing (c)buff

_____ 9. I don't have much _____ today. (a)energy (b)energetic (c)energized

_____ 10. Even though he is old, he is still very _____. (a)energy (b)energetic (c)energized

_____ 11. I joined a gym because I wanted to get in _____. (a)shape (b)shaping (c)shaped

_____ 12. Her hair was _____ like a flower. (a)shape (b)shaping (c)shaped

🖊 翻譯 Translation

1. 蒸氣室怎麼了？它為什麼沒蒸氣？

_____

2. 現在的台灣人喜歡結實的女性和肌肉男。

_____

3. 林黛玉型的纖細女人不再吸引(appeal to)台灣男人了。

_____

4. 我們頂級的Spa服務項目包括免費私人專屬訓練師和按摩師 (masseurs)。

_____

5. 下個月你要上瑜伽和有氧舞蹈課嗎？

_____

6. 這個月健身中心安排了(has scheduled)些什麼團體運動班？

_____

7. 這家健身房有些什麼設備？

_____

8. 藉著閃光和精力十足的音樂，這家健身房吸引了許多青少年。

_____

9. 你去過健身中心運動(work out)嗎？

_____

10. 許多上班族(office workers)每天到健身房健身(get in shape)和減壓。

_____

Diet Craze CD2 Track3

Influenced₁ by glamorous images of paper-thin models and actresses, many people in Taiwan, especially women, have joined the island's recent diet craze. Although some of these people are truly overweight and a few are even obese₂, most are just normally sized people who have become obsessed with losing weight₃.

In a culture where thinness equals beauty, many unscrupulous companies take advantage of the public's desire to be thin by promising quick and easy weight loss. Unfortunately, these promises are usually misleading₄, and some diet drugs can even be dangerous. Recently, the Department of Health has fined several companies that make diet products for false advertising₅.

Instead of relying on these diet drugs or fad diets, most people simply need a balanced diet and regular exercise to get in shape. Most importantly, we should realize that no matter what₆ fashion magazines suggest, fitness₇ is a better goal than thinness.

21 瘦身熱

　　許多台灣人，特別是女性，受了超級苗條名模和女明星光鮮亮麗形象的影響，喜歡趕最近台灣這股瘦身熱。儘管有些人真的過重，甚或少數人算是肥胖，不過大多數人體位均屬正常，他們只不過是迷上了瘦身而已。

　　當某種文化認為「瘦即美」時，不肖商家即利用一般人求瘦心切的心理，保證簡易又快速的瘦身良方，不幸的是這些保證常常誤導民眾，有的減肥藥甚至對人體有害。最近衛生署還針對做減肥藥不實廣告的商家施以罰款。

　　其實，與其靠減肥藥和流行的食療法，不如從均衡飲食和規律運動來改善體型，最重要的是，不管時尚雜誌建議什麼，以健康為目標總比以瘦身為目標來得好些。

✏ 生字 Vocabulary

1. glamorous 光鮮亮麗
   Actresses seem to live glamorous lives.
   女明星似乎活得亮麗光鮮。

2. paper-thin 超級苗條
   Many models are so paper-thin that they look unhealthy.
   許多模特兒超級苗條，她們看起來很不健康。

3. craze 熱潮
   Korean clothing has recently become a fashion craze in Taiwan.
   韓國服裝最近成了台灣的時裝熱。

4. overweight 超重
   Many women worry that they are overweight.
   許多女人擔心她們過重。

5. obese 肥胖的
   Because people eat so many more snacks than they used to, even some children are obese.
   人們吃的零食比從前多，甚至連兒童也過胖。

6. be obsessed with 熱中
   They are obsessed with investing money in the stock market.
   他們熱中玩股票。

7. unscrupulous 不講道德的
   Unscrupulous businessmen may lie to their customers to make extra money.

不法商人騙他們的顧客，以賺更多的錢。

8. weight loss 減重
Even thin high school students try products that promise weight loss.
連瘦瘦的高中生都試用保證可以減肥的產品。

9. misleading 誤導
Some politicians make misleading statements when they are running for office.
有的政治人物競選時說了一些誤導選民的話。

10. diet drug 減肥藥
If you are still taking diet drugs, stop taking them immediately. You need to make an appointment with your doctor.
如果你還在吃減肥藥，趕緊停掉，你需要去看醫生才行。

11. fine 罰款
They fined him NT$3000 for driving through a red light.
他們罰他闖紅燈3000元台幣

12. false advertising 不實廣告
The unbelievable claims that television commercials make are sometimes examples of false advertising.
電視廣告用些難以置信的廣告詞，是不實廣告的例子。

13. fad diets 流行食療減肥法
Fad diets sometimes require people to give up foods that are actually good for them.

流行食療減肥法有時要求人們放棄一些對他們身體有益的食物。

14. balanced diet 均衡飲食

Eating a balanced diet is a reasonable way to stay healthy.

飲食均衡是保持健康的合理方法。

15. get in shape 改善體型

Some people join gyms to get in shape.

有的人加入健身房使體型變好。

16. fitness 健康

Now that people live longer, fitness is especially important.

現在人們活得長，健康顯得特別重要。

✎ 課文重點分析 Analysis

1. Many people are influenced by glamorous images of models.

Many people have joined the island's recent diet craze.

這兩句的主詞都是many people，連成一句時可以把第一句的主詞(many people)去掉，動詞改用過去分詞：

Influenced by glamorous images of models, many people have joined the island's diet craze.

2. obese肥胖(形容詞)，obesity(名詞)。

More and more people are considered to be obese in Taiwan.

在台灣愈來愈多的人被認為過胖。

A diet high in fat may lead to obesity.

一個人的飲食含脂肪過多會導致肥胖。

3. lose weight減肥（動詞lose, lost, lost）She is obsessed with losing weight.（注意介系詞with後面動詞要加ing，lose→losing）。她熱中減肥。

   weight loss減肥（名詞）There are many weight loss resources on the Internet.網路上有許多減肥的資源。

4. mislead, misled, misled是「誤導」的動詞三態變化。

   Many politicians tried to mislead voters during the election.

   許多政治人物在選舉期間試著誤導選民。

   I was almost misled by the unscrupulous businessman who wanted to sell me a piece of fake jade.

   我幾乎被黑心商人誤導去買了一片假玉。

5. The Department of Health has fined several companies（that make diet products）for false advertising. that make diet products是形容companies的子句。for後面是指這些公司遭罰款的原因。

6. No matter how good you are...不管你有多好……

   No matter who you are...不管你是誰……

   No matter which book you bought...不管你買哪本書……

   No matter what he said...不管他說什麼……

   No matter when you come...不管什麼時候你來……

7. fitness健康（名詞），fit（形容詞）。

She likes to work out in the fitness center.

她喜歡在健身中心運動。

She likes to keep herself fit with diets and exercises.

她喜歡靠飲食和運動保持自己身體的健康。

✏ 克漏字 Cloze

> paper-thin, glamorous, balanced diet, get in shape, false advertising, unscrupulous, overweight, weight loss, fined, diet drugs

1. She takes some _____ medicine to lose weight.

2. Though she is a bit _____, many men think that she is a woman of great charm.

3. Many young Taiwanese work out in the gym two or three times a week to _____.

4. He was _____ for speeding yesterday.

5. Shh...Many people can hear what you are saying through this _____ wall.

6. Don't trust the _____ on TV commercials; you

can't never lose weight in three days.

7. Many _____ salespersons tried all kinds of tricks to rip off customers.

8. After reading news reports about the _____ issue, she realized she shouldn't rely on fad diets to lose weight.

9. If you have a _____, you can get all the nutrition you need.

10. Who can resist a _____ job and fame?

✎ 選擇適當的詞性 Multiple Choice

_____ 1. She was attracted to the _____ of Hollywood.
(a)glamour (b)glamorous (c)glamorously

_____ 2. Although the model's life was _____, she was unhappy. (a)glamour (b)glamorous (c)glamorously

_____ 3. Have you seen that _____ man who lives in our neighborhood? (a)obesity (b)obese (c)obesed

_____ 4. _____ has become a problem in many countries today. (a)Obesity (b)Obese (c)Obesed

_____ 5. The student was _____ with getting the highest

grade in his class. (a) obsessing (b) obsessed (c) obsession

_____ 6. Her _____ with Chinese opera is surprising. (a) obsessing (b) obsessed (c) obsession

_____ 7. He _____ his umbrella yesterday. (a) lose (b) lost (c) loss

_____ 8. Many weight _____ drugs are dangerous. (a) lose (b) lost (c) loss

_____ 9. Did you _____ any weight on that diet? (a) lose (b) lost (c) loss

_____ 10. The young girl was really too _____. (a) thin (b) thinness (c) thinned

_____ 11. In Taiwan, many people think _____ is attractive. (a) thin (b) thinness (c) thinned

_____ 12. Does Taiwan _____ any oil? (a) product (b) productive (c) produce

_____ 13. This _____ was made in France. (a) product (b) productive (c) produce

_____ 14. The woman was a very _____ writer. (a) product (b) productive (c) produce

✎ 翻譯 Translation

1. 健康(fitness)比瘦更重要。

___

2. 不管時尚雜誌建議什麼,我們都不要嘗試流行瘦身食療法 (fad diets)。

___

3. 你需要定期運動使體型改善。

___

4. 我從不羨慕(envy)超瘦型模特兒亮麗的形象。

___

5. 她雖是個正常體位的女孩,卻熱中減肥產品(diet products)。

___

6. 有些不實廣告保證快速容易的減肥(weight loss)。

___

7. 只要(as long as)你有個均衡的飲食,你會健康(fit)的。

___

8. 有些文化中肥胖等於美。

___

9. 與其靠流行食療法，一個人應該靠均衡的飲食。

---

10. 黑心商人利用大眾愛瘦心理賣他們的藥。

22　The Soothing Spa　CD2 Track4

As life has become increasingly hectic₁ in Taiwan, people are looking for ways to cope with the stress. Many people have turned to spas to relieve their tension. Located₂ in their own salons or in health clubs, spas pamper their customers with all kinds of treatments.

The most popular treatment is massage. A masseur or masseuse selects an appropriate massage style and essential oil fragrance for customers. Accompanied₃ by soft lighting and relaxing music, these massages are designed to please all of the senses.

Besides aromatherapy, other spa services can include hydrotherapy and facial treatments like peel-off masks and deep moisturizers. Although spa services can be quite expensive, loyal customers feel the psychological and physical benefits are worth every penny.

22 紓解壓力的Spa

當生活在台灣變得日益繁忙時,人們開始找法子應付壓力,去Spa紓緩壓力成為許多人的最愛。Spa設在自己的專店裡,或附設在健身中心裡,它用各種療法,撫慰顧客的身心。

最熱門的療法是按摩,由男女按摩師選擇適合顧客身體的精油香氣和按摩方式,搭配柔和的燈光和安神的音樂,這些按摩的設計,使所有感官得到快慰。

除了芳香療法外,其它Spa的服務項目還包括水療和用敷面膜和深層保濕膏做臉部保養。雖然Spa所費不貲,忠實的顧客還是覺得,花在使身心受益的Spa上,每一分錢都值得!

✎ 生字 Vocabulary

1. hectic 繁忙

   With his busy schedule, the businessman found that his life was very hectic.

   緊湊的行程使商人覺得自己的生活非常忙碌。

2. cope with 應付

   Exercise is a good way to cope with stress.

   運動是應付壓力的好方法。

3. spa 健康療程

   Spas have recently become a popular way to relax in Taiwan.

   健康療程最近在台灣已成了最風行的紓壓方法。

4. health club 健康中心

   Health clubs usually have a swimming pool, group exercise classes, and exercise machines.

   健康中心通常有游泳池、團體運動課程和運動器材。

5. pamper 撫慰、照顧

   Some people pamper their pets by giving them special treats and toys.

   有些人給寵物特殊的食物和玩具，溺愛他們的寵物。

6. massage 按摩

   A massage can help relieve the tension of people's daily lives.

   按摩可以幫助人們減輕每日生活的緊張。

7. masseur（男）or masseuse（女） 按摩師

In many hospitals in Taiwan a blind masseur or masseuse gives massages.

台灣許多醫院有男女盲按摩師給人按摩。

8. essential oil 精油

Essential oils are made from the flowers, leaves, and roots of plants.

精油是從植物的花、葉和根萃取而成。

9. fragrance 香氣

Her favorite fragrance was the scent of roses.

她最喜歡的香氣是玫瑰花香。

10. aromatherapy 芳香療法

Aromatherapy involves using essential oils for massages or baths.

芳香療法是用精油按摩和泡澡。

11. hydrotherapy 水療法

Hydrotherapy uses water as a form of massage.

水療法用水來按摩。

12. peel-off mask 敷面膜

A peel-off mask is supposed to tighten the pores on your face and remove impurities from your skin.

敷面膜是用來緊縮面部毛孔及移除皮膚上的污點。

13. moisturizer 保濕膏

A moisturizer can keep your face from looking too dry.

保濕膏讓你的臉看起來不要太乾。

14. psychological 心理的
Exercise and massage can have psychological benefits.
運動和按摩對心理也有好處。

15. physical 身體的
Daily physical activity is an important part of staying in shape.
每天從事與身體相關的活動是保持健康的要件。

✎ 課文重點分析 Analysis

1. hectic繁忙、快速的，是形容詞，如：a hectic schedule(繁忙的行程)。修飾形容詞要用副詞，如：an increasingly hectic pace of life(日益緊張繁忙的生活步調)。

2. 兩個相同主詞的句子可以合併在一起，例如：

Spas are located in their own salons or health clubs.

Spas pamper their customers with all kinds of treatments.

合為一句：Located in their own salons or health clubs, spas pamper their customers with all kinds of treatments.

3. 與上句Located...一樣，These massages are accompanied by soft lighting and relaxing music。與下句 These massages are designed to please all of the senses. 併為一句時，用過去分詞 Accompanied 開始。

🖊 克漏字 Cloze

> cope with, a peel-off mask, moisturizer, pamper, hectic, health club, massaged, aromatherapy, soothing, essential oil

1. In order to diminish wrinkles on her face, every night she applies _____ to her face with her fingertips.

2. The therapist gently _____ my back to help ease my backache.

3. She uses _____ once a week to remove impurities from her skin.

4. My recent _____ lifestyle has stressed me out.

5. Specializing in using _____ to help businessmen relax, this masseuse has gradually achieved fame and wealth.

6. I often use _____ music to help me fall asleep.

7. She used rose petals to make _____.

8. I don't know how to _____ the increasing number of emails.

9. She has recently joined a _____ to work out.

10. Don't try to _____ me. I don't want to be treated differently.

🖋 選擇適當的詞性 Multiple Choice

_____ 1. Students always feel _____ when school is over for the year. (a)relieve (b)reliefs (c)relieved

_____ 2. She took a big drink of water to _____ her thirst. (a)relieve (b)relief (c)relieved

_____ 3. At the meeting, everyone could feel the _____ in the room. (a)tense (b)tensed (c)tension

_____ 4. He is always _____ before an exam. (a)tense (b)tensed (c)tension

_____ 5. The cat _____ his muscles when he saw the dog. (a)tense (b)tensed (c)tension

_____ 6. Before it started to rain, we could already feel the _____ in the air. (a)moisture (b)moisturize (c)moisturized

_____ 7. The actress always keeps her face _____. (a)moisturizer (b)moisturize (c)moisturized

_____ 8. My mother told me to use a _____ on my face.

(a)moisturizer (b)moisturize (c)moisturized

_____ 9. He tries to get plenty of _____ exercise.

(a)physic (b)physical (c)physics

_____ 10. _____ is a very difficult science. (a)Physic

(b)Physical (c)Physics

_____ 11. After he graduated from medical school, he

became a _____. (a)physician (b)physicalist

(c)physist

✎ 翻譯 Translation

1. 最近我們的生活變得愈來愈(increasingly)繁忙。

_____

2. 你得找方法應付你緊張的生活。

_____

3. 最流行的治療法是芬香療法。

_____

4. 你知道在台北哪裡可以找到盲眼的男按摩師？

_____

5.　我們的服務包括水療和作臉部保養。

_____

6.　她不特別喜歡玫瑰的香氣。

_____

7.　他常用輕柔(soothing)的音樂紓解他的壓力。

_____

8.　你可以選擇最適合的按摩方式。

_____

9.　你喜歡我們健身中心的柔和燈光嗎？

_____

10.　我心理上很依賴(rely on)我的寵物。

_____

The Best of Both Worlds
CD2 Track5

While Taiwan has state-of-the-art Western-style medical care, many forms of traditional medical treatment are also covered by our National Health Insurance. More holistic than Western medicine, traditional treatment works gradually to get the whole body in balance$_1$.

Many Chinese medical doctors prescribe$_2$ herbal mixtures$_3$ that are drunk or eaten, but other forms of traditional medicine include many kinds of hands-on$_4$ therapies. Some of the best known in Taiwan are therapeutic massage, acupuncture, reflexology, cupping, and scraping.

Feeling that each type of medical care can be beneficial, some of Taiwan's doctors have integrated$_5$ Western and Chinese medicine. In the West, too, doctors and patients have recently turned to some traditional Chinese medical techniques. Thanks to open-minded doctors, we can all have the best of both worlds.

23 兼取中西醫之長

　　台灣有最先進的西醫療法，不過許多傳統療法也可以由健保給付。傳統療法比西醫更注重病人整體身心的健康，將病人全身慢慢調成平衡狀態。

　　許多中醫開中藥混合劑，供病人飲用或吞服，其他形式的傳統醫療還有用手的治療方法，其中最為人知的是推拿按摩、針灸、腳底按摩、拔火罐和刮痧。

　　台灣有些醫生覺得各種療法都對病人有益，所以將中西醫整合為一。在西方，醫生和病人最近也轉而採用一些傳統中醫的技術。還好有這些心胸開闊的醫生，我們可以擷取兩者之長。

🖉 生字 Vocabulary

1. **state-of-the-art** 最先進的
   His state-of-the-art computer was very expensive.
   他最先進的電腦所費不貲。

2. **cover** 涵蓋
   Her cosmetic surgery was not covered by insurance.
   她整型的費用不能由保險費給付。

3. **National Health Insurance** 健保
   Taiwan's National Health Insurance makes medical care available to many people.
   台灣健保讓許多人都能受醫療照顧。

4. **holistic** 全方位
   Doctors of holistic medicine consider the body as a whole.
   有全方位醫療概念的醫生把身體視為一個整體。

5. **balance** 平衡
   She tried hard to keep her work and family life in balance.
   她努力平衡她的工作與家庭。

6. **prescribe** 開處方
   The doctor prescribed a new kind of medicine for my father.
   醫生為我父親開了一種新藥。

7. **herbal medicine** 中藥（草藥）
   Even in the United States, many people now use herbal medicine.

即使在美國，許多人現在也用草藥。

8. hands-on 用手的
Massage is a hands-on therapy.
按摩是一種用手的醫療方式。

9. therapeutic massage 推拿按摩
Many people in Taiwan get a therapeutic massage every week.
許多在台灣的人每星期都讓人推拿按摩。

10. acupuncture 針灸
Acupuncture is not as painful as you might expect.
針灸沒有你想像的那麼疼痛。

11. reflexology 腳底按摩
Reflexology is supposed to restore the flow of energy in the body.
腳底按摩應該可以恢復你體內氣的順暢。

12. cupping 拔火罐
Cupping is an ancient Chinese medical technique that is still used today.
拔火罐是古代中國醫療技術，至今仍沿用。

13. scraping 刮痧
Scraping leaves bright red marks on the patient's skin that will last for several days.
刮痧留在病人皮膚上的紅印要過好幾天才會消。

14. integrated 整合

The teacher integrated several different teaching techniques into her lesson plans.

這位老師整合多種教學技術成為她自己的教案。

＊參考資訊

中醫 Chinese medicine；西醫 Western medicine；
中醫師 Chinese medical doctor；西醫師 Western doctor。

🖉 課文重點分析 Analysis

1. balance（動詞）、balance（名詞）、balanced（形容詞）：

He tried to balance his family values with his wild city nightlife.（動詞）

他試著在家庭價值觀與自己瘋狂的夜生活間找到一個平衡點。

Can you keep your mental and physical health in balance?（名詞）

你可以保持身心健康的平衡嗎？

She always has a balanced diet.

她的飲食均衡。

相反詞是an unbalanced diet。

2. prescribe（動詞）、prescription（名詞），例如：

The doctor prescribed a new medicine for me to try.

醫生開了一種新藥讓我試用。

I took the doctor's prescription to a drug store.

我拿著醫生的處方去藥房。

藥房通常有兩種藥，一種是prescription drugs處方藥，需要醫生的處方才能買得到，另一種是 over-the-counter drugs成藥，藥房架子上就可以買到。

prescription 還有一種特殊的用法：

She is wearing prescription sunglasses.

她帶著有度數的太陽眼鏡。

Prescription goggles are not very expensive.

有度數的泳鏡不貴。

3. mix（動詞）、mixed（形容詞）、mixture（名詞），例如：

He tried to mix water with milk powder.

他試著把奶粉跟水混在一起。

I have mixed feelings toward her.

我對她愛恨交雜。

I used the mixture of water, eggs, and flour to make pancakes.

我用水、蛋和麵粉的混合漿做蛋餅。

4. hands-on experience 實際動手的經驗

hands-on therapy 指用手按摩推拿的治療方法

5. integrate（動詞）、integrated（形容詞），例如：

She tried to integrate Western art and Chinese culture.

她試著整合西方藝術與中國文化。

These two systems are nicely integrated.

這兩種制度整合得很好。

✐ 克漏字 Cloze

state-of-the-art, cover, National Health Insurance, balance, prescribe, open-minded, integrated, holistic, therapeutic massage, acupuncture

1. The hospital's new equipment was _____.

2. The doctor refused to _____ any medicine since he didn't think the man was really ill.

3. I keep my _____ card with me at all times.

4. Doctors now use disposable needles for _____.

5. Does our insurance _____ surgery?

6. _____ can help relieve stress.

7. The _____ man always listened to other people's views.

8. Chinese medicine is more _____ than Western medicine because it treats the entire body.

9. With a busy schedule, it's hard to keep your life in
   _____.

10. The musician _____ classical music and jazz in
    his new CD.

🖉 選擇適當的詞性 Multiple Choice

_____ 1. In Taiwan, some doctors _____ herbal medicine.
(a) prescribe (b) prescription (c) prescriptive

_____ 2. The doctor gave her a _____ for some medicine.
(a) prescribe (b) prescription (c) prescriptive

_____ 3. We all need to _____ some relaxation into our
busy lives. (a) integrity (b) integrate (c) integrated

_____ 4. The honest man was known for his _____.
(a) integrity (b) integrate (c) integrated

_____ 5. The class _____ theory with practical advice.
(a) integrity (b) integrate (c) integrated

_____ 6. Taiwan's health insurance plan has many _____.
(a) benefit (b) beneficial (c) benefits

_____ 7. Studying a foreign language can be very _____.
(a) benefit (b) beneficial (c) benefited

_____ 8. She _____ from her father's reputation.
(a) benefit (b) beneficial (c) benefited

_____ 9. It is important to keep our lives in _____.
(a) balanced (b) balance (c) balancing

_____ 10. Everyone should eat a _____ diet. (a) balanced
(b) balance (c) balancing

_____ 11. The businessman had a hard time _____ his
expenses. (a) balanced (b) balance (c) balancing

✎ 翻譯 Translation

1. 這個最先進的醫療(medical treatment)不由健保給付。

_____

2. 傳統醫療使(keep)病人的全身保持平衡。

_____

3. 中醫比西醫更全方位。

_____

4. 這位中醫(Chinese medical doctors)開中藥混合劑給我飲
用。

_____

5. 有些醫生已經成功地整合中西醫學。

_____

6. 你試過了針灸、拔火罐和刮痧嗎？

_____

7. 我覺得腳底按摩對健康有益。

_____

8. 他懷疑中醫技術的效果(effectiveness)。

_____

9. 這位新聘人員(recruit)從來沒有任何實際動手的經驗。

_____

10. 只要我們心胸開闊，便可擷取中西方之長。

_____

Disasters
災難

24 Typhoons [CD2 Track6]

Most residents₁ of Taiwan have experienced the typhoons that sweep the island almost every summer. As soon as the Weather Bureau forecasts₂ the arrival of a typhoon, people begin to prepare.

Households store food and water and get out their matches, candles, and flashlights. Shops close and reinforce their windows with tape₃. Schools, offices, and financial markets close. Some people park their cars on highway overpasses₄ to avoid₅ flash flooding.

In the mountains, people have to watch for landslides. In low-lying areas, residents may have to be evacuated₆ to safer buildings. While some typhoons just bring heavy rain, severe ones can claim lives and damage property.

24　颱風

　　幾乎每年夏天颱風都會侵襲台灣，大多數的台灣居民也都有過颱風來襲的經驗。每當氣象局預報颱風來時，人們開始準備，

　　家家戶戶儲存食物和水，還把火柴、蠟燭、和手電筒拿出來。店家打了烊，還用膠帶強化窗戶。學校、辦公室和金融市場都關了，停止上課、上班和交易。有的人把車停在高架路上，避免突發的洪水。

　　在山區，人們得小心土石流；在低窪地區，居民疏散到較安全的建築物裡。颱風帶來大量雨量，劇烈的颱風還會奪走人命、危害居民的財產。

✏️ 生字 Vocabulary

1. resident 居民
   The local residents complained about the lack of parking spaces in this neighborhood.
   當地的居民抱怨附近缺少停車位。

2. typhoon 颱風
   Typhoons always bring rain and wind.
   颱風總是帶來風雨。

3. the Weather Bureau 氣象局；forecast 預報
   The Weather Bureau forecasts the weather, but it is not always correct.
   氣象局預報天氣，卻常常報得不準確。

4. flashlight 手電筒
   A flashlight can be very useful in a storm.
   手電筒在暴風雨時很有用。

5. reinforce 強化
   When she heard the typhoon was coming, she reinforced her windows with tape.
   當她聽到颱風要來時，用膠帶貼窗戶以強化玻璃(抗風力)。

6. financial market 金融市場
   The stock market is the best known financial market.
   股市是最廣為人知的金融市場。

7. overpass 高架橋、高架路

She parked her car on a highway overpass to avoid the flooded streets.

她把車停在高架橋上，以避開淹水的道路。

8. flash flooding 洪水

His car was washed away in the flash flooding.

他的車被洪水沖走了。

9. landslide 土石流

One village was destroyed by a landslide.

有一個村莊被土石流沖毀了。

10. low-lying area 低窪地區

Low-lying areas are flooded during typhoons.

颱風時低窪地區都會鬧水災。

11. be evacuated 被疏散

The old man refused to be evacuated even though he knew the storm was coming.

即使知道暴風雨要來，這位老先生還是拒絕疏散（到別的地方去）。

12. severe 厲害、嚴重

Their child has some severe learning difficulties.

他們的孩子有嚴重的學習困難。

13. claim 奪走

The Second World War has claimed millions of people's lives.

第二次世界大戰奪走了許多人的生命。

14. property 財產

This magazine is the property of the school library, so you can't keep it.

這本雜誌是學校圖書館的財產，你不能保有。

課文重點分析 Analysis

1. Most residents of Taiwan have experienced the typhoons that sweep the island almost every summer. 這句是談台灣居民的經驗，要用現在完成式。

2. forecast 動詞三態變化是forecast, forecast, forecast。

3. tape 可以當動詞：tape your voice（錄你的聲音）；tape the windows（用膠帶黏窗戶）。也可以當名詞：膠帶、卡帶。

4. highway overpass 車走的高架橋，pedestrian overpass 行人走的路橋。

5. avoid 後面的動詞要接動名詞，例如：I try to avoid shopping on Sundays.

6. evacuate 撤離：

   主動：The police evacuated local people to a safer place.

   警察遷離當地居民到較安全的地方。

   被動：Many people were evacuated from their homes.

   許多人被撤離出他們的家了。

✏ 克漏字 Cloze

residents, low-lying, reinforced, overpass, forecast, financial, properties, evacuated, household, severe

1. The weatherman _____ that there would be a pouring rain tonight.

2. Thanks to the firefighters' quick actions, tourists who got trapped in the building were _____ to a safer place.

3. I hope he can help his parents do some _____ chores when he has free time.

4. He has made some profits by investing some money in the _____ market.

5. People who live in _____ areas are worrying about the upcoming typhoon.

6. The family faced _____ damages after the earthquake.

7. The crumbling old house urgently needs to be _____ before the storm hits.

8. Taipei _____ are not happy with the lack of parking spaces.

9. He owns a lot of _____ in business districts.

10. My grandfather was afraid to drive on the highway

_____ .

✏ 選擇適當的詞性 Multiple Choice

_____ 1. My sister is a _____ of Seattle, Washington.

(a)residence (b)resident (c)residential

_____ 2. The prime minister's _____ was heavily guarded.

(a)residence (b)resident (c)residential

_____ 3. You should drive slower in _____ neighborhoods.

(a)residence (b)resident (c)residential

_____ 4. All of Ben's books were lost in the _____. (a)flood

(b)flooding (c)flooded

_____ 5. It was raining so hard that the basement was ____.

(a)flood (b)flooding (c)flooded

_____ 6. Living abroad is a very good _____. (a)experience

(b)experiencing (c)experienced

_____ 7. He is an _____ cook. (a)experience

(b)experiencing (c)experienced

_____ 8. I _____ the kitchen floor every week. (a)swept

(b)sweeping (c)sweep

_____ 9. You can sleep on the floor because it was _____ this afternoon. (a) swept (b) sweeping (c) sweep

_____ 10. Let's _____ the table for dinner. (a) prepare (b) prepared (c) preparing

_____ 11. Going camping takes a lot of _____. (a) prepares (b) preparation (c) preparing

_____ 12. Be _____ to know the vocabulary from the first three chapters of the textbook for the test tomorrow. (a) prepare (b) prepared (c) preparing

_____ 13. This pipe is leaking poisonous gases, so go ahead and _____ the building. (a) evacuating (b) evacuate (c) evacuated

_____ 14. The entire building was _____ in five minutes. (a) evacuating (b) evacuate (c) evacuated

✏ 翻譯 Translation

1. 你曾經歷過颱風橫掃台灣嗎？

_____

2. 我一儲存好食物和水時，颱風就來了。

_____

3. 住在低窪地區很危險。

    _____

4. 上回人們把車停在高架橋上避洪水。

    _____

5. 山區居民得注意土石流。

    _____

6. 週末金融市場都關了。

    _____

7. 我們被疏散到安全的地方去。

    _____

8. 上回颱風帶來大雨。

    _____

9. 上星期嚴重的地震奪走三條人命。

    _____

10. 你得關門和把窗貼膠紙以強化(玻璃)。

    _____

Fire Ant Invasion (CD2 Track7)

Fire ants have begun to invade Taiwan, attacking people and property. Originating₁ in Brazil, these unwelcome guests have dangerous venom that can cause painful₂ swelling₃ and sometimes even death. Furthermore, these pests can also damage crops, furniture, and electric cables.

If you are bitten by a fire ant, you should use a cold compress to stop the itchiness and swelling. Seek immediate medical treatments and be careful not to break the blister since that could lead to infection₄.

Officials are trying to destroy the ants' colonies, but it is very difficult to wipe them out completely. To be safe, people should not touch anthills and farmers should not work in the fields barefoot.

火蟻入侵

火蟻開始入侵台灣，攻擊人的身家財產。這群「不速之客」來自巴西，牠危險的毒液能使傷口紅腫疼痛，有時可致人於死，還有，這群害蟲會破壞農作物、家具和電纜。

如果你遭火蟻叮咬了，你得趕緊用冰敷，以免造成傷口發癢和紅腫。你得立刻找醫生治療，小心不要把傷口的水泡弄破了，以免感染。

官員們企圖摧毀火蟻族群，但要完全消滅火蟻並非易事。為了安全起見，一般人最好不要去碰觸蟻丘，農夫在田裡工作，也最好不要打著赤腳。

🖊 生字 Vocabulary

1. fire ant 火蟻

   The farmer was bitten by several angry fire ants.

   農夫被許多「生氣的」火蟻咬了。

2. invasion（invade動詞） 入侵

   The soldiers planned their invasion carefully to surprise their enemy.

   軍人小心計畫侵襲敵人，讓敵人驚慌失措。

3. originate 起源於

   Although some inventions originated in one country, they were developed in another country.

   雖然有些發明在某個國家先開始，卻在另一個國家發揚光大。

4. venom 毒液

   Snakes often have poisonous venom.

   蛇常有毒液。

5. swelling 腫脹

   The swelling on my arm was very painful.

   我手臂腫脹的部分很痛。

6. pest 害蟲

   Mosquitoes are common pests in most of Taiwan.

   蚊子是大部分台灣的常見的「害蟲」。

7. crop 農作物

   The main crop grown in Taiwan is rice.

台灣主要的農作物是水稻。

8. electric cable 電纜

Electric cables carry power to people's houses.

電纜將電輸送到每戶人家。

9. cold compress 冰敷用的軟布

My mother put a cold compress on my arm.

我的媽媽將冰毛巾敷在我的手臂上。

10. itchy 癢（itchiness是名詞）

If a mosquito or ant bites you, you will feel itchy.

如果一隻蚊子或一隻螞蟻咬了你，你馬上會覺得很癢。

11. treatment 治療

The doctor recommended a new treatment for his patient.

醫生建議病人一種新的治療方法。

12. blister 水泡

Walking in new shoes gave me a blister.

穿新鞋走路讓我腳磨出了一個水泡。

13. infection 感染

Washing your hands before you eat can help you avoid infection.

吃飯前先洗手讓你免於得傳染病。

14. colony 殖民地、昆蟲群

The British used to have many colonies all over the world.

英國人從前在世界各地有許多殖民地。

A colony of termites started to invade the wood floor in our living room.

白蟻群開始進攻我們客廳的木製地板。

15. wipe out 滅絕

It is very difficult to wipe out terrorism.

很難把恐怖主義完全消滅。

16. anthill 蟻丘

The workers even found anthills in Taipei City.

工人居然在台北市發現了蟻丘。

17. field 農田

Farmers often work long hours in their fields.

農夫常在田裡工作好幾小時。

18. barefoot 赤腳

In the summer, children like to be barefoot as often as possible.

在夏天，小孩子喜歡儘可能的打赤腳。

✎ 課文重點分析 Analysis

1. Fire ants originated in Brazil. Fire ants have dangerous venom.

以上兩個句子都在談 fire ants，可以將兩句合併，第一個動詞改為現在分詞(V+ing)：Originating in Brazil, fire ants have dangerous venom.

2. painful「令人感到痛苦的」而不是「人本身感覺痛苦」，通常放在名詞前面。例如：

He has a painful swelling on his ankle.

他腳踝腫得很痛。

This is a painful piece of news.

這是一則讓人痛心的新聞。

如果要形容人本身很痛，要用名詞 pain，例如：

I feel pain. I am in pain.

我覺得痛。

I feel some pain.

我覺得有些痛。

I feel great pain.

我覺得非常痛。

I feel no pain.（注意：（×）I feel painless.）

我覺得不痛。

3. swell（腫）的動詞三態變化如下：swell, swelled, swollen。

After I fell, my knee immediately started to swell up.

我跌倒後膝蓋馬上腫起來。

swelling是名詞，A cold compress will help the swelling go down.

冰敷可以幫助消腫。

4. infect（動詞）、infection（名詞）、infectious（形容詞）：

He infected at least five people with the SARS virus.

他把SARS病毒傳染了至少五個人。

Some infections can't be cured even by strong medicine.

有的感染下重藥也治不好。

Bird Flu is an infectious disease.

禽流感是一種傳染病。

克漏字 Cloze

> originated, barefoot, fire ants, venom, itchy, swelling, wipe out, infection, treatment, blister

1. Taiwan's humid weather makes my hands _____.

2. The game _____ in China.

3. If you don't keep your wound clean enough, it may lead to _____.

4. Don't expect that you can _____ fire ants all at once.

5. You'd better not walk _____ on the grass because you might get some insect bites.

6. Because there was no _____, the disease soon

spread quickly.

7. After breaking the ＿＿＿＿＿＿＿＿, you need to put some medicine on the wound.

8. The ＿＿＿＿＿＿ on my face subsided after I used a cold compress.

9. An army of ＿＿＿＿＿＿ started to invade our backyard.

10. Sometimes a snake's ＿＿＿＿＿＿ is strong enough to kill an elephant.

✎ 選擇適當的詞性 Multiple Choice

＿＿＿＿＿ 1. The mosquito bite led to a serious ＿＿＿. (a) infect (b) infection (c) infectious

＿＿＿＿＿ 2. Her positive attitude was very ＿＿＿＿. (a) infect (b) infection (c) infectious

＿＿＿＿＿ 3. His cut got ＿＿＿＿＿ when he touched it with his dirty hands. (a) infected (b) infecting (c) infectious

＿＿＿＿＿ 4. There was a ＿＿＿＿＿ of ants in his backyard. (a) colonize (b) colonist (c) colony

＿＿＿＿＿ 5. Many South American countries were ＿＿＿＿ by the Spanish in the sixteenth century. (a) colonize (b)colonized (c)colony

_____ 6. The doctor _____ his cold with medication.
(a)treat (b)treatment (c)treated

_____ 7. The bump on his head started to _____.
(a)swelling (b)swell (c)swollen

_____ 8. His eye was _____ so badly that he could not
see. (a)swelling (b)swell (c)swollen

_____ 9. They were the _____ members of the team.
(a)origin (b)original (c)originate

_____ 10. What is the _____ of this old saying?　(a)origin
(b)original (c)originate

_____ 11. Those ghost stories _____ in Africa.　(a)origin
(b)original (c)originated

_____ 12. They needed _____ to turn on the lights.
(a)electricity (b)electrical (c)electrically

_____ 13. He plugged the television into the _____ outlet.
(插座)(a)electricity (b)electrical (c)electrically

✎ 翻譯 Translation

1. 火蟻起源於巴西。

   _____

2. 這些不受歡迎的客人有很危險的毒液。

   _____

3. 火蟻的毒液能造成痛苦的腫脹。

   _____

4. 去年這些害蟲破壞穀物、家具和電纜。

   _____

5. 用一條冰敷巾可以止癢。

   _____

6. 你得找立即的醫藥處理。

   _____

7. 小心不要把水泡弄破了。

   _____

8. 你的傷口(wound)也許會導致感染。

   _____

9. 為了安全,你最好不要打赤腳(go barefoot)。

   _____

10. 火蟻很難完全消滅(wipe out)。

26 Devastating Tsunamis₁
CD2 Track8

In December 2004, as tourists were enjoying their holidays in tropical Asian resorts₂, and local people were going about their everyday lives, suddenly, with little warning, the most powerful earthquake in 40 years triggered a series of₃ devastating tsunamis.

While the earthquake's epicenter was just northwest of the Indonesian island of Sumatra, tidal waves caused catastrophic damage to many different countries. The nations hardest hit were Indonesia, Sri Lanka, India, and Thailand, but other Asian and even African countries were also affected₄. The United Nations estimates that the final death toll will be around 150,000. The survivors face severe problems, including food and water shortages, and epidemics.

In response to this natural disaster, governments, charities, and individuals have donated money, food, and clothing. Taiwan's government generously pledged US$50 million in aid, making Taiwan one of the world's top 10 donor countries. To prevent future disasters, scientists are working on improved₅ warning systems. Since Taiwan, too, is susceptible to earthquakes and tsunamis, we should upgrade our own emergency preparedness plans.

殺傷力驚人的海嘯

2004年12月，一群觀光客正在亞洲熱帶度假勝地歡度假期，當地人也正忙於每天的生活，突然幾乎沒有預警的情況下，四十年來威力最強的地震在當地引發一連串極具破壞力的大海嘯。

地震的震央在印尼蘇門達臘島的西北方，海嘯卻使許多國家遭受毀滅性的損失，受害最嚴重的國家有印尼、斯里蘭卡、印度和泰國。有些其他亞洲、甚或非洲國家也受到波及。聯合國估計，最後的罹難人數將在十五萬人左右。死裡逃生的人也面臨嚴重問題：包括食物和飲水的欠缺，還有傳染病的流行。

面對這次天然災害，政府、慈善機構和個人都捐輸錢財、食物和衣物。台灣政府也慷慨解囊，答應捐出五千萬美金援救災區，使台灣成為世界捐款排名的前十名。為了預防未來的災難，科學家正努力改善災難預警系統。台灣也同樣容易受到地震和海嘯的襲擊，我們應該提升危機處理的方案。

✎ 生字 Vocabulary

1. resort 度假勝地
During their winter vacations, many people travel to resorts to relax.
寒假期間許多人到度假勝地去放鬆一下。

2. trigger 引發
A typhoon can trigger a landslide.
颱風會引發土石流。

3. devastating 破壞性的、慘痛的
Taiwan's 921 earthquake was a devastating experience.
台灣921大地震真是經驗慘痛。

4. tsunami 海嘯
Japan has a well-developed tsunami warning system.
日本海嘯預警系統作得很好。

5. epicenter 震央
Many of Taiwan's earthquakes have epicenters on the east coast.
台灣許多地震的震央都在東岸。

6. Sumatra 蘇門達臘
With its tropical climate, Sumatra has many beautiful flowers and trees.
蘇門達臘屬熱帶氣候，花木十分美麗。

7. tidal wave 海嘯

A tidal wave can destroy an entire village in a short period of time.

海嘯可以在短時間內摧毀整個村莊。

8. catastrophic 毀滅性的、災難性的

Many people volunteer to help during a catastrophic flood.

許多人在大水災時自願幫忙。

9. death toll 罹難人數

The death toll continued to grow as authorities received more accurate reports.

當官方接到更多正確的報導時，罹難人數不斷攀升。

10. epidemic 流行傳染病

When water becomes contaminated, epidemics can easily break out.

水遭污染時，傳染病很容易爆發。

12. natural disaster 天然災害

Typhoons and earthquakes are the most common natural disasters in Taiwan.

颱風和地震是台灣最常見的天然災害。

13. pledge 承諾

The rich businessman pledged a large sum of money to the disaster relief effort.

這位有錢的商人答應捐筆鉅款救災。

14. susceptible 易受影響的

Young children are often susceptible to colds.

小孩很容易得感冒。

15. upgrade 提升

She upgraded her ticket to fly first class.
她把機票升級到頭等艙。

🖉 課文重點分析 Analysis

1. tsunami 是從日文「津波」而來，也可以稱為 tidal wave。許
多外來文字已為英文字典收為英文字，如：豆腐(tofu)、蘿蔔
(日文稱大根)(daikon)和卡拉OK(karaoke)。

2. resort 是度假勝地，as a last resort 的 resort 是指所有方法都
用盡之後，最後的解決法實或知道解決的人。如：
As a last resort, we could ask your grandpa to help.
說到最後解決之道，我們可以請你祖父幫忙。

3. a series of tsunamis 一連串的海嘯。也可以用在一系列的書 a
series of books。

4. affect 和 effect 很容易混淆。affect 是動詞，effect 是名詞，
effective(有效)是形容詞。如：
Her opinions did not affect my decision.
她的意見沒有影響我的決定。
Her opinions had no effect on my decision.
她的意見對我的決定沒有影響力。
This medicine was not very effective for my allergy.

這個藥對我的過敏沒有太大的效果。

5. improved warning system 是指這個預警系統已被改善。improved 是過去分詞。

✐ 克漏字 Cloze

> resort, epicenter, natural disaster, upgraded, trigger, catastrophic, death toll, pledged, susceptible, tsunami

1. The typhoon was a terrible _____.

2. They spent their holiday in an expensive _____.

3. A gas leak can _____ an explosion.

4. People living on the coast have to be prepared for a _____.

5. The _____ of the earthquake was in Nantou County.

6. The _____ from the storm was very high.

7. The mountains are _____ to landslides.

8. The government _____ to fight corruption.

9. After the fire, he faced _____ damage.

10. He _____ his seat on the flight to first class.

✎ 選擇適當的詞性 Multiple Choice

_____ 1. David's mom always _____ a snack for him when he comes home from school. (a) preparing (b) prepared (c) prepares

_____ 2. Too much time in front of the TV can _____ a person's vision. (a) affect (b) effect (c) affected

_____ 3. Tracy was a good role model and had a positive _____ on her sister. (a) affect (b) effect (c) affection

_____ 4. We have asked our friends to _____ to us by Tuesday to let us know if they will be attending our party. (a) response (b) responding (c) respond

_____ 5. The _____ to Joan's car was severe after she was hit by a truck. (a) damaging (b) damaged (c) damage

_____ 6. The roads were a _____ as soon as the traffic lights stopped working. (a) disaster (b) disastrous (c) disastrously

_____ 7. The heavy rain had _____ consequences for Taipei residents. (a) disaster (b) disastrous (c) disastrously

_____ 8. It is only _____ for parents to want what is best for their children. (a) nature (b) naturalist (c) natural

_____ 9. The pilot's _____ was correct and we landed on schedule. (a) estimating (b) estimation (c) estimate

_____ 10. The _____ to the charity auction (慈善義賣) was a great success as we raised a lot of money. (a) response (b) responding (c) respond

🖉 翻譯 Translation

1. 昨天當我正在看電視時，他打電話來。

   _____

2. 我最喜歡到墾丁的度假村去度假 (on vacation)。

   _____

3. 地震引發一連串的海嘯。

   _____

4. 昨晚地震的震央在花蓮東南方。

   _____

5. 一連串的戰爭對許多國家造成摧毀性的損傷。

   _____

6. 政府估計這次地震的最後死亡人數是472人。

_____

7. 人們得面對許多嚴重問題如水的欠缺和傳染病。

_____

8. 你捐錢、食物和衣物給受災戶了嗎？

_____

9. 許多公司答應幫助水災(flood)受災戶。

_____

10. 我們應該提升我們自己的危機處理方案。

_____

Food and Drinks
飲食

27 Yummy Taiwan CD2 Track9

As everyone who lives in Taiwan knows, food plays a major role in our country's culture. From business lunches to wedding banquets, food makes each occasion special. Thanks to Taiwan's geography and history, we can choose from a wide variety of mouthwatering dishes.

Since Taiwan is an island, seafood has long been a highlight₁ of Taiwanese cuisine. Taiwan's diet became more varied₂ when the KMT government and its followers retreated to Taiwan in 1949, bringing their cooking styles from different provinces₃ with them. Some well-known Chinese favorites include Peking duck, dim sum, and drunken chicken.

In addition to Chinese food, Taiwan also offers a diverse range of ethnic food. Because Japan occupied Taiwan for 50 years, Japanese food like sushi is still widely available. Recently, Taiwan's Southeast Asian foreign workers have introduced dishes that use exotic herbs and spices. Other restaurants specialize₄ in European food, especially French and Italian. With so many delicious choices, Taiwan is a food-lover's paradise!

台灣美食

　　台灣的人都知道，食物是我們文化裡很主要的一部份，從商業午餐到結婚酒席，食物使每個社交場合生色不少。由於台灣特殊的地理環境和歷史背景，我們可以選用多種令人垂涎三尺的好菜。

　　台灣是個小島，海鮮長久以來就是台菜最吸引人的部分。1949年國民政府和人民遷台，帶來各省口味的菜色，台灣的吃開始變得多樣化，有名的中華料理包括：北京烤鴨　廣式點心和醉雞。

　　除了中華料理外，台灣還有不同類別的外國食物，日本統治台灣50年，日本料理如壽司因而普及全台，近年來東南亞外勞引介的菜色，多用外國風味的香草和香料，有的餐館如法國菜和義大利菜則是以歐式料理為號召，台灣的吃有這麼多的選擇，無怪乎是老饕的天堂！

✎ 生字 Vocabulary

1. mouthwatering 令人垂涎
   Even though the restaurant is not famous, it serves mouthwatering food.
   這家餐館雖不太有名卻供應令人垂涎的菜色。

2. dish 菜
   Her favorite dish is fried eel.
   他最愛吃的一道菜是煎鰻魚。

3. highlight 特色、高潮
   The highlight of his American trip was his visit to New York.
   他美國行的重頭戲是去了紐約。

4. cuisine 料理
   French cuisine typically uses butter, cream, and wine.
   法國料理通常用牛油、奶油和葡萄酒。

5. province 省
   Each province in China has its own style of cooking.
   中國每省都有自己料理的方法。

6. Peking duck 北京烤鴨
   The restaurant's specialty is Peking duck.
   這家餐館的特色菜是北京烤鴨。

7. dim sum 廣式點心
   Hong Kong has many restaurants that serve dim sum.
   香港許多餐廳供應廣式點心。

8. drunken chicken 醉雞

The recipe for drunken chicken was originally from Shanghai.

醉雞的作法原創於上海。

9. diverse 多元的

Taiwan's population is now more diverse than it used to be.

現在台灣的人口比從前多元化。

10. ethnic food 不同種族的食物

Because Taiwan now has people who have moved here from many countries, more types of ethnic food are available.

因為台灣有許多人來自其他國家，所以可以買到更多樣的不同國家的食物。

11. sushi 壽司

Sushi is a convenient snack that you can buy all over Taiwan.

壽司是全台都買得到的方便小點心。

12. exotic 有趣的、外國的

When you travel abroad, you may have the chance to try some exotic food.

你到國外旅行時可以有機會嚐到許多外國的食物。

13. herb 香草

My grandmother grew her own herbs in a garden behind her house.

我的祖母在她家後面種了她自己的香草。

14. spice 香料

Indian food uses many spices that aren't common in Taiwan.

印度菜用了許多在台灣不常見的香料。

✏️ 課文重點分析 Analysis

1. highlight是動詞（強調）也是名詞（最好的部分）。例如：

I used a red pen to highlight the important part of the document.

我用紅筆把文件重要的部分劃出來。（主動）

The grammatical errors in the essay have been highlighted in red.

這篇文章中的文法錯處被用紅筆勾了出來。（被動）

The highlights of the movie will be shown on TV.（名詞）

這部電影中重要的部分會在電視上播放。

最近流行挑染頭髮也叫做highlight。例如：

Her hair has been highlighted in red.

她的頭髮被挑染成紅色。

2. vary（動詞）、varied（形容詞）、various（形容詞）、variation（名詞），例如：

Her interests vary from time to time.

她的興趣隨著時間而改變。

Nightlife in Taichung has become more varied.

台中的夜生活變得多采多姿。

This coffee shop offers first-rate espresso and various kinds of drinks.

這家咖啡店提供頂級義大利濃縮咖啡和各種飲料。

There is not much variation in Singapore's weather.

新加坡氣候的變化不大。

3. province（名詞）、provincial（形容詞）。例如：

How many provinces are there in China?

中國有幾省？

This type of music is a bit too provincial for my taste.

這類音樂對我而言太過地方性了（本土）。

4. special（形容詞）、specialty（名詞）、specialize（動詞）、specialist（名詞）。例如：

Her special hobby is collecting crabs' claws.

她特別的興趣是收集螃蟹的鉗子。

Stone carving is her specialty.

石雕是她的專長。

Today's specialty is rosemary lamb chops.

今天的特色菜是迷迭香羊排。

She specializes in research on political participation.

她專長於研究政治參與的議題。

He is a specialist in British history.

他是英國史專家。

✏ 克漏字 Cloze

mouthwatering, dish, cuisine, highlight, province, diverse, dim sum, spices, exotic, sushi

1. The waiter pushed around carts of food in the _____ restaurant.

2. When I went to Africa, I ate some _____ food that I can't find in Taiwan.

3. Chinese _____ is world famous.

4. She flavors her cooking with many different _____.

5. His grandfather was from Hunan _____.

6. The food my mother cooks is _____.

7. The United States has a very _____ population.

8. The restaurant's most famous _____ includes several kinds of seafood.

9. Even though _____ is Japanese, it is available in many countries.

10. Winning the lottery was the _____ of his life.

✒ 選擇適當的詞性 Multiple Choice

_____ 1. The restaurant serves a wide _____ of dishes.
(a) various (b) variety (c) vary

_____ 2. The store sells _____ kinds of books. (a) various
(b) variety (c) vary

_____ 3. Canada is divided into _____. (a) provincial
(b) province (c) provinces

_____ 4. The _____ office was much smaller than the national
office. (a) provincial (b) province (c) provinces

_____ 5. My mother uses many _____ in her cooking.
(a) spice (b) spices (c) spicy

_____ 6. Indian food is too _____ for me. (a) spice
(c) spices (c) spicy

_____ 7. She grows her own _____. (a) herbal (b) herbs
(c) herbalist

_____ 8. _____ medicine is popular in Taiwan. (a) Herbal
(b) Herbs (c) Herbalist

_____ 9. The man bought his wife a ring as a _____
gift. (a) specialist (b) specialized (c) special

_____ 10. These shops _____ in handmade furniture.

(a) specialist (b) specialize (c) special

_____ 11. His _____ was American literature.

(a) specialist (b) specialize (c) specialty

_____ 12. Taiwan's population is more _____ than it used to be. (a) diverse (b) diversity (c) diversify

_____ 13. _____ can make a country more interesting.

(a) Diverse (b) Diversity (c) Diversify

✎ 翻譯 Translation

1. 他喜歡吃各樣的餐飲 (meals)，從商業午餐到結婚酒席無一不愛。

   _____

2. 多虧台灣特別的地理和歷史，我們可以吃到各樣的好菜。 Thanks to...

   _____

3. 泰國菜 (Thai food) 用了許多外國香草和調味料。

   _____

4. 台灣是個海島，海鮮長久以來是台灣料理的一個重要的部分。

   _____

5. 你吃過北京烤鴨和醉雞嗎？

_____

6. 台灣有許多外國料理，例如：印度菜、泰國菜和義大利菜。

_____

7. 點心這家餐廳沒有 (not available)。

_____

8. 台灣是一個老饕的天堂。

_____

28 Chill Out with a Cold Drink
(CD2 Track10)

As Taiwan's weather heats up, thirst-quenching₁ cold drinks provide a great way to cool down. These ubiquitous treats₂ can be found in convenience stores, juice bars, vending machines, tea houses, and roadside stands throughout the island.

While some beverages like beer, sports drinks, and soft drinks are canned or bottled, others are freshly made from Taiwan's abundant supply of fruit. Papaya milkshakes and other blended drinks are popular favorites. Freshly squeezed₃ juice, often cooled with shaved₃ ice, is always refreshing.

Recently, Taiwan's cold tea drinks have also become very popular. Pearl milk tea, bubble tea, taro milk tea, green tea mixed with fruit juice, kumquat tea... you name it. When it comes to₄ satisfying₅ your taste buds, Taiwan's manufacturers are endlessly creative.

28 清涼舒爽靠冷飲

當台灣的天氣開始燠熱時，生津止渴的冷飲提供妙方使你頓生清涼，這些無所不在的「好康」可以在全台的便利商店、果汁店、自動販賣機、茶館和路邊攤買到。

有的飲料像啤酒、運動飲料和不含酒精的各種冷飲都用罐裝或瓶裝，有的飲料則直接從台灣豐富的水果取材，木瓜牛奶和其他混合飲料都很熱門。剛榨的新鮮果汁常加剉冰，喝起來讓人精神為之一振。

最近台灣的冰茶也開始流行，珍珠奶茶、泡沫紅茶、芋奶茶、綠茶加果汁、金桔茶……只要你說得出名字來的，無一不全。說到滿足你的味蕾，台灣商人點子可真不少！

✏ 生字 Vocabulary

1. chill out 輕鬆
   After all that heavy office work, you need to chill out.
   辦公室繁忙的工作完了後，你需要輕鬆一下。

2. thirst-quenching 生津止渴
   Thirst-quenching drinks are popular on hot days.
   大熱天生津止渴的飲料很當道。

3. ubiquitous 處處可見
   Motor scooters are ubiquitous in Taiwan.
   摩托車在台灣處處可見。

4. vending machine 自動販賣機
   You will find vending machines all over Taiwan.
   自動販賣機遍及全台。

5. roadside stand 路邊攤
   Many roadside stands sell fruits and vegetables in the summer.
   許多路邊攤在夏天賣水果蔬菜。

6. beverage 飲料
   Cold tea drinks are now very popular beverages.
   冰茶是當紅的飲料。

7. soft drink 不含酒精的飲料如汽水
   The cafe only sold soft drinks, not beer.
   這家咖啡店只賣汽水，不賣啤酒。

8. abundant 豐富的
Bananas are abundant in Taiwan.
台灣盛產香蕉。

9. papaya milkshakes 木瓜牛奶
The juice stand is famous for its papaya milkshakes.
這家果汁店以木瓜牛奶聞名。

10. squeezed 被榨成的
He will only drink freshly squeezed juice.
他只喝剛榨出來的果汁。

11. shaved ice 剉冰
Eating shaved ice is a good way to cool down.
吃剉冰是清涼的好方法。

12. refreshing 清爽的
Taking a cool shower can be refreshing during the summer.
夏天洗個冷水澡使人十分清爽。

13. pearl milk tea 珍珠奶茶
Pearl milk tea was invented in Taiwan.
珍珠奶茶是台灣的獨創。

14. bubble tea 泡沫紅茶
Bubble tea is not as well-known as pearl milk tea.
泡沫紅茶比不上珍珠奶茶有名。

15. taro 芋頭
Taro can be mixed with many different foods.

芋頭可搭配許多其他食物。

16. kumquat 金桔

Kumquats look like tiny oranges.

金桔看起來像小柳丁。

17. taste buds 味蕾

As people get older, their taste buds become less sensitive.

人愈老，味蕾就愈不敏感。

✎ 課文重點分析 Analysis

1. quench 是解(渴)的意思。例如：

   Iced tea can quench our thirst.

   冰茶可以解渴。

   thirst-quenching是形容詞，形容飲料可以生津止渴。如：

   thirst-quenching lemonade

   生津止渴的檸檬水。

2. treat是動詞也是名詞，當動詞用時，例如：

   I will treat my sister to a movie tonight.

   我今晚要請我妹妹去看場電影。

   I will treat myself to a new pair of jeans.

   我要買一條新的牛仔褲犒賞自己。

   當名詞用時意指請客或樂事、可喜的事。

   You paid for the meal, so dessert is my treat.

你付了飯錢，所以甜點由我來請。

Reading a novel is a real treat for a busy person.

讀本小說對一個忙碌的人來說，真是件賞心樂事。

3. squeezed juice, shaved ice都要用被動，因為果汁是被人榨的，剉冰是被人剉的。

4. When it comes to...提到某件事情時……

When it comes to the education of our children, many parents have a lot of complaints.

說到教育小孩，父母的抱怨可不少。

When it comes to games, today's are more complicated.

說到「遊戲」，今日的遊戲複雜多了。

5. satisfy(動詞)：

Pearl milk tea can satisfy my taste buds.

珍珠奶茶可以滿足我的味蕾。

satisfied(形容詞)：

I was satisfied with a glass of iced watermelon juice.

我對冰西瓜汁滿意極了。

It was satisfying to know that all my students had passed the exam.

很高興得知我所有的學生都通過了考試。

✏ 克漏字 Cloze

thirst-quenching, ubiquitous, vending machines, beverages, abundant, taste buds, squeezed, roadside stands, shaved ice, soft drinks

1. _____ provide a convenient way to get a quick drink or snack.

2. She always buys her fruit at _____.

3. Her _____ were very sensitive.

4. My mother _____ fresh orange juice for us this morning.

5. The supermarket has an _____ supply of fresh vegetables.

6. Convenience stores are _____ throughout Taiwan.

7. The shop sells several different kinds of cold _____.

8. _____ can be mixed with different kinds of fruit.

9. She never drinks alcohol, only _____ or juice.

10. The vendor sold many _____ drinks to the tourists.

🖊 選擇適當的詞性 Multiple Choice

_____ 1. My sister always has the best ideas because she is very _____. (a)create (b)creative (c)creativity

_____ 2. Mark's _____ helped him get into art school. (a)create (b)creative (c)creativity

_____ 3. The cook wanted her guests to try her latest _____. (a)creation (b)create (c)creativity

_____ 4. Pink and blue do not _____ together very well. (a)blended (b)blending (c)blend

_____ 5. This drink was _____ using only the best ingredients. (a)blended (b)blending (c)blend

_____ 6. Brian _____ a lemon every morning. (a)squeezing (b)squeeze (c)squeezes

_____ 7. Lisa enjoys the freshly _____ lemonade made by Brian. (a)squeezed (b)squeeze (c)squeezes

_____ 8. My father _____ his mustache every day. (a)shaving (b)shaved (c)shaves

_____ 9. John used to have long hair, but now his head is _____. (a)shaved (b)shaving (c)shave

_____ 10. I enjoy the _____ of riding a scooter instead

of walking. (a)convenient (b)convenience (c)conveniences

_____ 11. This bookstore is really _____ because it is open 24 hours a day. (a)convenient (b)convenience (c)conveniences

_____ 12. This orange is delicious because it is _____. (a)juice (b)juices (c)juicy

_____ 13. The glass _____ broke when I dropped it on the floor. (a)bottles (b)bottled (c)bottle

_____ 14. _____ drinks are more expensive than canned ones. (a)Bottles (b)Bottled (c)Bottle

_____ 15. The vegetables and fruit look very _____ today. (a)fresh (b)freshness (c)freshly

_____ 16. These _____ baked cookies are still warm. (a)fresh (b)freshness (c)freshly

_____ 17. He buys things without looking at their prices because he has an _____ of wealth. (a)abundant (b)abundances (c)abundance

_____ 18. Strawberries are cheap right now because they are so _____. (a)abundant (b)abundances

(c) abundance

翻譯 Translation

1. 你可以從一台自動販賣機買到各種冷飲。

   _____

2. 在台灣便利商店無所不在。

   _____

3. 現榨果汁加剉冰使人精神為之一振(refreshing)。

   _____

4. 端午節過後，台灣的天氣開始熱了起來。

   _____

5. 台灣的冰茶飲料包括珍珠奶茶、泡沫紅茶、芋奶茶和金桔茶。

   _____

6. 台灣商人的點子可真不少。

   _____

7. 木瓜牛奶是我最愛喝的冷飲。

   _____

8. 飲料如啤酒、運動飲料和汽水，都是罐裝或瓶裝的。

   _____

9. 我喜歡在路邊攤買冷飲。

_____

10. 台灣一年到頭(all year round)都供應豐富的水果。

_____

29 Night Markets `CD2 Track11`

Why do people still go to night markets when Taiwan now has so many sophisticated, modern stores? For their tasty snacks, bargain goods, and lively atmosphere, a night market beats$_1$ any store.

First of all, a night market is like a giant flea market that sells all sorts of food and goods. People line up at food stands to buy treats$_2$ like steamed$_3$ dumplings, oyster pastries, grilled$_3$ squid, stinky tofu, and coffin. At other stalls, customers can purchase items like DVDs, "designer" watches, stuffed$_4$ animals, and all sorts of trinkets. Bargaining can bring you a great price, but be careful since some of the goods are pirated$_5$. You should also watch out for pickpockets!

Besides shopping, people can also play games like net fishing and ring toss at many night markets. Other people enjoy meeting friends or family in the market's festive$_6$ atmosphere. Whatever you are looking for, chances are you can find it at a night market.

29 夜市

　　台灣已有許多精緻高雅的現代化商店，為什麼大家還是喜歡逛夜市？夜市有可口的小吃、可以討價還價的商品、加上活絡的氣氛，當然不輸任何商店！

　　首先，夜市賣各種商品和食物，簡直像個巨型的跳蚤市場。人們排隊在小吃攤前買蒸餃、蚵仔煎、烤花枝、臭豆腐和「棺材板」。在其他商家前，顧客可以買DVD和「設計師」設計的手錶、動物玩偶和各種各樣的小玩意兒。討價還價後可以討個便宜。不過得小心買到盜版貨，也得注意扒手。

　　除了買東西，人們還喜歡在夜市玩遊戲，如網魚、擲環。有的人則喜歡在夜市的節慶氣氛中與家人、朋友相聚。不管你要什麼，都可以在夜市找得到。

✐ 生字 Vocabulary

1. night market 夜市
   Night markets are good places to find snacks after work.
   夜市是下班後找小吃、零食的好地方。

2. sophisticated 老於世故的、精緻的、複雜的
   A sophisticated person is usually cultured, elegant, highly developed, and complex.
   一個世故的人通常有文化、高雅、有好教養，卻不單純。

3. snacks 小吃、零食
   Many Taiwanese like to eat night snacks which are no good for their health.
   許多台灣人喜歡吃無益於健康的宵夜。

4. lively atmosphere 活潑的氣氛
   Neighborhoods where college students live usually have a lively atmosphere.
   大學生住的地區通常氣氛活潑。

5. flea market 跳蚤市場
   In the United States, you can always find a bargain at a flea market.
   在美國你總是可以在跳蚤市場找到便宜貨。

6. food stand 小吃攤
   Next to the hospital, a row of food stands attracts patients.
   醫院隔壁有一排小吃攤吸引病人來(用餐)。

7. steamed dumpling 蒸餃
Students love to make steamed dumplings at their professors' houses.
學生喜歡在教授家做蒸餃。

8. oyster pastry 蚵仔煎（或叫做oyster omelet）
Oyster pastries are a traditional Taiwanese snack food.
蚵仔煎是傳統台灣小吃。

9. grilled squid 烤花枝
My favorite seafood snack is grilled squid.
我最喜歡的海鮮小吃是烤花枝。

10. stinky tofu 臭豆腐
Many foreigners cannot stand the smell of stinky tofu.
許多外國人受不了臭豆腐聞起來的味道。

11. coffin 棺材（指小吃棺材板）
Even though coffin has a scary name, it is a famous local snack in Tainan.
棺材板有個可怕的名字，但它卻是台南有名的地方小吃。

12. stall 小店、小吃攤
Her favorite place for lunch was a noodle stall near her house.
她最喜歡吃午餐的地方是她家附近的麵攤。

13. designer 設計家
Designer watches are very expensive.
設計家設計的表很貴。

14. stuffed animal 動物玩偶

He can't sleep without hugging his stuffed animal.

他不抱著他的動物玩偶無法入睡。

15. trinket 小玩意

She bought some small trinkets to give to her children.

她買了一些小玩意給她的孩子。

16. bargaining 討價還價

My mother can always get a great price since she is so good at bargaining.

因為我媽媽很會殺價，她總能用好價錢買到東西。

17. pirated goods 盜版貨

The criminal was caught with a truck full of pirated goods.

歹徒和一卡車的盜版貨被逮到了。

18. pickpocket 扒手

In a crowded area, you need to be careful about pickpockets.

人擠人的地方你得特別小心扒手。

19. net fishing 網魚

With net fishing, you can catch a fish even in the city.

用網抓魚，即使在都市裡你也可以抓到魚。

20. ring toss 擲環

Ring toss was originally a children's game, but people of all ages play it at the night market in my neighborhood.

擲環原本是孩子的遊戲，但在我住的附近，不同年齡層的人都在夜市玩擲環。

21. festive 節慶的

Chinese New Year is a festive holiday.

農曆新年是節慶的假日。

🖉 課文重點分析 Analysis

1. beat 是打敗(defeat)的意思。例如：

He always beats me at badminton.

他打羽毛球總是贏我。

The Red Sox beat the Yankees by 4-3.

紅襪隊以4比3勝洋基隊。

注意 beat 的動詞三態變化是 beat, beat, beaten。

2. treat 請客(可以當動詞，也可以當名詞。)

It will be my treat.

這次我付錢。

I will treat you this time.

這次讓我付錢。

a real treat是讓人心曠神怡的東西或事情。

3. steamed dumplings 和 grilled squid 都是被蒸、被烤的食物，所以要用過去分詞。

4. stuff(動詞)是填塞的意思，stuffed animals 是被填塞的小布偶，要用過去分詞。stuffing 是這些布偶裡面的填料，也可以是烤雞時雞肚子裡塞的香料。

5. pirated goods 是仿冒品，也可以說 counterfeit goods，這些東西都觸犯 (violate) 了智慧財產權 (intellectual property right，簡稱IPR)，作為現代公民，我們應該買原版的東西 (copyrighted goods)。

6. festive 節慶的 (形容詞)，festival 節慶 (名詞)，festivity 慶典活動 (名詞)。例如：festive holidays, the Moon Festival, the wedding festivity。

✐ 克漏字 Cloze

> bargaining, designer, sophisticated, lively, net fishing, night markets, pickpockets, pirated, steamed dumplings, stinky tofu

1. Many foreigners hate the smell of _____.

2. My grandmother never went downtown because she was afraid of _____.

3. The poor student can't afford to buy _____ brands.

4. He can always get a better price by _____.

5. If you make _____, you have to let the water boil three times.

6. He bought a cheap but expensive looking _____ watch in Hong Kong.

7. She loves to shop at _____.

8. The young boy was excited when he got to go _____ for the first time.

9. The _____ celebrity often lived abroad.

10. The _____ crowd cheered when the singer appeared.

✏ 選擇適當的詞性 Multiple Choice

_____ 1. _____ CDs are common in Taiwan. (a)Pirate (b)Piracy (c)Pirated

_____ 2. International law protects books and movies against _____. (a)pirate (b)piracy (c)pirated

_____ 3. The _____ party cheered everyone up. (a)festival (b)festivity (c)festive

_____ 4. Dragon Boat _____ is always a holiday in Taiwan. (a)Festival (b)Festivity (c)Festive

_____ 5. Her birthday celebration had an air of _____. (a)festival (b)festivity (c)festive

_____ 6. Children love these _____ snacks. (a)taste

(b) tasted (c) tasty

_____ 7. I love to _____ new foods. (a) taste (b) tasted (c) tasty

_____ 8. He carries a lot of _____ to school every day. (a) stuffs (b) stuffing (c) stuff

_____ 9. After the big meal, he felt _____. (a) stuffed (b) stuffing (c) stuff

_____ 10. The _____ in the sofa came out. (a) stuffed (b) stuffing (c) stuff

_____ 11. "Dinner is my _____ tonight," she said. (a) treats (b) treat (c) treatment

_____ 12. My friend _____ me to dinner last night. (a) treats (b) treated (c) treating

✏ 翻譯 Translation

1. 我最喜歡的小吃是烤花枝和臭豆腐。

_____

2. 好多人正在那家小吃店排隊(line up)買蚵仔煎。

_____

3. 除了買東西，人們還玩遊戲。

_____

4. 小心不要買到任何盜版貨。

_____

5. 注意！夜市有許多扒手。

_____

6. 這些設計師的洋裝是仿冒名牌(name-brand goods)。

_____

7. 他每次到國外旅行(travel abroad)都會買些小玩意送我。

_____

8. 有些外國人不習慣(be used to)討價還價。

_____

9. 雖然他是個大學生，他還是收集(collect)許多填充布偶。

_____

10. 你永遠不能打敗我。

_____

The Cozy Charm of Coffee Shops `CD2 Track12`

People who have never been to Taiwan may imagine us delicately sipping tea in traditional tea houses. While Taiwanese do drink plenty of tea, in the last few years, coffee has also become a wildly popular beverage, and coffee shops have sprung up all over the island. What explains this trend?

For some people₁, the appeal₂ is coffee itself. After all, coffee contains caffeine, which gives an energizing₃ buzz. But most coffee shops offer much more than plain black coffee. Fancy coffee drinks often include espresso, latte, mocha, and cappuccino. Those who can't handle so much caffeine can stick to decaf.

For others₁, the appeal of coffee shops has more to do with₄ their atmosphere. Young people, in particular, enjoy hanging out with friends in trendy coffee shops. Still others₁ linger for hours with a book, nursing a cup of coffee as they read and daydream. While tea will always be associated with Taiwan's culture, coffee is a welcome addition for many modern Taiwanese.

30 溫暖迷人的咖啡店

　　沒到過台灣的人也許會想像我們舉止優雅地在傳統的茶館裡輕啜著茶，沒錯，台灣人的確喝不少茶，不過，過去幾年來咖啡卻成了當紅飲料，咖啡店在島上如雨後春筍般的林立，這股熱潮，我們該如何解釋？

　　對某些人而言，咖啡之迷人在於咖啡的本身，畢竟它含有咖啡因，能使人精神為之一振。但另外的原因則是咖啡店賣的不只是平淡無奇的黑咖啡，講究一點的咖啡還賣義式濃縮咖啡、拿鐵、摩卡和卡布其諾。不能喝太多咖啡因的還可以專點低卡。

　　對其他人而言，咖啡店的魅力還來自它的氣氛，特別是年輕人喜歡跟朋友泡在時髦的咖啡店裡；還有一些人則捧著書耗在咖啡店裡好幾小時，一邊慢慢喝著咖啡，一邊讀著書、編織自己的白日夢。茶跟台灣文化有不可分的關係，對許多現代的台灣人而言，咖啡也成了另一種受歡迎的飲料。

🖊 生字 Vocabulary

1. sip 輕啜
   The woman slowly and carefully sipped her tea out of a delicate cup.
   這位女士緩緩、小心地輕啜著精緻杯裡的茶。

2. beverage 飲料
   In the winter, a hot beverage can warm you up.
   冬天來杯熱飲可以暖身。

3. spring up （出雨後春筍般）冒出
   Recently, new restaurants have been springing up in my neighborhood.
   最近新餐廳如雨後春筍般在我家附近出現。

4. appeal 吸引
   The new fashions appeal to college students.
   新的服飾吸引大學生的注目。

5. caffeine 咖啡因
   Too much caffeine can make some people feel jittery.
   喝太多咖啡因會讓人緊張。

6. buzz 振奮
   After two cups of strong coffee, he felt a pleasant buzz.
   兩杯濃咖啡下肚後，我的精神為之一振。

7. espresso 義式濃縮咖啡
   Espresso is usually served in a small cup because it is such a

powerful drink.
義式濃縮咖啡通常用小杯裝，因它太夠力了。

8. latte 拿鐵
He drinks a latte every afternoon during his break.
他每天下午休息時間會喝一杯拿鐵。

9. mocha 摩卡
She loved mocha because it reminded her of hot chocolate.
她喜歡摩卡咖啡因為摩卡使她想起熱巧克力。

10. cappuccino 卡布其諾
Cappuccino has become so popular that even some fast food restaurants serve it.
卡布其諾流行到連速食店都有販售。

11. stick to 堅持不變
Instead of buying fancy flavored drinks, he preferred to stick to black coffee.
他是黑咖啡的死忠，不喜歡喝花式加味咖啡。

12. decaf 低卡咖啡
If regular coffee makes you too nervous, you should switch to decaf.
如果普通咖啡讓你緊張，你該換成低卡。

13. hanging out 閒蕩
The girls enjoy hanging out at their friend's new house.
這些女孩喜歡耗在朋友的新房子裡。

13. linger 留連

He loves to linger in the bookstore until it closes.

他喜歡久待在書店裡直到打烊才走。

14. nurse 慢慢做某件事使時間拉長

Because it was raining heavily, the girl stayed in the coffee shop, nursing her drink to make it last as long as possible.

因為下著大雨，這個女孩待在咖啡店裡慢慢啜飲著飲料，能喝多久就喝多久。

🖊 課文重點分析 Analysis

1. 談三種不同類型的人或團體：

One... Another(one)... Still another(one)...

Some people... Others... Still others...例如：

One of my hobbies is collecting stamps. Another is surfing the Internet. Still another is singing at the KTV parlor.

我的一個嗜好是集郵，另一個嗜好是上網，還有一個嗜好是到卡拉OK唱歌。

Some students like to watch TV. Others like to play online games. Still others like to hang out in coffee shops.

有些學生喜歡看電視，有的愛玩網路電玩，更有的喜歡到咖啡店閒蕩。

2. appeal(動詞)吸引，例如：

Name-brand goods do not appeal to me at all.

名牌不吸引我。

appeal(名詞)吸引力,例如:

The appeal of the name-brand goods is the brand itself.

名牌的吸引力在品牌本身。

appealing(形容詞)吸引人的,例如:

I found that girl pretty appealing.

我發現那個女孩十分吸引人。

3. energy(名詞)精力,例如:

After finishing this project, I don't have any more energy to do other things.

完成這個計畫後,我再也沒有精力做其他的事情。

energetic(形容詞)精力充沛的,例如:

She always looks very energetic.

她看起來總是精力充沛。

energize(動詞)供應能量、激勵,例如:

My boss really knows how to energize her employees.

我的老闆真知道如何激勵她的員工。

4. have more to do with 跟……比較有關。例如:

This has nothing to do with him.

這件事跟他無關。

This has something to do with him.

這件事跟他有關。

This has more to do with him.

這件事跟他比較有關。

✎ 克漏字 Cloze

> sip, beverages, appeal, caffeine, lingers, hanging out,
> espresso, stick to, decaf, buzz

1. His mother doesn't want him ＿＿＿＿＿＿ with the other teenagers.

2. She likes to ＿＿＿＿＿＿ the same lunch every day.

3. That program does not ＿＿＿＿＿＿ to young people.

4. He took a small ＿＿＿＿ of the strong drink.

5. Cold ＿＿＿＿＿＿ are very popular in summer.

6. She often ＿＿＿＿＿＿ after school to talk to her friends.

7. ＿＿＿＿＿＿ is too strong for some people.

8. He drinks coffee for the ＿＿＿＿＿＿ it gives him.

9. ＿＿＿＿＿＿ is a drug even though it is legal.

10. After his heart attack, he had to switch to ＿＿＿＿＿＿

coffee.

🖎 選擇適當的詞性 Multiple Choice

_____ 1. Can you _____ winning the lottery?
(a) imagination (b) imagine (c) imaginary

_____ 2. The young child has an _____ friend.
(a) imagination (b) imagine (c) imaginary

_____ 3. That artist has a wild _____. (a) imagination
(b) imagine (c) imaginary

_____ 4. New stores _____ up on my street each month.
(a) spring (b) sprang (c) sprung

_____ 5. When the bell rang, the student _____ out of his
seat. (a) spring (b) sprang (c) sprung

_____ 6. The boat has _____ a leak! (a) spring (b) sprang
(c) sprung

_____ 7. Can you help me _____ this painting? (a) hang
(b) hung (c) hanging

_____ 8. The museum had _____ the painting upside
down before the artist pointed out. (a) hang (b) hung
(c) hanging

_____ 9. The river is very _____. (a)widen (b)width (c)wide

_____ 10. These shoes come in your _____. (a)widen (b)width (c)wide

_____ 11. The thrifty man can _____ one drink for several hours. (a)nursing (b)nurse (c)nursed

_____ 12. She is a _____ student. (a)nursing (b)nurse (c)nursed

✏️ 翻譯 Translation

1. 他正在傳統茶室裡輕啜著茶。

   _____

2. 你知道今天大部分的台灣人都愛喝咖啡嗎？

   _____

3. 這間咖啡店吸引我的地方在它溫暖的氣氛。

   _____

4. 咖啡因給我們一種鼓舞的力量(buzz)。

   _____

5. 他從不點黑咖啡，他總是忠於(stick to)拿鐵。

   _____

6. 最近在台灣咖啡店突然如雨後春筍般林立。

   _____

7. 這家咖啡店的成功跟它好的地點 (location) 比較有關。

   _____

8. 他坐在電腦前正慢慢啜飲著一杯咖啡。

   _____

9. 茶跟台灣傳統文化有相關聯。

   _____

10. 年輕人喜歡和朋友泡在時髦咖啡店裡。

   _____

Modern Technology
現代科技

"Talk to U Later" (CD2 Track13)

As the Internet has become increasingly popular, more and more people find themselves in chat rooms. On-line chat rooms offer many choices. Each user can create one or more on-line personas₁. For example, a teenaged boy in Taipei can have the profile₂ of a 30-year-old millionaire in New York or even a grandmother in France!

Once users have set up their on-line profiles, they are free to begin chatting, often in what looks like a special language full of slang, acronyms₃ (e.g.₄ brb for "be right back," U for "you," R for "are," and C for "see,") and emoticons (e.g. (:-* for kiss, (:-\ for very sad). Some popular subjects in Taiwan are horoscopes, blood types, and fortune telling, but topics are unlimited. Users can say whatever they want without fear of censorship₅.

Thanks to chat rooms, people can meet in a virtual₆ world where distance, status, and money are no longer barriers. How else can you meet people from across the world without leaving the comforts of your own home?

「待會兒再聊」

　　網路愈熱門就有愈多的人到「聊天室」聊天。網路聊天室提供使用者許多選擇，每位使用者可用不只一種身分，例如：一個台北的青少年可以在填寫個人資料時說自己是三十歲的紐約百萬富翁，甚或法國的老奶奶！

　　使用者建立了自己網上個人資料，就可以自由與人上網聊天，聊天時常用俚語、簡寫（例如：brb 代表「馬上回來」、U 代表「你」、R 代表「是」、C 代表「看」）和表情符號（例如：(:-* 代表接吻、(:-\ 代表很悲傷）。台灣聊天室流行的話題是星座、血型和算命，不過話題不限，使用者可以隨意交談也不怕被審查。

　　還好有網路「聊天室」，人們可以在虛擬世界彼此相會，在那裡距離、地位和金錢都不再是人和人交往的障礙，除聊天室外，還有什麼方法能使你不離開自己的安樂窩卻能與世界各地的人交往呢？

✏️ 生字 Vocabulary

1. **chat room** 聊天室
Although Mary was happy being a girl, she enjoyed changing her gender to talk like a man in chat rooms.
瑪麗雖然很高興自己身為女兒身，但是她還是很喜歡改自己的性別，像男的一樣，在聊天室跟人聊天。

2. **persona** 身分
Mr. Chang's chat room persona reflects the side of his personality he usually hides.
張先生聊天室的身分表現出他通常深藏不露的個性層面。

3. **profile** 個人資料
She thought carefully about writing her profile before she started visiting chat rooms.
上聊天室聊天之前，她小心考量如何填寫個人資料。

4. **set up** 建立、架設
He was eager to set up his new business.
他急著自己創業。

5. **slang** 俚語
Slang sometimes comes and goes at an amazing pace.
俚語通常來來去去，來去速度驚人。

6. **acronym** 首字母縮略字
TTYL is a popular acronym for talk to you later.
TTYL是很通用的首字母縮略字，代表「待會兒再聊」。

7. emoticon 表情符號
Her favorite emoticon looked like a smiling face.
她最喜歡的表情符號是張笑臉。

8. horoscope 星座
My superstitious grandmother reads her horoscope in the paper every day.
我迷信的祖母每天必讀報上她當天的星座（運勢）。

9. fortune telling 算命
Even in this modern age, many people still believe in fortune telling.
即使在現代，許多人還是相信算命。

10. censorship 審查制度
Countries without a free press often use censorship to control what people can read.
新聞不自由的國家常常使用審查制度控制人們的讀物。

11. virtual world 虛擬世界
The young man spent so much time in chat rooms that he was more comfortable interacting in their virtual world than he was meeting people face to face.
這個年輕人花很多時間待在聊天室，他覺得在虛擬世界裡與人互動，比真正見面與人交往來得自在。

12. status 地位
Teachers' social status is very high in many Asian countries.
許多亞洲國家的老師社會地位很高。

13. barrier 障礙

In the Middle East, there seem to be so many barriers to peace.

中東走向和平似乎還障礙重重。

✎ 課文重點分析 Analysis

1. persona 一個人的人格面貌。有的人 public persona 很害羞，私底下卻很活潑。許多上網交友的人明明不是健談、外向的人，卻選這種 persona 來呈現自己，以吸引網友注意。

2. profile 在課文中的意思是一段描寫本人性別、個性、興趣、家庭教育背景的短文。一般網路交友或線上聊天，就是根據 profile 的描寫內容，決定要不要開始一段新的「邂逅」。profile 也是人的側面，有的人覺得 Drawing profiles is easier than drawing the full face. (畫側面比畫正面容易。)。high-profile 曝光率很高，例如：He is a high-profile politician. (政治人物) 與 high-profile 相反的是 low-profile。有的人比較低調，不喜歡出鋒頭，例如：He tried to keep a low-profile. (他試著保持低調。)

3. acronym 首字母縮略字。例如：

AIDS is an acronym for "Acquired Immune Deficiency Syndrome."

AIDS 是「後天性免疫不全症候群」的英文縮寫。

WTO is an acronym for "World Trade Organization."

WTO 是「世界貿易組織」的英文縮寫。

WHO is an acronym for "World Health Organization."

WHO 是「世界衛生組織」的英文縮寫。

4. e.g.= for example 舉例來說，i.e.= that is 換句話說。

5. impose censorship 施行審查制度，例如：

The government has imposed censorship on the Internet.

政府對網路施行審查制度。

censor 審查、刪除 (動詞)：

The government has censored publications that promote sex.

政府禁止出版宣揚色情的出版品。

6. virtual world 虛擬世界，virtually 幾乎。

✐ 克漏字 Cloze

status, chat rooms, virtual world, persona, barriers, censorship, emoticons, set up, fortune telling, horoscope, slang

1. He checks his _____ in the newspaper every morning to see if he will have a lucky day.

2. When you use a chat room, you have the chance to create a

_____ that may be different from your actual personality.

3. Each generation has its own _____.

4. The computer science student was more comfortable in the _____ than in the real world.

5. _____ allow people to contact others with similar interests all over the world.

6. The generous father _____ a special bank account for his son.

7. _____ is very popular in Taiwan since many people want to ask questions about their futures.

8. Some countries with a strict _____ policy do not allow books to be published without government approval.

9. Social class and money are often _____ that separate people.

10. In many societies, doctors enjoy a very high _____.

11. She loves to use _____ to show her emotions in her e-mail messages.

✏ 選擇適當的詞性 Multiple Choice

_____ 1. As you get older, your parents may _____ your allowance. (a)increase (b)increasing (c)increasingly

_____ 2. With each passing day, he became _____ dissatisfied with his job. (a)increase (b)increasing (c)increasingly

_____ 3. That _____ brand of shoes can be found in almost every girl's closet. (a)popular (b)popularity (c)popularly

_____ 4. Due to the professor's _____, the class was oversubscribed. (a)popular (b)popularity (c)popularly

_____ 5. He made a _____ when he sold his stock options. (a)fortune (b)fortunate (c)fortunately

_____ 6. _____, nobody was seriously injured in the car accident. (a)Fortune (b)Fortunate (c)Fortunately

_____ 7. He was _____ that the burglar did not find his hidden money. (a)fortune (b)fortunate (c)fortunately

_____ 8. The _____ reality game was so realistic that I was surprised when it ended. (a) virtual (b) virtualized (c) virtually

_____ 9. The movie was so captivating that our eyes were _____ glued to the TV for the entire evening. (a) virtual (b) virtualized (c) virtually

_____ 10. He didn't realize that he had cut himself until he saw the _____ on his finger. (a) blood (b) bloody (c) bloodily

_____ 11. He managed to escape the fight with only a _____ nose. (a) blood (b) bloody (c) bloodily

✎ Translation 翻譯

1. 在台灣網路變得愈來愈流行。

_____

2. 網路 (online) 聊天室提供人們許多交友的機會。

_____

3. 一個在台灣的中年男士可以填資料為美國的少女。

_____

4. 在台灣最熱門的聊天話題是星座。

_____

5. 你對算命有興趣嗎？

_____

6. 多虧聊天室，寂寞的人們可以在一個虛擬世界相遇。

_____

7. 你一星期「訪問」聊天室幾次？

_____

8. 這本小說被查禁了。

_____

9. 我不知道她的血型是什麼。

_____

10. 當他跟我聊天時，我不瞭解他用的俚語。

_____

32 Internet Dating `CD2 Track14`

In the past₁, many couples met through a matchmaker or through a family friend. In today's busy world₁, however, the Internet often serves₂ as the matchmaker, allowing strangers to meet through Internet dating services or in chat rooms. Once₃ they meet online, a couple can go out on a date, which might be the first step toward a happy long-term relationship.

Other people, who are more interested in₄ the short-term excitement of cyber sex, use the Internet to meet partners for one-night stands. Sometimes money is exchanged for₅ sex, as in recent cases involving₆ young girls who met men online. These schoolgirls are not professional prostitutes; they are just looking for some spending money from a sugar daddy.

Internet dating can be not only "expensive" but also risky. In some cases, Internet acquaintances turn out to be liars, stalkers, or rapists. For fans of this new way of meeting, the excitement and convenience of Internet dating make it worth taking a chance. Risky or not, Internet dating is here to stay.

網路約會

　　過去很多對的婚姻是由媒人或朋友撮合而成，然而今日繁忙的社會，得靠網路充當媒人，網路讓陌生人經由網路約會站或聊天室的牽線，在網上「會面」，一旦他們在網路上搭上了線，便可約會外出，由此開始快樂愛情長跑的第一步。

　　如果有人對刺激的網愛露水姻緣有興趣，也可以利用網路約見對方，來段「一夜情」。像最近許多個案，是年輕女孩和男士從事網路援交，這些在學女生不是職業的性工作者，她們只想找個甜心老爹要點零用錢來花。

　　網路約會不但「得花錢」，還有風險。從一些個案顯示，網友後來成了騙子、跟蹤騷擾的無賴或性侵害者。不過這種新型交友方式的愛好者，覺得網路約會刺激又方便，還是值得一試，不管風險如何，網路約會還是會持續下去。

✎ 生字 Vocabulary

1. matchmaker 媒人
Traditional families often used a matchmaker to find a husband for their daughters.
傳統的家庭經常讓媒人給他們的女兒找個丈夫。

2. Internet dating service 網路交友服務
Internet dating services have become especially popular in the United States.
網路交友服務在美國變得特別風行。

3. chat rooms 聊天室
Chat rooms allow people with similar interests to talk online.
聊天室讓相同興趣的人上網聊天。

4. meet online 網路上相遇
Nowadays, many couples meet online.
當今許多伴侶是在網路上相遇的。

5. go out on a date 約會
The man wanted to go out on a date with the beautiful woman, but she refused.
這位男士想要跟這位漂亮的女士約會,但是她拒絕了。

6. long-term relationship 固定的戀情
After his divorce, he wasn't looking for another long-term relationship.
他離婚後不想另找固定的戀情。

7. cyber sex 網愛
The Internet has made cyber sex a popular term.
網路使「網愛」一詞變得很熱門。

8. one-night stand 一夜情
Whenever the businessman was in another city, he looked for a chance to have a one-night stand.
這位生意人每到另外一個城市出差，一定找機會來段一夜情。

9. prostitute 性工作者
The prostitute was arrested after she had sex with a policeman.
這位性工作者跟警察做愛後被逮捕了。

10. sugar daddy 甜心老爹
A sugar daddy is often old, but rich.
甜心老爹通常年紀雖大卻很有錢。

11. risky 有風險的
Keeping all your money in your pocket is risky in a crowded city.
在擁擠的都市裡，把所有的錢都裝在口袋裡是有風險的。

12. Internet acquaintances 網友
She met ten new Internet acquaintances last summer.
去年夏天她交了10個新網友。

13. stalker 跟蹤狂
Stalkers often follow their victims to find out their habits.
跟蹤狂常尾隨他們的受害者，以找出他們的生活習慣。

14. rapist 性侵害者

Many rapists already know their victims.

許多性侵害者早已認識他們的受害者。

15. fan 迷,「粉絲」

He was a big fan of American football.

他是美式足球迷。

✎ 課文重點分析 Analysis

1. In the past...In today's busy world...這是過去與今日繁忙社會的一個對比。

2. serve 通常意指提供食物或飲料,例如:

Do they serve meals in this coffee shop?

這家咖啡店供餐嗎?

這裡的 serve 意指當做(work),例如:

The committee has named Mr. Wong to serve as company's chief executive officer(CEO)and president.

理事會任命汪先生當公司的執行長和總裁。

3. Once...一旦

Once he falls in love with a girl, he won't let her go.

他一旦愛上一個女孩,他不會放她走。

4. be interested 還是 be interesting?

用 ed 還是 ing 形容詞常使人困惑,以這句為例:

The short-term excitement interests many people.

The short-term excitement is interesting.

Many people are interested in the short-term excitement.

因為露水姻緣的短暫刺激，所以許多人會對它感到興趣。

5. ... exchange for...用某樣東西交換另一樣東西，例如：

He exchanges money for love.

他用金錢來換取愛情。

exchange 也可以當名詞，例如:

He used money in exchange for love.

6. as in recent cases 是用最近一些個案來舉例說明網路援交，什麼樣的個案呢？後面有解釋：recent cases which involved young girls，什麼樣的女孩呢？girls who met men online。

✏️ 克漏字 Cloze

> chat rooms, stalker, one-night stands, sugar daddy, Internet dating service, matchmaker, cyber sex, Internet acquaintances, fans, going out on a date

1. Many young girls are not interested in finding a decent job; they would rather have a _____ to support them.

2. He has made many foreign _____, so he can

practice English with them online.

3. After his retirement, he decided to work as a _____,
helping people to find their ideal spouses.

4. Many lonely people enjoy the short-term sexual excitement
of _____ when they are surfing the Internet.

5. I can't get rid of that _____ who follows me all the
time.

6. Many Japanese middle-aged women are big _____
of a famous Korean movie star.

7. He can't find any long-term relationship, so he meets girls
in the bar for _____.

8. She knew that _____ with someone whom she'd
met online was rather risky, but she decided it worth taking
a chance.

9. You can meet someone who has similar interests through
an _____.

10. He flunked the course because he had spent too much time
chatting with friends in _____.

✎ 選擇適當的詞性 Multiple Choice

_____ 1. Next to my rich uncle, I felt like a poor _____.
(a) relation (b) relationship (c) relative

_____ 2. That couple has an excellent _____. (a) relation
(b) relationship (c) related

_____ 3. My grandmother's chief _____ is reading.
(a) interesting (b) interest (c) interested

_____ 4. He is _____ in gardening. (a) interesting
(b) interest (c) interested

_____ 5. Do you think that book is _____? (a) interesting
(b) interest (c) interested

_____ 6. Teaching is a respected _____ in Taiwan.
(a) professional (b) professionally (c) profession

_____ 7. He is a _____ baseball player. (a) professional
(b) professionally (c) profession

_____ 8. Having _____ with a stranger is not safe. (a) sexy
(b) sex (c) sexual

_____ 9. She was _____ harassed by her boss. (a) sexy
(b) sex (c) sexually

_____ 10. The actress looked _____ in her new outfit.

(a) sexy (b) sex (c) sexual

_____ 11. She is just an _____, not a close friend.

(a) acquaint (b) acquainted (c) acquaintance

_____ 12. I would like to get _____ with that handsome man. (a) acquaint (b) acquainted (c) acquaintance

🖉 翻譯 Translation

1. 許多人結婚是經由媒人的介紹。

_____

2. 現今網路常充當媒人。

_____

3. 網路約會站讓兩個陌生人在網上「相遇」。

_____

4. 我對跟我的網友約會沒有興趣。

_____

5. 目前我還沒有找到一個固定的戀情。

_____

6. 她總是找機會來一段一夜情。

_____

7. 用金錢交換性風險太大。

_____

8. 有些個案裡甜心老爹變成騙子。

_____

9. 網路交友雖有風險還是值得一試。

_____

10. 她不是職業性工作者，她只是找些零用錢來花。

_____

33   Taiwan Goes Mobile `CD2 Track15`

What tiny gadget lets you call your friends, take pictures, listen to music, and surf the Internet? A cell phone, of course. Now that Taiwan has more cell phones than people, these handy machines$_1$ are an inescapable feature of our everyday$_2$ lives.

These ultimate all-in-one toys offer more features all of the time. You can use your mobile phone$_3$ as a calculator, a calendar, and an alarm clock. Cell phones also let you play games, send text messages, and even watch movies. In many ways, cell phones can replace a computer, a PDA, and an MP3 player. On a more practical note, these phones enable parents to stay in touch with their children and people to get help in an emergency.

Not everyone loves cell phones, however. They can be very annoying$_4$ when they ring in public, especially in a theater or a meeting. Even worse, some people rudely hold loud, personal conversations$_5$ no matter where they are. While we are enjoying the conveniences cell phones bring us, we should also watch our cell phone etiquette$_6$.

手機響遍台灣

　　什麼小電器用品能讓你打電話給朋友、照相、聽音樂和上網路？答案當然是「手機」！現在台灣的手機數量比人還多，這個方便的小機器在我們每天生活中是不可或缺的東西.

　　這個集各種功能於一身的高級「玩具」總是能提供更多的功能，你可以用手機當計算機、日曆和鬧鐘，手機還可以讓你玩遊戲、發簡訊，甚至看電影。在很多方面，手機可以取代電腦、掌上型電腦和MP3音樂盒。實用方面，手機使父母能夠跟孩子隨時保持聯絡，也可以在緊急時得到援助。

　　不過，不是每個人都喜歡手機。手機有時在公共場所，尤其是戲院或開會時響起，令人生厭。更差勁的是，有些人一機在手，不管在哪裡，就粗魯地大聲談私事。當大家享受手機的方便時，更應該注重使用手機的禮節。

✎ 生字 Vocabulary

1. **mobile phone** 手機
   A mobile phone can save your life in an emergency.
   手機可以在緊急狀況時救你的命。

2. **gadget** 機電物件
   That shop specializes in all sorts of electronic gadgets.
   這家店專賣各種輕巧的電子產品。

3. **surf the Internet** 上網
   Many students prefer to surf the Internet instead of reading a book for pleasure.
   許多學生寧可上網也不以讀書為樂。

4. **inescapable** 不可避免的
   In a big city, noise and pollution sometimes seem inescapable.
   在大城市噪音和污染似乎不可避免。

5. **ultimate** 最上乘的
   A trip to Hawaii was my parents' ultimate dream.
   我父母最大的願望是到夏威夷一遊。

6. **all of the time** 永遠、總是
   You can fool some of the people all of the time, all of the people some of the time, but you cannot fool all of the people all of the time.
   你總能騙過某些人，有時也能騙過所有的人，但你不能總是騙過所有的人。

7. calculator 計算機
A calculator can help you keep track of your expenses.
計算機可以讓你隨時計算你的花費。

8. text message 簡訊
My brother loves to send text messages to his friends.
我的哥哥愛發簡訊給朋友。

9. PDA(Personal Digital Assistant) 掌上型電腦
A PDA can take the place of an address book.
PDA可以取代地址本。

10. MP3 player 放送音樂的電子盒
MP3 players are popular gifts for young people who like music.
MP3播放器是送給愛樂年輕人最熱門的禮物。

11. on a more practical note 實際而言、實用方面來說
On a more practical note, are your employees making more money for you than they cost?
實際而言，你的雇員幫你賺的錢比你付他們的薪水還多嗎？

12. enable 使……能夠
The Internet enables people to gather information from all over the world.
網路可以使人們從世界各地取得資訊。

13. annoying 可厭的、惱人的
He finds the sound of barking dogs very annoying.
他覺得狗吠的聲音很可厭。

14. rudely 粗魯地

She rudely pushed the elderly man out of her way.

她粗魯地把這位老人從她前面推開。

15. etiquette 禮節

Parents should teach their children proper etiquette.

父母親應該教小孩正當的禮儀。

✎ 課文重點分析 Analysis

1. machine 機器。修理機器，如修汽車的人叫 car mechanic。machinery 一組機器。

2. everyday 是形容詞，如 everyday English（生活英語）。如果說 I go to school every day. 就不能用 everyday。

3. 美式英文的 cell phones 就是英式英文的 mobile phones。

4. annoying 和 annoyed 用法很容易混淆。前者主動，後者被動。例如：

Cell phones' ring tones annoy me.

手機鈴聲煩我。

Cell phones' ring tones are annoying.

手機鈴聲真討厭。

I am annoyed by cell phones' ring tones.

我被手機鈴聲煩。

5. 英文字裡有許多搭配出現的字，如 turn on the air conditioner

不能說成 open the air conditioner。conversation 這個字可以搭配的動詞有：carry on a conversation, make conversation, hold a conversation。

6. etiquette 禮節，例如：dining etiquette 用餐禮節，e-mail etiquette 伊媚兒禮節，Internet etiquette 網路禮節，telephone etiquette 電話禮節。

🖉 克漏字 Cloze

> annoying, calculator, enable, etiquette, gadgets, mobile phone, MP3 player, rudely, surf the Internet, ultimate

1. The clerk used a _____ to figure out the price.

2. My brother loves to _____ after school.

3. The sound of traffic can be very _____.

4. She always carries her _____ with her.

5. The waiter spoke _____ to the customer.

6. He loves to collect all sorts of new _____.

7. A college degree should _____ you to find a better job.

8. She asked her mother the proper _____ for holding

a party.

9. Winning the lottery is her _____ fantasy.

10. Most students who like music have an _____.

✏️ 選擇適當的詞性 Multiple Choice

_____ 1. The new washing _____ is expensive.
(a)machinery (b)machine (c)mechanic

_____ 2. The _____ repaired my old car. (a)machinery
(b)machine (c)mechanic

_____ 3. Most of this factory's _____ is very old.
(a)machinery (b)machine (c)mechanic

_____ 4. She used a computer program to _____ her
students' grades. (a)calculating (b)calculated
(c)calculate

_____ 5. She _____ that the trip would cost NT $9,000.
(a)calculating (b)calculated (c)calculate

_____ 6. I used a _____ to figure out my taxes.
(a)calculating (b)calculator (c)calculate

_____ 7. Those tourists were very _____. (a)rude
(b)rudeness (c)rudely

_____ 8. He _____ interrupted my conversation. (a)rude (b)rudeness (c)rudely

_____ 9. Everyone noticed their _____. (a)rude (b)rudeness (c)rudely

_____ 10. Barking dogs _____ us every night. (a)annoying (b)annoyed (c)annoy

_____ 11. Mosquitoes are _____ pests. (a)annoying (b)annoyed (c)annoy

_____ 12. The longer I listened, the more _____ I became. (a)annoying (b)annoyed (c)annoy

_____ 13. Even though my grandmother is very old, she is still _____. (a)mobile (b)mobility (c)mobilized

_____ 14. After her accident, she lost some _____ in her arm. (a)mobile (b)mobility (c)mobilized

翻譯 Translation

1. 她喜歡各種電器精巧產品。

_____

2. 你每天上網幾小時？

_____

3. 你可以用你的手機當成計算機。

_____

4. 你可以用你的手機當成鬧鐘嗎？

_____

5. 有些人用手機大聲談天 (hold conversations)。

_____

6. 你最好注意你的手機禮貌。

_____

7. 死亡和疾病不能避免的。

_____

8. 手機鈴聲十分可厭。

_____

9. 我每天發一封簡訊給我的女朋友。

_____

10. 手機讓父母可以隨時跟子女保持聯絡 (stay in touch)。

_____

Religions and
Folk Beliefs
宗教和民間信仰

34 One Country, Many Faiths

(CD2 Track16)

In many parts of the world, religious differences frequently lead to conflict. In Taiwan, however, different faiths co-exist harmoniously. Currently, Taiwan has 13 registered₁ religions, including Buddhism₂, Taoism, various Christian₃ denominations, and Islam.

In addition to these well-known sects, many people worship a combination of religions or folk religions. In many temples, for instance, people can burn incense for gods and goddesses from different religions. Besides worshipping at temples, most Taiwanese also keep a family shrine that contains ancestral tablets. People make daily offerings to their ancestors and hold special ceremonies for them during holidays.

What all these religions have in common is the idea that spiritual forces are a part of our lives. Thanks to Taiwan's tradition of religious tolerance₄, all these groups are free to worship as they wish.

一國多教

世上許多地方由於宗教不同常引發爭端，在台灣不同的信仰卻能和諧共處。目前在台灣登記的宗教有13個，其中包括佛教、道教、不同支派的基督教和回教。

除了一些著名的教派外，許多人還拜眾教合一的宗教和民間信仰。許多廟裡，信徒燒香拜不同宗教的眾神，除了在廟裡祭拜外，台灣人家裡還擺設供奉祖先牌位的神龕，人們每日用供品祭拜祖先，節慶還舉辦一些特別儀式。

這些宗教相通處在於相信神靈是我們生活的一部份。感謝台灣有宗教包容的傳統，使各派信徒可以自由敬拜他們所愛之神。

✏️ 生字 Vocabulary

1. **faith** 信仰
People of many different faiths helped victims of the 921 earthquake.
各派宗教人士都來幫助921地震的受害者。

2. **Buddhism** 佛教
Buddhism originated in India.
佛教源於印度。

3. **Taoism** 道教
Taoism teaches acceptance of our fate.
道教教導我們接受自己的命運。

4. **Christian denominations** 各派基督教
Taiwan has over 60 different Christian denominations.
台灣有超過60種不同的基督教派。

5. **Islam** 回教
Islam is the primary religion in the Middle East.
回教是中東主要的宗教。

6. **sect** 教派
Which religious sect do you belong to?
你屬於哪一教派？

7. **folk religion** 民間信仰
Many believers in folk religions fear ghosts.
許多有民間信仰的人怕鬼。

8. burn incense 燒香

Her grandmother frequently went to the Taoist temple to burn incense.

她的祖母經常去道觀燒香。

9. god 神

Taoist temples often have shrines for several different gods.

道觀常有供奉多神的神龕。

10. goddess 女神

Many fishermen in Taiwan worship Matsu, the Goddess of the Sea.

台灣許多討海人拜媽祖——海洋守護女神。

11. worship 祭拜

On holidays, you can see many people worshipping at Taipei's Long Shan temple.

節慶時你可以看到許多人在台北龍山寺拜拜。

12. family shrine 家庭神龕

She puts fresh flowers on the family shrine every day.

她每天都放鮮花在家中神龕上。

13. ancestral tablet 祖先牌位

He keeps his ancestral tablet in a special shrine with the family gods.

他將祖宗牌位和家中神明安放在特別的神龕裡。

14. offerings 祭品

She places offerings in front of her ancestors' tombs.

她將祭品放在祖墳前。

15. ancestor 祖先

Worshipping one's ancestors is an important part of Taiwan's religious tradition.

拜祖先是台灣宗教傳統的重要的一部分。

16. spiritual forces 神靈

Most people in Taiwan believe in spiritual forces that we cannot see.

大部分台灣人相信看不見的神靈。

17. religious tolerance 宗教包容性

Many countries lack an atmosphere of religious tolerance.

許多國家缺乏宗教包容的氣氛。

✐ 課文重點分析 Analysis

1. register (主動)，registered (被動)，例如：

I registered the house in my name.

我將房子註冊在我的名下。

a registered letter 掛號信

a registered religion 登記合法的宗教

2. Buddha 釋迦摩尼，Buddhism 佛教，Buddhist 佛教徒、佛教的。例如：

A statue of Buddha 釋迦摩尼雕像

She converted to Buddhism last year.

她去年改信了佛教。

He is a firm Buddhist and vegetarian.

他是虔誠的佛教徒和素食者。

We visited a Buddhist temple last weekend.

上個週末我們去了一座佛教寺廟。

3. Christian 基督教的，是形容詞，也是名詞（基督教徒）。

Christianity 基督教，是名詞。例如：

Christianity has many denominations.

基督教有許多宗派。

He is a firm Christian.

他是個虔誠的基督教徒。

Christmas is a Christian holiday.

聖誕節是基督教的節日。

4. tolerate（動詞）、tolerance（名詞）、tolerant（形容詞）、
tolerantly（副詞）例如：

I can't tolerate him any longer.

我再也受不了他了。

The government has encouraged tolerance of different ethnic
groups.

政府鼓勵族群容忍。

The government is tolerant of dissidents.

政府容忍異議份子。

After listening to my complaint, she smiled tolerantly.

聽了我的抱怨後，她容忍地微笑著。

克漏字 Cloze

> gods, goddess, worship, family shrine, offerings, ancestors, Islam, Buddhism, spiritual, burn incense

1. She placed _____ of fruit in the temple.

2. Believers in _____ face the east to pray.

3. She asked the _____ of Mercy to help her son.

4. When he converted to _____, he quit eating meat.

5. His _____ came from Fujian Province many years ago.

6. Their _____ is on the top floor of their house.

7. Many people in India have deep _____ beliefs.

8. On special holidays, many people at that temple _____ Matsu.

9. Many Taiwanese believe in several different _____.

10. The temple was full of smoke because so many people had come to _____.

✏️ 選擇題 Multiple Choice

_____ 1. Many people began to lose _____ in the government after the scandal was revealed. (a) faithful (b) faith (c) faithfully

_____ 2. On their wedding day, Bob made a vow to remain _____ to his wife for the rest of their lives. (a) faithful (b) faith (c) faithfully

_____ 3. I explored Christianity, Taoism, and Islam before deciding that Buddhism was the _____ that best suited me. (a) religiously (b) religious (c) religion

_____ 4. Desperate to lose weight, Tina became _____ in following the rules of health and dieting. (a) religiously (b) religious (c) religion

_____ 5. To avoid conflict, we must show patience and _____ for one another's differences. (a) tolerate (b) tolerated (c) tolerance

_____ 6. Although she was very saddened by her mother's

death, Judy felt better knowing that her mother's
_____ had gone on to a better place. (a)spiritual
(b)spirit (c)spiritually

_____ 7. The crowd went crazy when they announced who
had been chosen as the new _____ leader
of the Catholic Church. (a)spiritual (b)spirit
(c)spiritually

_____ 8. After a lot of practice, the orchestra learned how
to play in perfect _____. (a)harmony
(b)harmonious (c)harmoniously

_____ 9. We all hope there will soon be a _____
end to the war. (a)harmony (b)harmonious
(c)harmoniously

_____ 10. Scientists say that bees are a perfect example of
many individuals working _____ together.
(a)harmony (b)harmonious (c)harmoniously

_____ 11. Growing up in a _____ household, Emily
was forced to follow very strict rules. (a)Christ
(b)Christian (c)Christianity

_____ 12. When Tom was diagnosed with cancer, he turned
to _____ and his belief in Jesus gave him

strength and courage.　(a)Christmas　(b)Christian
(c)Christianity

🖉 翻譯 Translation

1. 許多人們到廟裡為諸神燒香。

   _____

2. 我的祖母準備每天的供品給她的祖先。

   _____

3. 在台灣許多信仰和諧並存。

   _____

4. 神靈是我們生活的一部份。

   _____

5. 在台灣佛教、道教、回教和基督教都是登記合法的宗教。

   _____

6. 許多人拜萬教合一的宗教和民間信仰。

   _____

7. 我們應該學習如何包容不同的宗教。

   _____

8. 我們家裡沒有放家庭神龕。

_____

9. 不同的宗教團體可以自由敬拜他們所愛之神。

_____

10. 宗教的不同常導致爭端。

_____

Global Fortune Telling

CD2 Track17

　People might expect₁ that a modern country like Taiwan would reject fortune telling as old-fashioned₂. However, thanks to technology and globalization, this ancient art has become more popular than ever. With TV and radio call-in₃ shows, Internet sites, and mobile phone services, your fortune is just a touch away.

　Many of the traditional Chinese forms of fortune telling like divination with eight characters, face reading, palm reading₄, and finding lucky names₅ are still widely practiced. Some people visit psychics or mediums who go into a trance to learn about their previous lives. Others buy good luck charms or go to temples for predictions.

　As Taiwan has become more internationalized, some fortune tellers have turned to Western fortune telling techniques like crystal balls and tarot cards. Western astrology and aura interpretations₆ are also popular. Whether we believe in traditional Chinese or New Age methods, fortune telling seems here to stay.

35 全球算命

　　人們也許以為像台灣這麼現代化的國家會視算命為老掉牙的玩意兒，然而由於科技和全球化的推波助瀾，這項古老的「藝術」比以往更為風行。藉著電台和電視的扣應節目、網站和手機服務，你的命運近在咫尺。

　　許多傳統中國算命如算八字、看面相、手相和找好名字仍廣為流行，有人找通靈人和靈媒讓他們進入半昏迷狀態以得知自己的前世。另有人買護身符，或到廟裡預知未來。

　　當台灣變得國際化時，許多算命的轉向西洋相術，如水晶球和塔羅牌，西洋星座和氣運解析也很流行。不管你相信傳統中國或新世紀的相術，算命都將永存台灣。

✐ 生字 Vocabulary

1. **fortune telling** 算命
   Fortune telling always becomes more popular when a society feels uncertain about its future.
   當整個社會覺得對未來不太確定時，算命便開始流行。

2. **globalization** 全球化
   Because of globalization, many products from other countries are available in Taiwan.
   由於全球化的關係，許多其他國家的產品在台灣都可以買得到。

3. **call-in** 扣應
   She listens to a radio call-in show every morning in her car.
   她每天早上都在車上聽收音機的扣應節目。

4. **a touch away** 很近
   With so many self-study websites available online, learning English is just a touch away.
   隨著許多網路自學網站的架設，學習英文十分近便。

5. **divination** 推算、卜卦
   An ancient form of Chinese divination used turtle shells.
   中國古代用龜殼卜卦。

6. **eight characters** 八字
   Traditional fortune tellers use eight characters to predict a person's future.
   傳統中國算命師用八字預知一個人的未來。

7. face reading 看面相
    Many people believe that face reading can tell a person's character.
    許多人相信面相可以看出一個人的個性。

8. palm reading 看手相
    According to my palm reading, I will live a long life.
    根據我的手相，我會活得很長。

9. psychic 通靈人
    In some countries, police consult psychics to help solve crimes.
    有些國家連警察都向通靈人討教，以幫助破案。

10. mediums 靈媒
    The medium helped the man get in touch with his grandfather's spirit.
    靈媒幫這個人跟他祖父的靈魂搭上了線。

11. trance 恍惚
    When she went into a trance, she began speaking a different language.
    當她進入昏迷狀態，開始用不同的語言說話。

12. previous life 前世
    The fortune teller said that I was a Chinese general in a previous life.
    算命的說我的某個前世是位中國將軍。

13. good luck charm 護身符

The grandmother insisted that her grandson wear a good luck charm every day.

阿嬤堅持她的孫兒每天得帶護身符。

14. internationalized 國際化

In the past 15 years, Taiwan has become increasingly internationalized.

過去十五年間,台灣變得愈來愈國際化了。

15. crystal ball 水晶球

Some people believe that crystal balls have special powers.

有人相信水晶球有特殊的力量。

16. tarot cards 塔羅牌

My friend sometimes uses her tarot cards to tell her own fortune.

我的朋友有時用塔羅牌為她自己算命。

17. astrology 星座

Many Americans believe in the Western form of astrology.

許多美國人相信西洋星座。

18. aura 氣

Some especially sensitive people can see the auras that surround others like a band of energy.

有些特別敏感的人可以看到有股像帶狀的氣,環繞在他人四周。

19. New Age 新世紀

The term "New Age" was around in the 60's and used by American sociologists to describe the younger generation's fascination with alternative spiritual beliefs.

六〇年代美國社會學家用「新世紀」這個詞描述年輕世代迷戀另類的信仰方式。

✎ 課文重點分析 Analysis

1. expect（動詞）、expectation（名詞）、expected（形容詞）、expectancy（名詞）。例如：

I didn't expect that he would show up tonight.

我沒想到他今天晚上會出現。

Taiwanese parents always have high expectations for their kids.

台灣的父母總是對小孩的期望很高。

I felt sorry that I couldn't live up to my parents' expectations.

我對自己無法達到父母的期望感覺遺憾。

life expectancy 平均壽命

The life expectancy of an average Taiwanese person has increased by almost two years in the past decade.

台灣人的預期平均壽命過去十年來幾乎增加了兩歲。

2. as old-fashioned 視為老古板、老掉牙，是常用的詞，它的原意為：

People reject fortune telling as old-fashioned.

人們拒絕算命，視它為老掉牙的東西。

I know that my ideas are sometimes portrayed as old-fashioned.

我知道我的想法常被描繪為老掉牙。

Many of us are terrified of being thought of as old-fashioned.

我們很多人都怕被人認為太老古板。

3. call in（動詞）：

Many people called in to her program yesterday.

昨天許多人扣應她的節目。

call-in（形容詞）：

I don't like the call-in program she hosts.

我不喜歡她主持的扣應節目。

4. face reading, palm reading是名詞，指兩種算命的方法。動詞的用法為：

I had a fortune teller read my palm last night.

昨晚我找了個算命的幫我看了手相。

She read my face and told me something I needed to be careful about.

她看了我的面相，告訴我一些我應該注意的事項。

5. 所謂 find a lucky name，對中國人而言，就是算名字的筆劃（count the strokes of your name's three characters）。有的筆

劃數字比較吉利，所以許多人習慣為剛出生的嬰兒取名時，一定要算筆劃。

6. aura interpretation 解釋一個人的「氣」。

An aura is a feeling or character that a person or place seems to have.

aura 可以說是一個人或一個地方擁有的特殊的氣氛或氣質。

例如：

This room seems to have an aura of mystery.

這間房間好像有股神秘之氣。

There is an aura of peace about her.

她有股平和之氣。

✐ 克漏字 Cloze

> fortune telling, call-in, globalization, face reading, psychics, trance, previous lives, astrology, predictions, aura

1. Roses have added an _____ of romance to this restaurant.

2. For every election, the newspaper makes _____ about the winners.

3. There are many _____ booths near Long Shan

Temple in Taipei.

4. Some people think that _____ causes many economic problems.

5. That _____ show lets people express their views about politics.

6. When he went into a _____, he could talk to spirits.

7. My friend and I think we were sisters in our _____.

8. According to _____ theory, his large nose is a good trait.

9. Western and Asian _____ are both based on when a person was born.

10. Some _____ claim they can read other people's minds.

✐ 選擇適當的詞性 Multiple Choice

_____ 1. She _____ to graduate next year. (a) expect (b) expectation (c) expects

_____ 2. Winning the lottery was beyond his _____. (a) expects (b) expectations (c) expected

_____ 3. The rainy weather was _____. (a) unexpecting

(b)unexpectedly (c)unexpected

_____ 4. She _____ to receive a good grade on her report.
(a)expecting (b)expected (c)expectations

_____ 5. The life _____ for people in Taiwan has increased. (a)expecting (b)expectancy (c)expectation

_____ 6. The new book sold _____ well. (a)unexpecting (b)unexpectedly (c)unexpected

_____ 7. The main _____ in this story is an old man. (a)character (b)characteristic (c)characterize

_____ 8. One _____ of Taiwanese culture is its friendliness. (a)character (b)characteristic (c)characterize

_____ 9. American universities have many _____ students. (a)international (b)internationalized (c)internationally

_____ 10. The _____ of business has changed the world's economy. (a)international (b)internationalized (c)internationalization

_____ 11. The local conflict became _____ when

a Japanese reporter was shot. (a) international
(b) internationalized (c) internationalization

✏️ 翻譯 Translation

1. 多虧現在科技，算命變得比以往更流行。

_____

2. 看面相、看手相、找個幸運的名字仍然廣為運用 (widely practiced)。

_____

3. 最近他迷上了新世紀音樂。

_____

4. 當這位通靈人進入一種半昏迷狀態，他的身體不斷地抖動。
   (kept shaking)

_____

5. 她那股迷人的 (charming) 神秘氣息令人著迷。

_____

6. 我覺得沒有安全感如果我忘了帶 (wear) 我的護身符。

_____

7. 這位靈媒告訴我我的前世是像什麼樣的。

_____

8. 只要輸入(key in)你的生日,你的運勢就會近在咫尺。

_____

9. 他常常用塔羅牌預測他自己的未來。

_____

10. 算八字是傳統中國的算命形式之一。

_____

Superstitions₁ Connected with Language (CD2 Track18)

Since ancient times, every culture has tried to prevent bad luck and encourage good. These attempts to control fate₂ have led to many superstitions and taboos. In Taiwan, many superstitions are connected₃ to the way words sound, either in Mandarin or Taiwanese.

For instance, the number four is unlucky because it sounds like the word for death₄. Similarly, never give someone a clock because in Mandarin "giving a clock" sounds exactly the same as "holding a funeral" for that person. An umbrella is also an unlucky gift because it sounds like the character meaning "to separate."

On the other hand, some objects have auspicious names. In Taiwanese, the term for radish sounds like "good fortune," and pineapple sounds similar to "something prosperous is coming." Even though many people no longer fully believe these superstitions, they don't dare risk jinxing themselves by ignoring them.

迷信和語言

古早以來，每個文化都試著驅惡迎善，企圖掌握命運，以致許多迷信和禁忌大為流行。在台灣，許多迷信跟國語或台語字的發音方法有關。

舉例來說，「四」之所以不吉利，因其聽起來與「死」這個字相近似，另外，絕對不送鐘給人家，因為國語「送鐘」聽起來和幫某人「送終」一模一樣。同樣地，傘也是不吉利的禮物，因為「傘」聽起來像「散」這個字。

相反地，有的東西卻有個吉祥的名字。「菜頭」這個台語名稱聽起來像「彩頭」，台語「鳳梨」聽起來像「旺來」。即使許多人不完全相信這些迷信，他們可不敢冒著惹禍上身的危險，置迷信於不顧。

✐ 生字 Vocabulary

1. fate 命運
   My grandmother believes that people cannot change their fate.
   我的祖母相信你不能改運。

2. superstition 迷信
   Many superstitions have to do with increasing your luck.
   許多迷信與增添好運有關。

3. taboo 禁忌
   There are many taboos associated with the first day of the lunar New Year.
   許多禁忌與農曆大年初一有關。

4. Mandarin 國語、普通話
   Mandarin is the official language of Taiwan and mainland China.
   國語（普通話）是台灣和大陸的官方語言。

5. funeral 喪事
   When the popular singer died in a car accident, her fans held a very large funeral for her.
   當這位廣受歡迎的歌星因車禍去世時，她的影迷為她舉辦了一個盛大的葬禮。

6. character 中文字
   Many foreigners find that learning how to write Chinese characters is very difficult.

許多外國人覺得學寫中文字真困難。

7. auspicious 吉利

She wanted to get married on an auspicious day.

她希望在良辰吉日結婚。

8. radish 蘿蔔

Radish cake is a popular dish in Taiwan during the lunar New Year holidays.

蘿蔔糕是農曆新年受歡迎的年菜。

9. pineapple 鳳梨

Hawaii is famous for its delicious pineapples.

夏威夷以產可口的鳳梨出名。

10. prosperous 繁榮

His new business has attracted many customers and seems very prosperous.

他新店開張顧客盈門，生意看來十分興隆。

11. jinx 帶來厄運

The superstitious man was careful to avoid jinxing himself.

這位迷信人士小心謹慎，以避免帶給自己厄運。

🖋 課文重點分析 Analysis

1. superstition（名詞）、superstitious（形容詞）、superstitiously（副詞），例如：

According to a Western superstition, walking under a ladder

will bring you bad luck.

根據西方的迷信，從梯子下走過會招厄運。

He is very superstitious about the seat numbers he books.

他對劃位的號碼很迷信。

Tourists rubbed this stone superstitiously, hoping they would get some luck.

觀光客迷信地摸這塊聖石，希望能得到好運。

2. fate（名詞）、fatal（形容詞），例如：

It must be fate that brought us together again.

一定是命運讓我們重新在一起。

Cancer is not always a fatal illness any more.

癌症已不是致命的疾病。

3. connect（動詞）、connection（名詞）、be connected to。例如：

May I connect my computer to your printer?

我可以把我的電腦接到你的印表機上嗎？

My computer has been connected to her printer.

現在我的電腦和她的印表機已接好了。

She has built many social connections in the past few years.

過去幾年她建立了不少人脈。

He doesn't know how to connect with people.

他不知道如何跟人相處。

4. die（動詞）、died（過去式、過去分詞）、dying（動名詞）、death（名詞）、dead（形容詞）、deadly（致命的，形容詞）例如：

My dad died of a heart attack.

我的父親死於心臟病。

He is taking care of his dying wife.

他正在照顧垂死的太太。

Her dying words were, "I see a light from heaven."

她臨死的話是「我看到一道光從天而降。」

Do you believe in life after death?

你相信死後還能重生嗎？

Is Bin Laden alive or is he dead?

賓拉登到底活著還是死了？

I can't believe there is market for deadly weapons.

我不相信致命的武器居然會有市場。

✎ 克漏字 Cloze

fate, superstition, taboo, characters, pineapple, prosperous, jinxing, radishes, funeral, auspicious

1. His new office is in a very _____ neighborhood in Taipei.

2. Talking about death is a _____ in many cultures.

3. The fortune teller said the man had an _____ face.

4. When the former president died, he was given a very expensive _____.

5. Most people in China can only write Chinese in simplified _____.

6. _____ shrimp is one of her favorite dishes.

7. Avoiding the number four is a Chinese _____.

8. _____ are a root vegetable.

9. She blamed her bad luck on her _____.

10. When his luck turned bad, he thought someone was _____ him.

✏ 選擇適當的詞性 Multiple Choice

_____ 1. Johnny believed that _____ brought him and his new wife together. (a) fate (b) fatal (c) fateful

_____ 2. The news reported a _____ car accident in

which two people were killed. (a) fate (b) fatal (c) fateful

_____ 3. To believe that the number thirteen is unlucky is a common Western _____. (a) superstition (b) superstitious (c) superstitiously

_____ 4. Caroline is very _____ and will never do anything that she believes will bring bad luck. (a) superstition (b) superstitious (c) superstitiously

_____ 5. It is important to _____ with your audience. (a) connect (b) connected (c) connection

_____ 6. Individuals often feel the need to be _____ to the outside world through telephone, Internet and even television. (a) connect (b) connected (c) connection

_____ 7. Kerry felt a strong _____ with Matt, as if they had known each other in a previous life. (a) connect (b) connected (c) connection

_____ 8. Don't _____ anything Melissa says because she always tells lies. (a) belief (b) believe (c) believable

_____ 9. Many people support the idea of an afterlife, but

others refute the _____ that anything could exist after death. (a) belief (b) believe (c) believable

_____ 10. Caroline has lived a very _____ life; she has always had everything she wanted. (a) prosper (b) prosperous (c) prosperity

_____ 11. Julia's _____ was a result of good market timing. (a) prosper (b) prosperous (c) prosperity

_____ 12. We are not sure whether he is _____ or not, but we are sure that he is injured. (a) died (b) dead (c) death

_____ 13. His parents _____ when he was four years old. (a) died (b) dead (c) death

_____ 14. Don't be scared. It's not a _____ virus. (a) died (b) dead (c) deadly

🖉 翻譯 Translation

1. 人們常常試著防止厄運同時助長好運。

_____

2. 今年我進大學的企圖失敗了。

_____

3. 在台灣許多迷信與字的發音方式有關。

___

4. 數字「四」之所以不吉利，因其聽起來與「死」這個字相近似。

___

5. 國語「送鐘」給人聽起來與「送終」（幫那個人辦喪事）完全一樣。

___

6. 一把傘是不吉利的禮物，因為它聽起來好像中文字意思是「分散」。

___

7. 在台灣有的東西有吉利的名字。

___

8. 用台語說「菜頭」聽起來像「好彩頭」。

___

9. 「鳳梨」聽起來跟「旺來」（興旺的事情來了）很相似。

___

10. 我可不敢冒帶給我自己厄運的危險，忽視迷信。

___

Unit 1

克漏字

1. travel agent　2. tour group　3. visa　4. five-star
5. package deal　6. sightseeing　7. formalities　8. itinerary
9. budget motel　10. Spring Festival

選擇適當的詞性

1. b　2. c　3. a　4. a　5. c　6. a　7. b　8. a　9. b　10. c　11. a
12. c

翻譯

1. I prefer independent travel to a tour group.
   I like traveling independently instead of joining a tour group.
2. Travel agents will help you apply for a visa and purchase airplane tickets.
3. I hate to deal with the formalities of traveling abroad.
4. I think a tour group will suit my parents better.
5. He prefers a tour since everything is nicely arranged.
6. She doesn't like a tour guide accompanying her while she is sightseeing or shopping.
7. Have you ever stayed in a five-star hotel?
8. I can't decide whether to stay in a luxury resort or a budget motel.
9. Despite the ease of a tour, I still prefer the freedom of independent travel.
10. Every time I dine out, I always choose a greasy spoon.

Unit 2

克漏字

1. lion dance　2. Fireworks　3. rooster　4. symbolizes
5. lantern fair　6. sticky-rice balls　7. zodiac animal　8. mark
9. are absorbed in　10. was stuffed

選擇適當的詞性

1. c　2. b　3. a　4. b　5. c　6. a　7. c　8. b　9. a　10. c　11. a
12. a　13. b　14. b

翻譯

1. My favorite dish is chicken stuffed with sticky rice.
2. How many days do we have for this year's springtime celebration?
3. Lantern Festival falls on the 15th day of the first lunar month.
4. Lantern Festival marks the end of the New Year celebration.
5. She got her English name from a famous movie star's middle name.
6. Every Lantern Festival evening, children carry lanterns under the full moon.
7. Did you eat sticky-rice balls during Lantern Festival?
8. What was last year's Chinese zodiac animal?
9. What is your Chinese zodiac sign?
10. I was born in the year of the tiger.

Unit 3

克漏字

1. bouquet　2. pruning shears　3. annual　4. departed　5. dust pan
6. shovel　7. bond　8. Tomb Sweeping Day　9. a barrel of
10. manual

選擇適當的詞性

1. b　2. c　3. b　4. c　5. b　6. a　7. c　8. b　9. a　10. c　11. b
12. c

翻譯

1. My grandpa uses a broom and a dust pan to sweep the floor every day.
2. I use the solar calendar instead of the lunar one.
3. Except for my sister, this year everybody went to sweep our ancestors' burial grounds.
4. One last touch is to arrange a bouquet of flowers in a vase.
5. We used a shovel to dig out weeds yesterday afternoon.
6. Besides digging out weeds, we trimmed the overgrown trees.
7. We prayed for our ancestors' continued protection.
8. He waters plants with a barrel of water every day.
   He uses a barrel of water to water plants every day.
9. Did you burn ghost money and incense?
10. Unlike him, I like to do manual labor.

Unit 4

克漏字

1. Dragon Boat Festival　2. grab　3. decorated　4. spectacular
5. Corruption　6. medicinal herbs　7. discourage　8. team
9. course　10. Wrapping

選擇適當的詞性

1. b　2. a　3. c　4. b　5. c　6. a　7. a　8. b　9. b　10. c　11. c
12. b　13. a　14. b

翻譯

1. My mom taught me how to wrap zong zi yesterday.

2. I am not familiar with Taiwanese holiday customs.
3. Did you see the spectacular dragon boat race on TV?
4. Which team grabbed the flag at the end of the course?
5. During Dragon Boat Festival did you successfully stand an egg on its end at noon?
6. Her house was decorated like a palace.
7. Everyone at the party is dancing to drum beats.
8. Children wrote articles to memorialize their father.
9. My grandfather often picks medicinal herbs in the mountains.
10. Hanging this picture on the front door is to prevent evil.

Unit 5

克漏字

1. Besides 2. took place 3. memorialize 4. matchmaker
5. jewelry store 6. reunion 7. romantic 8. commercialized
9. owner 10. Western

選擇適當的詞性

1. a 2. c 3. a 4. c 5. c 6. b 7. b 8. b 9. a 10. c

翻譯

1. I go to the matchmaker temple to pray for peace.
2. This flower shop's owner is very romantic.
3. I look forward to having the once-a-year high school reunion.
4. I don't have any other boyfriend besides him.
5. I asked a matchmaker to help me find an ideal companion.
6. This temple has become increasingly commercialized.
7. He is very lucky because his candy store has very good business.

8. Celebrating Chinese Valentine's Day is not very popular yet.
9. Have you ever gone to the temple to pray for marriage?
10. Chinese Valentine's Day takes place on the 7th day of the 7th lunar month.

Unit 6

克漏字

1. underworld　2. on hold　3. ghost money　4. lunar calendar
5. wedding　6. sacrifices　7. dine on　8. wandering　9. souls
10. dos and don'ts

選擇適當的詞性

1. a　2. b　3. c　4. a　5. b　6. a　7. b　8. c　9. a　10. b　11. a
12. c

翻譯

1. When you take the college entrance exam, remember the following dos and don'ts.
2. Because the typhoon hit Taiwan, the exam had to be put on hold. (the typhoon struck Taiwan..., the typhoon swept Taiwan... 皆可)
3. He has prepared a lot of sacrifices to please the gods.
4. The best way to treat these wandering souls is to burn ghost money.
5. Because I was sick, I had to put my wedding on hold.
6. Last week I offered food and drinks for ghosts to dine on.
7. Next month ghosts will come out from the Gates of Hell.
8. Water lanterns light the way for the souls of the drowned.
9. Ghosts are wandering in the living world.

10. During Ghost Month, moving should be put on hold.

Unit 7

克漏字

1. brutal 2. elixir 3. legend 4. barbeque 5. season 6. Grilled
7. racks 8. moon cakes 9. take 10. Pomelos

選擇適當的詞性

1. b 2. a 3. b 4. a 5. c 6. b 7. a 8. c 9. c 10. b 11. a

翻譯

1. How are you going to celebrate the Moon Festival this year?
2. It's better not to take any medicine when you catch a cold.
3. Houyi was a brutal emperor.
4. According to the Chinese legend, Chang E was a beautiful fairy.
5. I don't like the flavor of that moon cake.
6. He is grilling pork chops on the rack.
7. Are you going to hold a barbeque on Moon Festival night?
8. I don't believe that a magical elixir exists.
9. Pomelos are in season during fall.
10. He flew to America last night.

Unit 8

克漏字

1. committed suicide 2. victims 3. stress 4. At your age
5. recognize 6. warning signs 7. deal with 8. statistics
9. lacks 10. tragic

選擇適當的詞性

1. c　2. a　3. b　4. c　5. b　6. c　7. a　8. c　9. b　10. c　11. b

翻譯

1. An average of nine people per day dies by suicide.
2. The strawberry generation cannot deal with life's pressures.
3. His death did not have any warning signs at all.
4. Teenagers should know how to handle stress.
5. Many suicide victims are teenagers.
6. I need adults' guidance and emotional support.
7. Taiwan's standard of living is much higher than it was before.
8. I could hardly recognize his voice.
9. His mother didn't know how to deal with his depression.
10. According to official statistics, Taiwanese students have a lot of stress.

Unit 9

克漏字

1. characters　2. self-esteem　3. tummy tuck　4. face reading
5. fairy tales　6. auspicious　7. graduation present
8. plastic surgery　9. transformed　10. double eyelid surgery

選擇適當的詞性

1. c　2. a　3. b　4. b　5. c　6. a　7. c　8. b　9. a　10. b　11. a
12. c

翻譯

1. I read a lot of fairy tales when I was a child.
2. Last year this vocational school was transformed into a college.

3. After the double eyelid surgery, her eyes have become larger and rounder.
4. Did you notice that he had had a nose job?
5. In order to increase her self-esteem, she is willing to go under the knife.
6. He chose an auspicious date to get married.
7. Do you think that cosmetic surgery will improve your career opportunities?
8. What all these women have in common is that they are not interested in having breast augmentation.
9. Why do so many Taiwanese value appearance?
10. Thanks to moving to the city, I started to have my own social life.

Unit 10

克漏字
1. domestic violence　2. Mandarin　3. foreign bride
4. second- class citizens　5. hotline　6. language barrier
7. social prejudice　8. legal aid　9. submissive　10. legal barrier

選擇適當的詞性
1. a　2. c　3. b　4. a　5. b　6. c　7. a　8. c　9. a　10. b　11. c
12. b　13. a

翻譯
1. Their marriage was arranged by an agency.
2. Approximately 30% of college graduates are unable to (can't) find a job.
3. He feels like a second-class citizen.

4. We should treat foreign brides with respect.
5. How many foreign brides are the victims of domestic violence?
6. Due to big language and cultural barriers, they finally got divorced.
7. Many new Taiwanese suffer learning difficulties in school.
8. He just wanted to marry a submissive woman.
9. This organization provides services like legal aid and hotlines.
10. Do you want to join free Mandarin classes and child care workshops?

Unit 11

克漏字

1. ATM card　2. ransom　3. account　4. Gullible　5. transfer
6. suspicious　7. text message　8. tax refund　9. scams
10. swindle

選擇適當的詞性

1. b　2. c　3. a　4. c　5. a　6. c　7. c　8. b　9. c　10. b　11. b
12. c　13. b　14. c

翻譯

1. Please transfer NT$10,000 into my account.
2. If you want your child back, you'd better pay the ransom.
3. He has become the victim of a fake kidnapping.
4. You should never, ever push the confirm button.
5. His savings have been transferred to a swindler's pocket.
6. In less than a minute, her savings disappeared.
7. Elderly people are often gullible victims of scams.

8. Yesterday I was informed to collect the tax refund.
9. Have you ever received a bogus text message?
10. Be suspicious about phone calls from strangers.

Unit 12

克漏字

1. election results 2. banners 3. Voter turnout
4. Independent candidates 5. rallies 6. bombarded 7. citizens
8. cast their ballots 9. polling station 10. count the vote

選擇適當的詞性

1. b 2. c 3. c 4. a 5. a 6. c 7. c 8. a 9. b 10. b

翻譯

1. When will the next legislative election be?
2. Can you guess how many seats independent candidates will win in the legislature?
3. Supporters held rallies for their candidates.
4. How many more days are we going to be bombarded with campaign ads?
5. Voter turnout for this election was only 43%.
6. By four o'clock this afternoon you have to cast your ballot at your local polling station.
7. When are they going to count the vote?
8. I don't know when they are going to announce the election results.
9. This candidate was accused of vote buying.
10. During the campaign season, colorful banners lined the streets.

Unit 13

克漏字

1. slim 2. stall 3. temple 4. random 5. striking 6. jackpot
7. lottery 8. pray 9. swept 10. fever

選擇適當的詞性

1. b 2. a 3. a 4. c 5. b 6. b 7. a 8. c 9. b 10. a 11. c
12. a 13. b

翻譯

1. Although the odds of hitting the jackpot were slim, many people still stood in line to buy lottery tickets.
2. I have never played Big Lotto.
3. I want to take a chance to see if I can hit the jackpot.
4. I prayed to God to help me pass the exam.
5. Last year lottery fever swept Taiwan.
6. Did you buy your lottery tickets at this lottery stall?
7. She chose a student at random to be the class leader.
8. I never dreamed that I could strike it rich.
9. Did you buy a lottery ticket?
10. The idea of winning a lot of money is appealing

Unit 14

克漏字

1. narcotics 2. decent 3. critic 4. Betel nut 5. cash crop
6. Environmentalists 7. sleazy 8. stain 9. erosion
10. oral cancer

選擇適當的詞性

1. a 2. c 3. b 4. b 5. a 6. b 7. a 8. a 9. c 10. b 11. a

12. c　13. c　14. a

翻譯

1. Have you ever chewed betel nut?
2. Computers are widely used throughout the world.
3. Various kinds of fruit contribute enormously to Taiwan's economy.
4. Environmentalists claim that growing so many betel palms causes erosion.
5. Taiwan's high rate of oral cancer worried doctors.
6. Rice is one of Taiwan's major cash crops.
7. Owners of the betel nut stall insisted that being a betel nut beauty was a decent job.
8. Wearing skimpy clothing, this betel nut beauty is working in a glass booth.
9. Don't spit on the sidewalk.
10. The controversy over chewing betel nut is not going to go away anytime soon.

Unit 15

克漏字

1. bride　2. newlyweds　3. wedding gown　4. groom
5. honeymoon　6. engagement party　7. rituals　8. engaged
9. proposal　10. worth every penny

選擇適當的詞性

1. c　2. b　3. b　4. c　5. a　6. c　7. a　8. b　9. c　10. a　11. c
12. b　13. b

翻譯

1. When did you get engaged?
2. John popped the question last week.
3. I can't decide whether I should accept his proposal.
4. The bride and groom just rented a formal wedding gown and suit.
5. The newlyweds decided to go to Hong Kong on their honeymoon.
6. Even though their wedding cost a fortune, they felt that it was worth every penny.
7. Everyone dreams of living happily ever after with his/her lover.
8. It took me three years to pay all the bills for the wedding.
9. The newlyweds spent a lot of money on wedding photographs.
10. The traditional wedding involves many rituals that a couple has to follow.

Unit 16

克漏字
1. credit cards　2. spending spree　3. charge　4. regulates
5. account　6. Interest rates　7. cash　8. handy　9. plastic money
10. bankruptcy

選擇適當的詞性
1. b　2. a　3. c　4. c　5. a　6. b　7. b　8. a　9. a　10. c　11. b
12. c

翻譯
1. If you don't have enough cash, you can pay with your credit card.

2. The bank will automatically deduct money from your account.
3. Cash cards allow you to borrow money through ATMs.
4. With a card on hand, you no longer need to bring much cash.
5. If you use your credit card wisely, you should never have a problem.
6. Credit cards often have high interest rates.
7. Every month when I receive the credit card bill, I pay off the entire balance.
8. Last month he only made the minimum payment.
9. The government passed stricter rules to regulate credit card advertising.
10. After he won the lottery, he went on a spending spree right away.

Unit 17

克漏字
1. recommendations 2. top choice 3. admitted 4. test scores
5. entry rate 6. attend 7. take 8. placement 9. options
10. record number

選擇適當的詞性
1. b 2. a 3. c 4. c 5. b 6. c 7. a 8. b 9. c 10. a 11. b
12. c

翻譯
1. What is your major? What are you majoring in?
2. In spite of how high my test scores are, my mom is still unhappy.
3. This year a record number of students took the college

entrance exam.

4. I attended college in 1970.
5. Because of his special talent, he was accepted by Taiwan University (he was admitted to Taiwan University).
6. I don't know the placement results yet.
7. When are you going to apply to that graduate school?
8. I don't have any other options but majoring in history.
9. How many times have you taken the college entrance exam?
10. That college is not my top choice.

Unit 18

克漏字

1. new recruit 2. standardized tests 3. connections 4. Critics
5. all walks of life 6. record-breaking 7. competitive
8. Life-long learning 9. criteria 10. globalization

選擇適當的詞性

1. a 2. c 3. b 4. a 5. c 6. c 7. b 8. c 9. a 10. c 11. b
12. a

翻譯

1. Have you taken the high-intermediate level of the GEPT?
2. In Taiwan people from all walks of life are obsessed with this book.
3. He is too young to take the GEPT.
4. Are you ready for the age of globalization?
5. Don't push your kid to take the elementary level of the GEPT.
6. The new recruits' English proficiency is not good enough.
7. My English oral proficiency is only at the intermediate level.

8. Based on his personal connection with the boss, he got this job.
9. This company doesn't have standard hiring criteria.
10. Many employers require staff to participate in life-long learning.

Unit 19

克漏字

1. hobbies　2. tips　3. bulky　4. articulate　5. resents
6. limitations　7. weary　8. intensive　9. beneficial　10. encounter

選擇適當的詞性

1. c　2. a　3. b　4. c　5. b　6. a　7. c　8. b　9. a　10. a　11. c
12. c　13. a　14. c　15. b

翻譯

1. Cram schools are beneficial to students, but they have their limitations.
2. Cram schools only cram some testing tips into students' brains.
3. Today I spent a full day in school.
4. I resent the test-oriented teaching style.
5. Although he is the most articulate teacher in the cram school, he has his limitations.
6. I don't like the canned music in this coffee shop.
7. Students complained that they had no free time for relaxation.
8. I can't stand the intense cold in this air-conditioned classroom.
9. If you only rely on cram school teachers, you will never be an active, independent learner.

10. This intensive training did improve students' test scores.

Unit 20

克漏字

1. toned　2. treadmill　3. sauna　4. personal trainer
5. weight machines　6. Yoga　7. fitness center　8. work out
9. Aerobics　10. delicate

選擇適當的詞性

1. b　2. c　3. c　4. b　5. a　6. b　7. c　8. a　9. a　10. b　11. a
12. c

翻譯

1. What happened to the steam room? How come it doesn't have any steam?
2. Now Taiwanese like toned women and muscular men.
3. Delicate maidens do not appeal to Taiwanese men any more.
4. Our deluxe spa services include free personal trainers and masseurs.
5. Are you going to take yoga and aerobics next month?
6. What kind of group exercise classes has the fitness center scheduled this month?
7. What kind of equipment does the gym have?
8. With flashing lights and high-energy music, this gym has attracted many teenagers.
9. Have you ever gone to the fitness center to work out?
10. Many office workers go to the gym to get in shape and reduce stress.

Unit 21

克漏字

1. diet drugs　2. overweight　3. get in shape　4. fined
5. paper-thin　6. false advertising　7. unscrupulous
8. weight loss　9. balanced diet　10. glamorous

選擇適當的詞性

1. a　2. b　3. b　4. a　5. b　6. c　7. b　8. c　9. a　10. a　11. b
12. c　13. a　14. b

翻譯

1. Fitness is more important than thinness.
2. No matter what fashion magazines suggest, we should not try fad diets.
3. You need regular exercise to get in shape.
4. I never envy glamorous images of paper-thin models.
5. Although she is a normally sized girl, she is obsessed with diet products.
6. Some false advertising promises quick and easy weight loss.
7. As long as you have a balanced diet, you will be fit.
8. In some cultures obesity equals beauty.
9. Instead of relying on fad diets, one should rely on a balanced diet.
10. Unscrupulous businessmen took advantage of public's desire to be thin to sell their drugs.

Unit 22

克漏字

1. moisturizer　2. massaged　3. a peel-off mask　4. hectic

5. aromatherapy　6. soothing　7. essential oil　8. cope with
9. health club　10. pamper

選擇適當的詞性
1. c　2. a　3. c　4. a　5. b　6. a　7. c　8. a　9. b　10. c　11. a

翻譯
1. Recently our lives have become increasingly hectic.
2. You have to look for ways to cope with your stressful life.
3. The most popular treatment is aromatherapy.
4. Do you know where I can find a blind masseur in Taipei?
5. Our services include hydrotherapy and facial treatments.
6. She doesn't particularly like the rose fragrance.
7. He often uses soothing music to relieve his tension.
8. You can select the most appropriate massage style.
9. Do you like the soft lighting in our health club?
10. I rely on my pet psychologically.

Unit 23

克漏字
1. state-of-the-art　2. prescribe　3. National Health Insurance
4. acupuncture　5. cover　6. Therapeutic massage
7. open-minded　8. holistic　9. balance　10. integrated

選擇適當的詞性
1. a　2. b　3. b　4. a　5. c　6. c　7. b　8. c　9. b　10. a　11. c

翻譯
1. This state-of-the-art medical treatment is not covered by National Health Insurance.
2. Traditional medical treatment keeps the patient's whole body

in balance.
3. Chinese medicine is more holistic than Western medicine.
4. This Chinese medical doctor prescribed herbal mixtures for me to drink.
5. Some doctors have successfully integrated Western and Chinese medicine.
6. Have you ever tried acupuncture, cupping, and scraping?
7. I think that reflexology is beneficial to my health.
8. He doubted the effectiveness of Chinese medical techniques.
9. This new recruit doesn't have any hands-on experience.
10. As long as we are open-minded, we can have the best of both worlds.

Unit 24

克漏字
1. forecast 2. evacuated 3. household 4. financial 5. low-lying
6. severe 7. reinforced 8. residents 9. properties 10. overpass

選擇適當的詞性
1. b 2. a 3. c 4. a 5. c 6. a 7. c 8. c 9. a 10. a 11. b
12. b 13. b 14. c

翻譯
1. Have you ever experienced the typhoons that sweep Taiwan?
2. As soon as I stored food and water, the typhoon arrived.
3. Living in low-lying areas is very dangerous.
4. People parked their cars on overpasses to avoid flash flooding.
5. Residents in the mountains have to watch for landslides.
6. Financial markets close on weekends.

411

7. We were evacuated to safer places.
8. The last typhoon brought heavy rain.
9. Last week the severe earthquake claimed three lives.
10. You should close the door and reinforce the windows with tape.

Unit 25

克漏字
1. itchy 2. originated 3. infection 4. wipe out 5. barefoot
6. treatment 7. blister 8. swelling 9. fire ants 10. venom

選擇適當的詞性
1. b 2. c 3. a 4. c 5. b 6. c 7. b 8. c 9. b 10. a 11. c
12. a 13. b

翻譯
1. Fire ants originated in Brazil.
2. These unwelcome guests have very dangerous venom.
3. Fire ants' venom can cause painful swelling.
4. Last year these pests damaged crops, furniture, and electric cables.
5. Using a cold compress can stop the itchiness.
6. You have to seek immediate medical treatment.
7. Be careful not to break the blister.
8. Your wound may lead to infection.
9. To be safe (For your own safety), you had better not go barefoot.
10. It is very difficult to wipe fire ants out completely.

Unit 26

克漏字

1. natural disaster　2. resort　3. trigger　4. tsunami　5. epicenter
6. death toll　7. susceptible　8. pledged　9. catastrophic
10. upgraded

選擇適當的詞性

1. c　2. a　3. b　4. c　5. c　6. a　7. b　8. c　9. b　10. a

翻譯

1. Yesterday as I was watching TV, he called.
2. I like to go to resorts in Kenting on vacation.
3. The earthquake has triggered a series of tsunamis.
4. Last night the earthquake's epicenter was southeast of Hualien.
5. A series of wars have caused catastrophic damage to many countries.
6. The government estimated the final death toll of this earthquake was 472.
7. People have to face severe problems such as water shortages and epidemics.
8. Have you donated money, food, and clothing to the victims?
9. Many companies pledged to help the victims of the flood.
10. We should upgrade our own emergency preparedness plans.

Unit 27

克漏字

1. dim sum　2. exotic　3. cuisine　4. spices　5. province
6. mouthwatering　7. diverse　8. dish　9. sushi　10. highlight

選擇適當的詞性

1. b 2. a 3. c 4. a 5. b 6. c 7. b 8. a 9. c 10. b 11. c
12. a 13. b

翻譯

1. He likes to eat all kinds of meals from business lunches to wedding banquets.
2. Thanks to Taiwan's special geography and history, we can eat a wide variety of dishes.
3. Thai food uses a lot of exotic herbs and spices.
4. Since Taiwan is an island, seafood has long been a highlight of Taiwanese cuisine.
5. Have you ever eaten Peking duck and drunken chicken?
6. Taiwan has a lot of ethnic food. For example, Indian cuisine, Thai cuisine, and Italian cuisine.
7. Dim sum is not available in this restaurant.
8. Taiwan is a food-lovers' paradise.

Unit 28

克漏字

1. Vending machines 2. roadside stands 3. taste buds
4. squeezed 5. abundant 6. ubiquitous 7. beverages
8. shaved ice 9. soft drinks 10. thirst-quenching

選擇適當的詞性

1. b 2. c 3. a 4. c 5. a 6. c 7. a 8. c 9. a 10. b 11. a
12. c 13. c 14. b 15. a 16. c 17. c 18. a

翻譯

1. You can buy all kinds of cold drinks from a vending machine.
2. In Taiwan convenience stores are ubiquitous.

3. Freshly squeezed juice with shaved ice is very refreshing.
4. After Dragon Boat Festival, Taiwan's weather begins to heat up.
5. Taiwan's cold tea drinks include pearl milk tea, bubble tea, taro tea, and kumquat tea.
6. Taiwan's manufacturers are endlessly creative.
7. Papaya milkshake is my favorite cold drink.
8. Beverages like beer, sports drinks, and soft drinks are canned or bottled.
9. I like to buy cold drinks at roadside stands.
10. Taiwan has an abundant supply of fruit all year round.

Unit 29

克漏字

1. stinky tofu　2. pickpockets　3. designer　4. bargaining
5. steamed dumplings　6. pirated　7. night markets　8. net fishing
9. sophisticated　10. lively

選擇適當的詞性

1. c　2. b　3. c　4. a　5. b　6. c　7. a　8. c　9. a　10. b　11. b
12. b

翻譯

1. My favorite snacks are grilled squid and stinky tofu.
2. Many people are lining up at that food stand to buy oyster pastries.
3. Besides shopping, people also play games.
4. Be careful not to buy any pirated goods.
5. Watch out! There are many pickpockets at night markets.

6. These "designer" dresses are pirated name-brand goods.
7. Every time he travels abroad, he will buy some trinkets for me.
8. Some foreigners are not used to bargaining.
9. Though he is a college student, he still collects stuffed animals.
10. You can never beat me.

Unit 30

克漏字
1. hanging out　2. stick to　3. appeal　4. sip　5. beverages
6. lingers　7. Espresso　8. buzz　9. Caffeine　10. decaf

選擇適當的詞性
1. b　2. c　3. a　4. a　5. b　6. c　7. a　8. b　9. c　10. b　11. b
12. a

翻譯
1. He is sipping tea in a traditional tea house.
2. Did you know that today most Taiwanese like to drink coffee?
3. What makes this coffee shop appealing to me is its cozy atmosphere.
4. Caffeine gives us an energizing buzz.
5. He never orders black coffee. He always sticks to latte.
6. Recently, coffee shops have suddenly sprung up in Taiwan.
7. The success of this coffee shop has more to do with its good location.
8. He is nursing a cup of coffee, sitting in front of the computer.
9. Tea is associated with traditional Taiwanese culture.
10. Young people like to hang out with friends in trendy coffee shops.

Unit 31

克漏字

1. horoscope   2. persona   3. slang   4. virtual world
5. Chat rooms   6. set up   7. Fortune telling   8. censorship
9. barriers   10. status   11. emoticoms

選擇適當的詞性

1. a 2. c 3. a 4. b 5. a 6. c 7. b 8. a 9. c 10. a 11. b

翻譯

1. In Taiwan the Internet has become increasingly popular.
2. Online chat rooms offer many chances for people to make friends.
3. A middle-aged man in Taiwan can have the profile of an American teenaged girl.
4. In Taiwan the most popular subject for chatting is horoscopes.
5. Are you interested in fortune telling?
6. Thanks to chat rooms, lonely people can meet in a virtual world.
7. How many times a week do you visit chat rooms?
8. This novel has been censored.
9. I don't know what her blood type is.
10. When he chatted with me, I didn't understand the slang he used.

Unit 32

克漏字

1. sugar daddy   2. Internet acquaintances   3. matchmaker
4. cyber sex   5. stalker   6. fans   7. one-night stands

8. going out on a date　9. Internet dating service　10. chat rooms

選擇適當的詞性

1. c　2. b　3. b　4. c　5. a　6. c　7. a　8. b　9. c　10. a　11. c
12. b

翻譯

1. Many people get married through the introduction of a matchmaker.
2. Nowadays, the Internet often serves as a matchmaker.
3. Internet dating services allow two strangers to meet online.
4. I am not interested in going out on a date with my Internet acquaintances.
5. I haven't had a long-term relationship yet.
6. She always looks for a chance to have a one-night stand.
7. Using money to exchange for sex is too risky.
8. In some cases, sugar daddies turn out to be liars.
9. Although Internet dating is risky, it is worth trying.
10. She is not a professional prostitute; she is just looking for some spending money.

Unit 33

克漏字

1. calculator　2. surf the Internet　3. annoying　4. mobile phone
5. rudely　6. gadgets　7. enable　8. etiquette　9. ultimate
10. MP3 player

選擇適當的詞性

1. b　2. c　3. a　4. c　5. b　6. b　7. a　8. c　9. b　10. c　11. a
12. b　13. a　14. b

翻譯
1. She likes all kinds of electronic gadgets.
2. How many hours do you surf the Internet every day?
3. You can use your cell phone as a calculator.
4. Can you use your cell phone as an alarm clock?
5. Some people use cell phones to hold loud conversations.
6. You had better watch your cell phone etiquette.
7. Death and illness are inescapable.
8. Cell phones' ring tones are annoying.
9. I send a text message to my girlfriend every day.
10. Cell phones enable parents to stay in touch with their children.

Unit 34

克漏字
1. offerings　2. Islam　3. Goddess　4. Buddhism　5. ancestors
6. family shrine　7. spiritual　8. worship　9. gods
10. burn incense

選擇題
1. b　2. a　3. c　4. b　5. c　6. b　7. a　8. a　9. b　10. c　11. b
12. c

翻譯
1. Many people go to the temple to burn incense for gods and goddesses.
2. My grandma makes daily offerings to her ancestors.
3. Different faiths co-exist harmoniously in Taiwan.
4. Spiritual forces are a part of our lives.
5. Buddhism, Taoism, Islam and Christianity are registered

religions in Taiwan.

6. Many people worship a combination of religions or folk religions.
7. We should learn how to tolerate different religions.
8. We don't keep a family shrine in our house.
9. Different religious groups are free to worship as they wish.
10. Religious differences frequently lead to conflict.

Unit 35

克漏字

1. aura　2. predictions　3. fortune telling　4. globalization
5. call-in　6. trance　7. previous lives　8. face reading
9. astrology　10. psychics

選擇適當的詞性

1. c　2. b　3. c　4. b　5. b　6. b　7. a　8. b　9. a　10. c　11. b

翻譯

1. Thanks to the modern technology, fortune telling has become more popular than ever.
2. Face reading, palm reading, and finding lucky names are still widely practiced.
3. Recently he has been obsessed with New Age music.
4. When the psychic went into a trance, his body kept shaking.
5. Her charming aura of mystery fascinates many people.
6. I feel very insecure if I forget to wear my good luck charm.
7. This medium told me what my previous life was like.
8. Just key in your birthday, and your fortune will be just a touch away.

9.　He often uses tarot cards to predict his own future.
10. Divination with eight characters is one of the traditional Chinese forms of fortune telling.

Unit 36

克漏字
1. prosperous　2. taboo　3. auspicious　4. funeral　5. characters
6. Pineapple　7. superstition　8. Radishes　9. fate　10. jinxing

選擇適當的詞性
1. a　2. b　3. a　4. b　5. a　6. b　7. c　8. b　9. a　10. b　11. c
12. b　13. a　14. c

翻譯
1.　People often try to prevent bad luck and encourage good luck.
2.　This year my attempt to enter the university failed.
3.　In Taiwan, many superstitions are connected to the way words sound.
4.　The number four is unlucky because it sounds like the word for death.
5.　In Mandarin, "giving a clock" to a person sounds exactly the same as "holding a funeral" for that person.
6.　An umbrella is unlucky gift because it sounds like the character meaning "to separate."
7.　In Taiwan, some objects have auspicious names.
8.　In Taiwanese, radish sounds like "good fortune."
9.　Pineapple sounds similar to "something prosperous is coming."
10. I don't dare risk jinxing myself by ignoring superstitions.

Linking English系列
用英文說台灣

2005年9月初版　　　　　　　　　　　　　定價：新臺幣380元
2012年5月初版第十二刷
有著作權・翻印必究
Printed in Taiwan.

著　　者	文　庭　澍
	Catherine Dibello
發 行 人	林　載　爵

出　版　者	聯 經 出 版 事 業 股 份 有 限 公 司	叢 書 主 編	何　采　嬪
地　　　址	台 北 市 基 隆 路 一 段 1 8 0 號 4 樓	校　　對	林　慧　如
台北聯經書房	台 北 市 新 生 南 路 三 段 9 4 號	封 面 設 計	翁　國　鈞
電話	(0 2) 2 3 6 2 0 3 0 8		
台 中 分 公 司	台 中 市 健 行 路 3 2 1 號		
暨 門 市 電 話	(0 4) 2 2 3 7 1 2 3 4　e x t . 5		
郵 政 劃 撥 帳 戶 第 0 1 0 0 5 5 9 - 3 號			
郵 撥 電 話	(0 2) 2 3 6 2 0 3 0 8		
印　刷　者	世 和 印 製 企 業 有 限 公 司		
總　經　銷	聯 合 發 行 股 份 有 限 公 司		
發　行　所	台北縣新店市寶橋路235巷6弄6號2F		
電話	(0 2) 2 9 1 7 8 0 2 2		

行政院新聞局出版事業登記證局版臺業字第0130號

本書如有缺頁，破損，倒裝請寄回台北聯經書房更換。　ISBN　978-957-08-2916-7 (平裝附光碟)
聯經網址 http://www.linkingbooks.com.tw
電子信箱 e-mail:linking@udngroup.com

國家圖書館出版品預行編目資料

用英文說台灣 / 文庭澍、Catherine
Dibello 合著 . --初版 . --臺北市 .
聯經，2005 年(民 94)
440 面；14.8×21 公分 .（Linking English）
ISBN 978-957-08-2916-7(平裝附光碟)
〔2012年5月初版第十二刷〕
1.英國語言-讀本

805.18   94016990

紐約時報英文解析

透過「悅」讀優質文章 轉化建構聽、說、寫的能力

「悅」讀優質文章、提昇英語文能力

《紐約時報》是全美、也是全球最具權威性的報紙。它的內容廣泛、立場超然,深具指標性與影響力。除此以外,《紐約時報》用字嚴謹、結構紮實有力、內容新穎實用,文章裡的新字新詞也跟現代生活環環相扣。《紐約時報英文解析》從選文、分析、評鑑等過程,都經過嚴謹的分析和討論,每一篇文章均有特殊的跨領域代表性。

希望讀者經由閱讀、聆聽CD範讀,融會聽說讀寫的語言能力。在領略精采文章之際,獲得預期中的學習效益。

最堅強解析團隊

對於李振清教授能主導整個團隊,我們感到十分難能可貴。解析團隊均是一時之選,在繁重的學術工作中撥冗為文,藉由導讀解析,讓讀者細細體會文章肌理。充分展現團隊對《紐約時報》的一份熱誠與堅持。

李振清:世新大學人文社會學院院長、前教育部國際文教處處長
胡耀恆:世新大學英語系客座教授、前國立台灣大學外文系教授兼系主任
彭鏡禧:國立台灣大學外文系及戲劇系教授兼文學院院長
梁欣榮:國立台灣大學外文系教授
賴慈芸:國立台灣師範大學翻譯研究所助理教授
李文肇:美國舊金山州立大學外文系副教授